G

TMW Marv

LIZZIE

Although William Chalmers loves Lizzie Immerson, he is engaged to her sister Bessie. Lizzie, a widow with a young daughter, marries Lewis Gilbert to ensure her security and William returns to Scarborough, heartbroken. Then fate takes a hand, and William discovers his feelings for Lizzie are reciprocated, but in order to achieve his heart's desire, William must fight for the woman he loves. Only one thing is certain—Lizzie will be worth the battle ahead ....

LIZZIE

LIZZIE

by

Louise Brindley

Magna Large Print Books
Long Preston, North Yorkshire,
England.

British Library Cataloguing in Publication Data.

Brindley, Louise
  Lizzie.

A catalogue record for this book is
available from the British Library

ISBN 0-7505-1396-9

First published in Great Britain by Severn House Publishers
Ltd., 1998

Published in Large Print 1999 by arrangement with Severn
House Publishers Ltd.

Magna Large Print is an imprint of
Library Magna Books Ltd.
Printed and bound in Great Britain by
T.J. International Ltd., Cornwall, PL28 8RW.

All situations in this publication are fictitious and any resemblance to living persons is purely coincidental.

For my parents, Elizabeth and William Hembrough, whose love affair lasted a lifetime, and is still going on, for all I know.

My thanks are due to Mr Chris Lloyd, the Features Editor of *The Northern Echo,* for his book *Memories of Darlington,* on which my research was based.

PART ONE

PART ONE

ONE

Bessie Donen was on a stepladder cleaning the front room window when she saw the young man turn the corner into Parker Street. (Nosy Parker Street, some folk called it.) He must have arrived at Bank Top Station on the half-past two train, she reckoned, judging by the hefty leather suitcase he was carrying.

Moisture from the washleather she was holding ran up her arm unnoticed as she watched him coming towards her. She felt bemused, the way she often did at the theatre, clutching her usherette's torch, gawping at the stage, wearing what her mother described as her 'milch cow' expression, adding, 'You'll come a cropper one of these days, my girl, if you don't buck your ideas up and think what you're doing'.

That prediction very nearly came true as, screwing her head round to follow the man's progress, the ladder creaked under her weight, the leather fell to the ground, she lost her balance and, 'Ooooo!' she wailed from the circle of her full red lips.

'Here, allow me!' Plonking down his

suitcase on the pavement, the man grasped her arm and helped her to the ground. Overwhelmed by his touch, the blushing Bessie looked up at him appealingly.

'Oh, ta ever so much,' she said breathlessly. 'I might have sprained my ankle, if it hadn't been for you.'

'Dangerous things, stepladders.' The young man smiled disarmingly. 'Sure you're all right?'

Bessie's blush deepened, thinking what a lovely speaking voice he had, and such gentlemanly manners. Only a real gent would have raised his hat to her as he continued on his way. But Bessie wasn't about to let go of him so easily.

'My name's Bessie Donen,' she called out unashamedly. 'What's yours?' Heart fluttering, she held up her skirts and took a series of quick, skittering steps after his retreating figure.

Turning, he smiled politely at the hefty girl teetering in his wake. 'Chalmers,' he said. 'William Chalmers.'

'I just wondered if you was going anywhere in particular? I mean, if you was looking for someone ...?' Bessie's voice faltered, knowing her mother would kill her if she happened to pop her head round the front door at that moment.

'Well, yes, as a matter of fact.' The girl seemed harmless enough, William decided.

Just a kid really, holding the washleather he had picked up for her; letting the water drip down her skirts held high enough to reveal an inch or two of petticoats above her chubby, black-booted ankles. 'I'm seeking a Mrs Maude Thompson. Do you know where she lives?'

Bessie sniffed disdainfully. Everyone in Parker Street knew Maudie Thompson, the widow who kept the corner shop. 'Why? Is she a friend of yours?'

'Not exactly. I'm going to lodge with her.'

Miserably aware of some women having all the luck, others none at all, 'You want to be over yonder at the corner shop,' Bessie said huffily, turning back to her window cleaning, wondering if what the neighbours said about Mrs Thompson being no better than she should be, was true. If so, it seemed a sin that the wicked should flourish like the green bay tree, whatever *that* meant. And flourish she had, since her husband had got himself killed in the war. Now Mrs Thompson was making money hand over fist, what with the shop and taking in lodgers. *Lodgers,* indeed!

Squaring his shoulders, the challenge William had hungered for since his demobilisation from the Army, was here at last. Not that he had seen much action.

The war with Germany had been all over bar the shouting when he joined up, to his great disappointment. Even so, his first taste of freedom away from home had whetted his appetite for more.

Savouring rough and ready male companionship after so many female apron-strings, his horizons had broadened to the extent of not wanting to return to the dominating influence of his mother and two sisters, nor his old job in civvy street. His army pals would have hooted in derision had they known he dressed women's hair for a living. Joining up, he'd named his profession as 'Barber' which sounded far more manly than 'Ladies' Hairdresser'.

Above all things, William wished to be regarded as manly, a status denied him when, leaving school, his mother—the owner of a ladies' hairdressing salon in Scarborough—had drummed him into the family business forthwith as an apprentice to learn the art of singeing, shampooing, and Marcel waving, despite his protestations that he would far rather be a fireman or an engine-driver.

'Nonsense,' she'd said, in that high-handed way of hers, 'of course you must enter the family business'. And he had been too much under her thumb to rebel.

Now, hunching into his coat collar against the keen wind whistling down Parker Street bringing with it a flurry of hailstones, hurrying towards the haven of Mrs Thompson's corner shop where early-lit gasmantles illuminated the windows on this cold February afternoon. William recalled the expression of shocked disbelief on his mother's face when he told her that he had decided to leave home.

The confrontation had taken place in the over-furnished drawing room above the salon one evening after supper, with the letter William had received from his old school pal Fred Willis, burning a hole in his pocket ... *It's all fixed, Billy Boy, I've had a word with old Schiller, and the job's yours if you want it ...*

Then all William had to do was break the news to his mother that he'd been offered employment as a barber's assistant in Darlington, and hand her a week's notice. Easier said than done.

'Are you out of your mind?' had been Clara Chalmers' immediate reaction. 'You mean to tell me that having taught you all you know about ladies' hairdressing, you are about to plunge a dagger into my heart!'

His sisters, Nell and Louisa, had been seated on a sofa at the time, embroidering opposite corners of the same tablecloth.

The sharp-tempered Nell, also an unwilling victim of her mother's despotism, had said tartly, 'Oh, let him go! If all he wants from life is lathering men's chins, sweeping up hair clippings and cleaning washbasins, why worry? He hasn't been pulling his weight in the salon for some time now, Ma, and you know it!'

'I also know who's responsible for this sorry state of affairs,' Clara had retorted, 'that commercial traveller friend of William's—what's his name? Fred Willis! A common little creature if ever there was one, whom I hold entirely responsible for leading my son astray!'

Rounding fiercely on William, 'I *am* right, am I not, in thinking *he* put you up to this? Well, deny it, if you can!'

William couldn't deny it, nor did he wish to do so. Fred had talked him into the idea of leaving home one evening in the George Hotel, over a couple of pints of beer.

'God-dammit, Billy Boy,' he'd said, wiping the foam from his flourishing ginger moustache with the back of his hand, 'life's for living. Why muck about doing a job you hate just to please your old lady?'

'I know, but I'll need a job and I'm not qualified for anything else except hairdressing.'

'Good God, man, you can scrape the beard off a bloke's chin, can't you? Look, I'm off to Darlington tomorrow, lodging with Maudie Thompson.' Fred's eyes had twinkled. 'What a woman! Well, I'll have a word in her shell-like; see what she can come up with. At least you'd be away from this dump, earning a bob or two till you find your feet. What do you say?'

'Yes. Why not?'

Fred's ebullience had rubbed off on him. He'd felt suddenly uplifted as he usually did in his pal's company.

'Great! I'll see what I can do, then. Darlington's a fine town. Plenty of pubs and billiard halls, a couple of theatres, lots of good-looking women.'

Fred was right. Alighting from the train at Darlington's Bank Top Station, William had experienced an overwhelming feeling of freedom. Breathing in the smoky atmosphere of a sprawling industrial town —as different from a seaside resort as chalk from cheese—he felt the way he had as a schoolboy smoking his first cigarette behind the bike-sheds: excited and nervous at the same time.

The corner shop door was set obliquely between two small windows plastered with Reckitt's Blue, Virol, and Robin's Starch adverts. The bell pinged as he entered.

His nostrils were assailed by the curiously blended aromas of cheese, bacon, malt vinegar and firelighters. A narrow counter fronted a curtained doorway leading to the living quarters, gaslight shone down on shelves of tinned goods and sweet-jars of pear-drops, mint imperials and aniseed balls. Cards of dummies, Carter's Little Liver Pills, clay pipes and hard-skin ointment dangled from a brass rail above the counter, behind which stood a youth wearing a flat cap and braces.

Sidestepping an obstacle course of buckets, scrubbing brushes and mousetraps, William approached the counter hopefully not looking as foolish as he felt. 'Good afternoon,' he said politely. 'I—er, that is, I'd like to see Mrs Thompson. I'm her new lodger.'

'Oh.' Turning awkwardly, the lad twitched back the curtain and bellowed, 'Ma, it's someone for you. The new lodger.'

A disembodied voice floated from the upper region. 'All right, Charlie, tell him I'll be down in a minute. Let him through to the passage. And Charlie, remember to mind your manners!'

Lifting the counter-flap, Charlie jerked his head and said unnecessarily, 'She'll be down in a minute. You're to wait in the passage.'

'Thanks.' Squeezing himself and his

suitcase through the narrow aperture, William faced a flight of stairs framed with looped-back lace curtains. Awaiting the appearance of his landlady, he recalled the twinkle in Fred Willis's eyes whenever her name cropped up in conversation. The minute he clapped eyes on her, he knew why.

A well-corseted woman in her early forties, Maudie Thompson exuded a warm sensuality which left him almost breathless with admiration. Everything about her radiated health and *joie de vivre*. Her mouth, full-lipped and smiling, revealed a set of strong white teeth stopped here and there with discreet gold fillings. The tightly-fitting blouse and skirt she wore emphasised her hour-glass figure. Red-gold hair framed a soft-featured face with a dazzling pink and white complexion. In short, Maudie Thompson was a work of art.

'So, you are Freddie's friend? My, aren't you handsome?' She looked at William admiringly. 'You're welcome, I'm sure. Now, come upstairs, dear. Leave your case where it is. Charlie will bring it up later, won't you, Charlie?'

'Yes, Ma.' The lad sighed deeply and returned to his counter. Another prisoner of the apronstrings, William thought fleetingly, feeling sorry for the youth.

Maudie's drawing room reflected her comfort-loving personality. A plump, cushion-strewn sofa was set in front of a blazing coal fire. Firelight gleamed on the brass fender and fire-tongs. There were innumerable gimcrack ornaments on the mantelpiece and many side-tables against the walls of the room; pictures, mirrors and photographs galore. Next to the fireplace stood a tall blue and white vase containing a collection of peacock feathers.

Maudie laughed. 'I know, what you're thinking. Peacock feathers are supposed to be unlucky, but I don't believe in that kind of superstitious nonsense. People make their own luck, that's what I think. Come now, Billy, take off your hat and coat and make yourself at home. You don't mind if I call you Billy? And you must call me Maudie. Now, I'll just go through to the kitchen and make us a nice cup of tea. Smoke if you want to.'

Lighting a cigarette, William stretched his feet to the fire, sighed deeply with satisfaction, and blew smoke rings at the ceiling. Awaiting his landlady's reappearance with the tea, he thought about home—his mother lording it over the restrictive world of her salon; of Nell and Louisa incarcerated in their narrow cubicles, dreading the sound of Clara's footsteps whenever she creaked downstairs to exert her authoritarian influence over members of her staff—her daughters included. Forever fault-finding and complaining about this or that; reducing to nervous wrecks the apprentices in her employ.

Thank God he was free at last, his own man, William thought. And standing on his own two feet. He grinned suddenly, aware of the solecism, feeling the heat from Maudie Thompson's fire burning the soles of his shoes.

Stubbing out his cigarette, he rose swiftly to his feet when Maudie came in with the tea-tray.

Maudie chuckled. 'Fred told me you were a proper little gent,' she remarked. 'Now, you just sit beside me on the sofa whilst I do the pouring.'

The sofa cushions billowed about her plump derrière as she sat down. Lifting the teapot, she said, 'You know, Billy, you remind me of my late husband. Jim had lovely manners, too. Thought the world of me, he did. Poor Jim. Killed on the Somme, he was. Milk and sugar, dear?'

'Yes, thank you.'

William felt he ought to utter a word or two of consolation, but Maudie rattled on, 'It wasn't easy making a living after Jim went, I can tell you, what with the

25

war and all and goods for the shop being in short supply. That's when I decided to take in lodgers to supplement my income. I had my son to think of, you see, to clothe and feed, and that was no easy task, believe me. Charlie being the way he is. Well, you know what I mean?'

'No, I'm not sure that I do,' William said cagily, aware that his hostess's posterior was now touching his, and feeling uncomfortable as a result.

Maudie sighed deeply, 'Somehow I never imagined that Jim and I would produce a ... Oh well, never mind, eh? It's just that poor Charlie is not quite like other boys of his age, a bit of a misfit. All he's really interested in is that gramophone of his; that blasted record "The Sheikh of Araby", which I swear I'll smash to smithereens one of these days! Besides which, Charlie isn't the least bit interested in—girls.'

'Neither was I, at his age,' William remarked, feeling suddenly hot and bothered by the close proximity of Maudie's thigh nestling against his, the touch of her hand on his knee. 'He's just going through a phase, that's all; missing his father, I dare say.'

'What an understanding young man you are! But I'm sure your aversion to girls didn't last long, and I bet they liked *you?*'

Anxious to change the subject, 'I'd like to thank you for putting in a good word for me with Mr Schiller,' William said.

'Oh, that? Think nothing of it. Poor old Maurice needs a hand in the shop. Not that trade's all that good nowadays since the war, and with him being in a prison camp all that time. Made no difference that he'd been in this country for twenty-five years or more, he was still classed as an enemy agent, being a German.'

She paused, 'More tea, dear? He used to cut Jim's hair, that's how I came to know him. Jim said he was the best barber in Darlington. Course there are people who still won't go near his shop, but I've never been one to hold grudges. Life's too short. Live, love and laugh is my motto.' She laughed. 'Ever had your fortune told, dear?'

Picking up William's cup, she swirled the dregs and cradled it in her plump beringed hands. 'A beautiful woman is about to enter your life,' she said dramatically. 'A widow perhaps, with a child to support.'

William stirred uneasily. 'Anything else?'

'Ah yes. I foresee success in some business venture, but beware of a dark-haired girl who has designs on you.' She burst out laughing, 'I saw you talking to Bessie Donen,' she said. 'Oh, Billy, if you could see your face! No need to look so serious, it's just a bit of fun, though you should take care about the Donen girl. Not get too friendly with her, I mean.'

Charlie clumped into the room at that moment, lugging the suitcase and wanting to know if he should take it upstairs to the spare room.

'Well, we certainly don't want it in here, do we?' Maudie said impatiently.

Glad of the interruption, William got up from the sofa to retrieve his outdoor things. Maudie took the hint, 'I'd best show you your room, then,' she said. 'I expect you'll want to unpack and get settled before supper?'

'Yes. Thank you, Mrs Thompson.'

His bedroom window overlooked Parker Street. His landlady's cosy influence was evident in the furnishings: the puffy rose pink eiderdown, matching bedspread and curtains; colourful hooked rugs scattered on beige lino floor covering; lavender-sachets in the mahogany wardrobe. A biblical text, *'Thou, God, See'st Me'*, above the marble-topped washstand.

'I hope it's to your liking, that you'll feel comfortable here?' Maudie fussed.

'Yes, it's fine. Very nice indeed.' He smiled at Charlie, hovering in the doorway. 'Thanks for carrying my case upstairs.' The lad blushed, and promptly disappeared.

William wished devoutly that his mother would do the same. He breathed a deep sigh of relief when she finally went away, closing the door behind her, chirruping that supper would be ready at six and she was going to cook something special for him.

When he'd finished his unpacking, he crossed to the window and stared down at the street—a very long street lit with wavering lamplights casting weird shadows on the ice-filmed pavements—wondering if he'd made a mistake in turning his back on his old life with scarcely a backward glance. He'd have been glad, in that moment of loneliness, to have seen Bessie Donen on her stepladder, but she'd have gone indoors ages ago.

The street wasn't entirely deserted, however. Two women stood gossiping on the opposite corner, risking pneumonia in the biting wind, wearing aprons and shawls, arms folded. His mother would be horrified if she saw them. Nice women did not gossip on street corners; a common habit peculiar to the lower classes, in her opinion. But this was a working-class area, William thought, and in no way comparable with Scarborough's upper-crust South Cliff where 'nice' women would meet one another for morning coffee or afternoon tea in the privacy of their drawing rooms—to gossip just as avidly, he imagined.

Then two men appeared, obviously workmen coming home from a hard day's labour judging by their heavy-duty clothing and the bait boxes they had with them, whereupon the two women parted company and went indoors with their respective menfolk to give them their suppers.

It was then he saw a girl, pushing a pram, walking down the street from the direction of the station; a painfully thin young woman shabbily dressed in a brown coat with an upturned collar, a pale, heart-shaped face beneath the brim of an unfashionable brown felt hat.

Not that he could discern her features clearly from a distance, but there was something about her that riveted William's attention—the way she walked, perhaps, as if she had the weight of the world on her shoulders.

Watching her intently, William saw her hesitate momentarily on the doorstep of the Donen house as if considering whether or not to go inside. Then, squaring her shoulders, obviously deciding not to, she walked past it to a house a few doors away where she stood still for a little while before entering—as if she was afraid to enter—as if something terrible awaited her behind that closed front door.

TWO

Despite the five children she had given birth to, Emily Donen's figure remained as slim and supple as a girl's. Apart from a sprinkling of grey hairs, a hint of blurring about her throat and chin, she had changed very little from the way she appeared on her wedding day twenty-five years earlier walking up the aisle of St Cuthbert's Church wearing a tailored grey costume and carrying a prayer-book instead of flowers.

Never one for falderal, she had flatly refused to waste good money on a white dress and veil which she would never wear again. Even then, Emily had possessed that strong core of common sense which Jack Donen found so attractive, filling him with a sense of wonder that he'd managed to woo and win so lovely a woman, a good six inches taller than himself, and far better educated.

Asked why she had chosen to marry him when she could have taken her pick of any number of suitors, 'You have a kind heart', was all she would say.

After the wedding, they had moved into

23 Parker Street, spending the money Emily had refused to squander on a white wedding and honeymoon on paint and wallpaper for their home.

Ten months later, Emily had given birth to their first child. Elizabeth, nicknamed Lizzie. A year later their only son, Richard, put in an appearance, followed at yearly intervals by Madge, Elsie and Bessie. A family for any man to feel proud of, Jack Donen realised, and yet ...

Seated at the kitchen table, watching his wife busy about her preparations for supper, hearing hailstones pattering against the back-room window, Jack Donen's thoughts returned inevitably to his favourite daughter Madge, his reckless wild rose of a girl; reopening an old wound, wondering if she was happy, if they would ever hear from her again?

Thinking about her brought back the intensity of pain, the bitterness he harboured against the man who had ruined an innocent girl's life. If he knew the name of that man he would beat the living daylights out of him—which was precisely why Madge stubbornly refused to name the father of the child she was carrying.

Tossing her head, 'It was my fault as much as his,' she'd cried defiantly. 'I knew I was playing with fire. Well, I got burnt, that's all.'

'We'll see about that!' Playing the heavy father. 'I'll find out his name right enough, and when I do—'

'It's no use, Pa! Wild horses wouldn't drag it out of me!' Her voice had broken in a sob. 'In any case, he's married to someone else.'

Emily had taken over then. Gathering the weeping girl into her arms, 'Too late for tears now,' she'd said calmly, 'and you, Jack, had best save your breath to cool your porridge. Our girl's in trouble so it's up to us to help her as best we can. Just one thing, Madge, I want your word of honour that you will never see this man again.'

'I promise, Ma. Never again!'

And so Emily had stood proudly beside their wayward daughter; had walked with her the length of Parker Street, head held high, ignoring the wagging tongues of the neighbours at the so-called 'respectable' end of the street where the women religiously sandstoned their doorsteps and hung out their washing first thing on a Monday morning—unlike the slatterns at the lower end, whose homes in close proximity to the Ox public house were filthy with neglect; women to whom unwanted pregnancies were a fact of life. But Emily had known, as she ran the gauntlet of unsympathetic eyes, that

33

even those less-inhibited denizens of Lower Parker Street derived a grim satisfaction from the downfall of a lass from the snobby end of the street.

All that was in the past now. Just as well perhaps that Madge's baby had been stillborn, that their girl would not be lumbered with her mistake. Jack Donen consoled himself. Given time, he was sure Madge would forget the tragedy which had overshadowed her young life. But he was wrong. Pale and listless, Madge had hung about the house like a ghost, a shadow of her former happy self.

Then, out of the blue, she had begged him to write to her uncle and aunt in America; asking them if she could stay with them for a while—a few months at the most.

'*America?*' Dumbstruck. 'Have you any idea how much that would cost?' Jack had demurred. 'No, it's out of the question. Emily, *you* talk to her, try to make her see sense.'

But the clear-sighted Emily came straight to the heart of the matter. Seemingly impervious to Madge's tears, she'd said calmly, 'That man, the father of your child, has started pestering you again, hasn't he?'

'*Yes!* Yes, he has if you must know! If I don't get far enough away from him, no telling what might happen!'

'In which case, Jack,' Emily had decreed, 'you must write to Phil and Flo at once. We'll scrape up the fare somehow.'

And so Madge had gone to America, wearing a new dress and coat her mother had made for her, a steamship ticket to New York in her handbag. Jack, who had escorted her to Southampton, would never forget that leavetaking, the lump in his throat, the tears in his eyes as he kissed her goodbye; his last lingering glimpse of her standing near the ship's rail as the vessel left harbour.

At first everything had seemed fine. Madge wrote that Uncle Phil and Aunt Flo were taking good care of her, and she loved New York: Central Park, Coney Island, the El-trains, the bright lights of Broadway. Moreover, she had found herself a job as a saleswoman in a downtown department store.

But the idyll was shortlived. Three months later there came a letter from Jack's brother, Phil, breaking the news that Madge had cleared off to California without a word of explanation, apart from a brief note left on the dressing table in her room saying where she was going and telling them not to worry about her, she'd be fine, just fine.

'*My belief is*', Phil had written, '*she had*

met some man or other she'd taken a shine to. Flo said I was crazy, but I'm not too sure. She'd started acting mysterious, going out, not telling us where she was going; coming in late. I'm sorry, Jack, believe me. Flo and I did our best for her'.

None of them had heard another word from Madge from that day to this.

Emily knew all too well what was on her husband's mind as she plopped suet dumplings into the simmering stew-pot on the kitchen range. Worry over Madge was making him ill, herself too, but life went on. It had to. She was equally worried about poor Lizzie, with a nine-month-old baby and a sick husband to take care of.

Elsie Donen entered the room at that moment. 'Lizzie passed here a few minutes ago,' she volunteered. 'I thought she was going to stop, but she didn't. Happen Tom's feeling poorly again,' she added smugly.

'And if he is, what business is that of yours?' Emily demanded tartly. 'Where's Bessie?'

'Where do you think? Mooning about in the bedroom as usual, looking at herself in the mirror. Honestly, Ma, the way she carries on! It just isn't fair!'

'What isn't fair?'

'Well, *you* know! Working at the Theatre

36

Royal, meeting lots of interesting people, while I'm stuck away in that rotten old milliners' shop on the High Row.'

'There's nothing rotten about a good steady job, my girl, and don't you forget it! Now, just make yourself useful for once, instead of moaning. You can start by setting the table!'

Moving quickly to the foot of the stairs, Emily called up, 'Come down this minute, Bessie! You too, Dicky! Supper's nearly ready, and don't forget, my lad, the coal scuttle needs filling.'

'Coming, Ma!' Dicky Donen, the apple of his mother's eye, glissaded softly down the stairs, flung his arms about her, kissed her soundly on the cheek and hurried off whistling to the coal shed in the yard. Emily smiled to herself, wishing her other offspring were more like him.

Heaving coal into the skep, conscious of his own strength and vigour, Dicky thought of his girl, Beulah, of their becoming engaged when he had saved up enough money for a ring.

The trouble was, his mother did not approve of Beulah. Bringing her to tea the other Sunday afternoon had been a mistake, he knew that now, as if poor Beulah was to blame for what went on in the public bar of the King's Head Hotel. As if it was her fault she'd been on duty the day of the christening, when Lizzie's husband had drunk himself into a stupor.

God, what a shambles that had been! Lizzie, left literally holding the baby, not knowing her husband's whereabouts after the ceremony. He'd been beside her one minute, gone the next, and there was poor Lizzie worried sick, wondering what had become of him. But Dicky knew what had become of Tom right enough, and where to find him. Lizzie had gone back to the house with the christening party to eat the food set out in the front room: sandwiches, sausage rolls and the cake Emily had provided, whilst he and Pa hurried round to the King's Head in search of Tom Imerson.

The day had been ruined. No one except Elsie and Bessie had done justice to the grub. When Jack and Dicky had managed to haul Tom to his mother's house, they'd put him to bed to sleep off the effects of the booze. 'This would happen today of all days,' Jack had said. 'You'd best fetch Lizzie and Mrs Imerson. Ask your mother to take care of the baby for a while and, son, don't make too much of it in front of the others. Just say that Tom's feeling a bit under the weather.'

William was in his room when Charlie

knocked at the door.

'Ma sent me to tell you supper's ready,' he said awkwardly.

'Thanks. I'm coming.'

The lad had removed his headgear to reveal a crop of fair frizzy hair standing above his narrow face like a busby. No wonder the poor kid hadn't a girlfriend, William thought. Poor Charlie was no oil painting, and girls could be cruel to the Charlie Thompsons of the world, just as people could be cruel to enemy aliens like Maurice Schiller.

Maudie had set the table near the bay window with a white cloth and numerous cork mats. 'We usually have our meals in the kitchen apart from Sundays,' she said. 'But this being a special occasion ...' Leaving the sentence unfinished, she glanced at him flirtatiously. 'Well, you know what I mean? Our first evening together.'

William's heart sank. The last thing he'd envisaged was sharing his landlady's quarters. He'd imagined a small residents' sitting room where he could be alone to read, write letters, or simply relax. The thought of spending his evenings tête-à-tête with Mrs Thompson was more than he could bear.

No use beating about the bush, he realised. He said lightly, not wishing to cause offence yet determined to settle the matter there and then. 'The fact is, I usually go out in the evenings for a drink and a game of billiards. Which reminds me, have you a spare key?' He smiled disarmingly. 'I wouldn't dream of disturbing you if I happen to come in late.'

Maudie's charm deserted her momentarily. 'All my lodgers have spare keys,' she said huffily. 'Not all of them make a habit of coming in late. I hope you won't prove an exception to the rule. This, need I remind you, is a respectable house, and Charlie and me keep respectable hours, with the shop opening early and all.'

'I never meant to suggest otherwise,' William said mildly. Changing the subject adroitly, 'By the way, something smells good.'

'Yes, well, I do keep a good table though I do say so myself,' Maudie replied, somewhat if not entirely mollified by his reference to the smell of liver and onions floating through from the kitchen. 'Now, where's Charlie got to? I shall need a hand with the dishing up!'

'Perhaps I could help?' William suggested, but Maudie wouldn't hear of it.

'No, you sit down and wait. I'll give him a shout ... Char*lie!*' she bellowed up the stairs, 'come down here at once!'

William sat down, as requested. Presently, Maudie appeared from the kitchen with the plates of liver and onions, followed by Charlie carrying tureens of steaming vegetables which he plonked on the table missing the cork mats by a mile, to his mother's scarcely concealed irritation.

'How many times do I have to tell you not to put hot dishes on the cloth?' Maudie berated him. 'What do you suppose the cork mats are for?'

Charlie blushed to the roots of his unfortunate hairstyle. 'They was burning me fingers,' he muttered. 'Sorry, Ma.'

All charm once more, 'Charlie's got such a sensitive skin,' she explained, dolloping mashed potatoes, carrots and gravy onto the plates. 'He favours me in that respect, don't you love?'

The boy flinched. Maudie rattled on. 'His colouring is mine too. Funny really, his father's hair was quite dark, and he was ever so handsome ...'

Glancing across the table at the boy's downcast face, William realised the depth of Charlie's humiliation that he in no way resembled his father, and experienced an overwhelming sense of pity for the lad.

Suddenly, Charlie pushed away his plate, splattering the tablecloth with gravy, and rushed out of the room. Maudie smiled. She said calmly, 'He always gets upset

when I talk about hs father. I can't
think why.'

William knew why. It must be sheer
hell for a lad of his age to be constantly
compared, to his detriment, with the late
lamented Jim Thompson, none of whose
genes—colouring, physique, intelligence or
good looks—he had inherited.

Maudie returned from the kitchen with
a home-made apple pie and a jug of
custard. 'The trouble with Charlie is
that he likes nothing better than to draw
attention to himself. Knowing him, he'll
come downstairs later to finish his supper,
the artful young monkey. I just wish I
knew what to do about those awful spots
of his.'

'I had acne at his age,' William said.
'It was about the time I was beginning to
shave.'

'Beginning to shave?' Maudie burst into
peals of laughter. 'Who? Charlie? Why, he
wouldn't know one end of a razor from
the other!'

It was then William decided that
he'd had enough of Maudie Thompson's
company for the time being and requested,
politely, the door-key she'd promised him.

The unease, the restlessness he'd experienced in the cloying warmth of Mrs
Thompson's drawing room, fell away from

William as he walked quickly to the less salubrious end of Parker Street, gulping in fresh air like a man starved of oxygen for the past twenty-four hours. Despite the bitter wind blowing in his face, all he knew or cared about was the blessed feeling of being alone at last in a new environment: free to come to terms with himself, to explore the possibilities of a town where the night sky was stained red from the furnaces of steelworks, from which sprung the town's industrial wealth and security.

At the lower end of Parker Street, he noticed the lights of a public house spilling onto the ice-filmed pavement; heard the sound of music and laughter, of people having a good time. But the pub looked seedy, with peeling paintwork and a dirty doorstep, and he turned away again.

Walking on, he came to an iron bridge spanning a turgid stream. Lingering a while near the parapet, gazing down into the dark, slowly moving water, he thought about Mrs Thompson and her son Charlie, wondering how soon he could decently move away from the corner shop. Move to where? Perhaps, when he'd got his bearings, he might rent a cheap room somewhere; look after himself for a change, do his own washing, cooking and cleaning, please himself entirely. Come and go as he wished? Yes, he'd like that very much.

A woman sidled up to him. 'Lookin' for a bit of company are you, dearie?' she asked. 'You'd find it well worth your while, I'm sure.'

Startled, 'I, er, that is, thank you, but I'm meeting someone,' he lied desperately.

'Oh? Not good enough for yer, am I? Well bugger off then. See if I care.' The woman turned away.

'No, please. Here, treat yourself to a drink.' William gave her a shilling, hating to see anyone down on their luck.

Crossing the bridge towards a market square and a church, he suddenly remembered the girl with the pram he had seen that afternoon.

The High Row, described by Fred Willis as the finest street he had come across in the trail of northern towns that marked his territory, came as a disappointment to William at first sight.

No signs of bustling atmosphere were apparent on this freezing cold night, but there were some fine buildings and a unique architectural feature inasmuch as the street was built on two levels: the shops and houses on the upper level linked to the lower by a series of steps running the length of the thoroughfare.

Well, what had he expected to see? Crowds of merrymakers abroad on a chill winter evening? What he needed was a drink in a warmly-lit atmosphere, which he intended to have, recalling Fred's fondness for the public bar of the King's Head Hotel.

The barmaid polishing glasses spotted him the moment he walked in: wondered who he was and where he had sprung from? He wasn't one of her regulars whom she made a point of calling by name. Men, in her experience, liked that touch of flattery, especially the old buffers who enjoyed a mild flirtation with a pretty young girl across the beer pumps.

The barmaid knew she was pretty. She had only to look at herself in the mirror behind the bar to convince herself of that, to catch sight of her pert young face, lustrous eyes, abundant dark, upswept hair, and the firm contours of her breasts beneath the high-collared white blouse she habitually wore on duty.

'You're new here, aren't you?' she asked William, pulling him a pint of beer, her approach friendly, direct, but not too forward. 'I mean, you ain't one of my regulars. I know most of them by name. Mind if I ask yours?'

Enjoying the encounter, the atmosphere of warmth and camaraderie after the coldness of the world outside, he said jokingly, 'My name's Billy.'

'Mine's Beulah. Beulah Cammish, for the time being at any rate. Me and my fellah are getting married next summer, God willing. My name'll be Beulah Donen then, if the big soft ha'porth saves up enough money for the ring.'

'Donen?' William's interest quickened.

'Yes. Why? Don't tell me you know him? A big fair-haired chap? Works at The Forge? Lives in Parker Street?'

'No, but I think I've met his sister.'

'Which one?' Resting her elbows on the bar, 'He's got four of them, you know?'

'The one called Bessie.'

'Oh *her!* The fat one!' Beulah sniffed disdainfully. 'Goes after every man she meets, does Bessie! Works as an usherette at the Theatre Royal. Thinks she's God's gift to mankind!'

'What about the other three sisters?' William asked as casually as he could, despite the swift beating of his heart as he remembered the girl with the pram who had hovered momentarily on the Donens' doorstep.

A gossip by nature, Beulah warmed to the subject. 'Well, there's Elsie who works in a hat-shop on the High Row—a right miserable little cat if ever there was one, forever complaining about this and that, and as plain as a pikestaff into the bargain.

46

'Then there was Madge, the one who got herself into trouble with a married man and went off to America to get over the shame of it, though where she is now is anyone's guess. The last they heard of her, she'd gone to California to live with some bloke or other, I shouldn't wonder.

'Mind you,' Beulah lowered her voice confidentially, 'it's poor Lizzie Imerson I feel sorry for. The one with the baby. I was here on duty, you see, the day of the christening, when her husband, Tom Imerson, came into the bar about lunchtime to drink himself blotto, the silly sod!

'What a shemozzle *that* caused you wouldn't believe! Dicky and his pa, Jack Donen, had a devil of a struggle with him, I can tell you, before they managed to drag him out of here, cursing and blinding like a trooper, the poor bloke.

'Dicky told me afterwards they'd had to put him to bed. And all the time there was poor Lizzie at her mother's house at the christening party for friends and neighbours, not knowing what had become of him, why he had disappeared from the church the way he did, without a word of explanation.

'She found out soon enough, poor lass, that her husband was an alcoholic. Any other girl in her right senses would have

47

left him then and there, I dare say. But
not Lizzie ... Oh, if you'll excuse me for
just a minute, there's a customer needs
serving.' Beulah tripped away to the other
end of the bar counter, pausing to check
her appearance in the mirror, to smooth
back a stray wisp of hair and straighten
the collar of her blouse.

When, in due course, she returned to
William's end of the bar to continue
her discourse on the Donen family's
misfortunes, all she found there was a
half-empty beer glass.

Walking out into the cold night air, pausing
momentarily to look up at the stars shining
like diamonds in a red velvet sky, William
thought about Bessie Donen's sister, the
one called Lizzie, whose husband had
drunk himself into oblivion on the day
of their baby's christening.

THREE

Maudie's complexion looked far less dazzling
by the kitchen's glass-shaded gas-mantles
and the even colder light of a winter
morning filtering through the white lace
curtains.

She had slept badly and came down to cook breakfast in a bad temper, fuming over William's cavalier treatment of her the night before. She had gone to no end of trouble cooking him a tasty supper, and had planned a cosy evening together in front of the fire with a nice bottle of sweet sherry to loosen his inhibitions, and all he had done was make a fuss about a door-key and gone out for a drink and a game of billiards, leaving her high and dry. A slap in the face if ever there was one, the ungrateful young pup.

Charlie had already had his breakfast and gone downstairs to open the shop in readiness for the first customers of the day, mainly workmen wanting cigarettes; an encounter which had added to her rising feeling of irritation at her son's appearance, his acne-scarred face beneath that ridiculous flat cap he insisted on wearing to hide his busby of frizzy fair hair, the way he had wolfed down his food without a word, not even a civil 'good-morning' or a 'thank you'.

Soon William would be wanting *his* breakfast, Maudie thought, glancing at the clock. Well, he could sit and wait for it for all she cared, and serve him damn well right if he was late for work on his first morning. Even so, she had her reputation as a caring landlady to maintain, besides which he was a friend of Fred's and devilishly handsome to boot; in need of guidance from an experienced older woman, perhaps, to file down his rough edges? If only she'd had time, earlier on, to apply her Velouty-de-Dixor face cream, Bourjois rouge and Snowfire powder. Too late now to repair the ravages wrought by a sleepless night. She had, at least, had time to put on her corsets and brassiere, stockings, and her new pink peignoir, a seductive garment if ever there was one.

When William entered the kitchen as hungry as a hunter, anticipating a good breakfast, he stared first at Maudie Thompson's pink peignoir, then, with a sinking heart, at the dried-up egg, burnt sausages and two wizened strips of bacon on the plate she set before him, not knowing where to begin to tackle the abomination.

'So, William, where did you get to last night?' Maudie asked, pouring him a cup of stewed tea. 'Anywhere in particular?'

Chivvying the grub round his plate, speaking through a mouthful of leathery egg which he could scarcely bring himself to swallow, 'Well yes,' he explained, 'I discovered the whereabouts of Mr Schiller's shop in Skinnergate for one thing, which seemed a sensible thing to do in the circumstances.'

'I could have shown you the way myself, if only you'd asked me to accompany you,' Maudie reminded him, sniffing becomingly into a lace-edged hanky retrieved from the pocket of her peignoir. 'I felt so deeply wounded, so humiliated that you didn't want my company after all I'd done to make you feel welcome in my home.'

Strung on the horns of a dilemma, unsure of what to do or say to placate the tearful Maudie, William took the coward's way out. Glancing at the clock, he said, 'I really must be off now if I'm to get to work on time.'

'But you haven't finished your breakfast!'

'No, well I'm not all that hungry.' Laying down his knife and fork. 'Now, if you'll excuse me.' He rose to his feet in a hurry.

But Maudie Thompson, like Bessie Donen, was not prepared to let go of him that easily. Blocking his exit from the kitchen by the simple expedient of standing in front of him and laying her hands on his shoulders, 'Please kiss me goodbye, Billy,' Maudie whispered intently, 'just to show there's no ill feeling.'

A man of the world would have known how to deal with the situation. But then, a man of the world might have been inured

51

to being clung to by a half-dressed woman in the early hours of the morning, eyes closed, holding up her face to be kissed. By no means a man of the world, William took fright.

Thrusting her hands aside he rushed out of the house by the side door as if the devil was after him, struggling into his overcoat and jamming on his hat as he ran the gauntlet of women clearing snow from their doorsteps who stared at him as though he had taken leave of his senses. Deeply humiliated that he had handled a tricky situation so badly and dreading a recurrence, he knew that he must get away from the corner shop and his predatory landlady as soon as possible, but if he did leave Parker Street he might never see Lizzie Imerson again. Why this seemed important to him he had no clear idea, he simply knew that it did.

He arrived ten minutes late for work. Maurice Schiller, grey haired, slightly built, of dapper appearance, regarded him coldly. Taking out his pocket watch, 'You are late. On your first morning, you are late,' he said. 'Perhaps you think this old German is not worthy of correct timekeeping?' His accent betrayed his origins, and he pronounced his w's as v's, the word is as iss.

'No, Mr Schiller, I'm sorry, I meant no disrespect. I missed my way. It won't happen again.'

'Very well then. Now hang up your coat in the cupboard, put on your overall and make a start on the basins.'

William looked stricken. In his headlong flight from Maudie's embrace he had forgotten his overall, comb, scissors and clippers, which he had left upstairs in his room. For the second time within minutes he found himself apologising to his employer, thinking the rate he was going he might well be given the sack before he'd even started work.

'What is it you have on your shoulders, a head or a turnip?' the old man asked, his voice heavy with sarcasm. 'What is going on in your mind, if you have one? I think I can guess, this old man is a foreigner, therefore a fool, *nicht wahr?*' So saying, shaking his head, he went through a door marked 'Private' which he closed firmly behind him.

The shop was small and chilly. Dampness hung in the air: a smell of mouldiness and disuse. The floor was covered with shabby green oilcloth, the walls painted a depressing shade of green. There were two shampoo basins, two barber chairs, a showcase containing dusty bottles of Bay Rum and hair tonic. The shampoo sprays lay dull and inert, like flaccid snakes, in the grimy basins. The place reeked of neglect. Rolling back his sleeves, William set to work.

Finding cloths, a bucket and a block of bathbrick in the cupboard, first he cleaned the basins and sprays with hot water from the geyser, scraping away a detritus of congealed soap from the corners of the basins where it had lodged. That done, he washed the shaving mugs and brushes and dusted the showcase. He was on his hands and knees washing the floor when Schiller reappeared from his private quarters.

'Wilhelm,' he said quietly, 'I have the apology to make. I make you feel small, yes? I want that you should forgive me. The war is to blame. So much mistrust there is in the world today. Come, stop what you are doing. I have prepared for you the coffee.'

Drying his hands, William followed Schiller into a small room furnished with a table, a camp-bed, chairs, several pictures and photographs and a gas-ring on which stood an enamel pan containing a bubbling liquid almost black in colour, the smell of which permeated the tiny apartment.

Pouring the coffee into chipped enamel mugs, one of which he handed to William, 'You will find it too strong, perhaps?' the old man said quizzically, 'but this is the way I prefer it. The way we used to drink it many years ago in Germany, when I was a boy of your age.'

Taking a sip, 'No, it's fine, sir, thank you.' William would have been glad of anything at that moment to dispel the gnawing hunger pains in his stomach.

'So, you are staying with Mrs Thompson?' A teasing smile quirked Schiller's lips. 'An attractive woman, yes?'

'You could put it like that, I suppose.' William said cagily.

The old man snorted derisively, 'She is a man-eater, that one: Tell me, Wilhelm, did you sleep with her last night?'

'Good God, no!' William spluttered his coffee. 'The thought never entered my head!'

'I imagine it entered hers,' Schiller chuckled. 'Possibly you will do so tonight?'

'Certainly not! Why, she's old enough to be my mother!'

'What has age to do with it?' Schiller cocked his head enquiringly. 'Would it surprise you to know that I have slept with her, and I am old enough to be her grandfather?' He paused. 'I should not have told you perhaps? I did so for a reason. You are young, Wilhelm. In time you will come to understand the loneliness of growing old, the need of human warmth, as I have done. This is true also of the Frau Thompsons of the world, faced with the fear of losing their youth and beauty, in constant need of assurance that this is not so. You understand what I am trying to tell you?'

'I think so, but I came here to make a new life for myself, to get away from—women.' William smiled ruefully, 'Three of them to be exact: my mother and my two sisters. The last thing I want is another "keeper".' He paused awkwardly, 'I'm sorry, Herr Schiller, but I am not prepared to be eaten alive just yet.'

'Then what do you intend to do about it?'

'I'm not quite sure. Find a place of my own to live, I suppose, when I've got my bearings. I have a little money of my own: my Army gratuity, so I'm not entirely skint.'

'Skint? What is skint?'

'Well, you know, broke, on my beam ends? What I mean is, I could afford to get a room somewhere, if I could pluck up enough courage to tell Mrs Thompson I was leaving. She'd be dreadfully upset and so would I.'

'Ach yes, I understand perfectly your dilemma,' the old man said shrewdly. 'Now I think it is time you went back to work.'

'Yes, of course. Thanks for the coffee.'

When William had gone, Schiller picked up a framed daguerrotype of a young man taken many years ago, discerning a fleeting resemblance between two young men born years apart and in different countries, who nevertheless had a great deal in common.

The morning dragged abominably. Not one customer had entered the shop. Why Herr Schiller felt in need of an assistant, William had no idea. Even so he kept himself busy stropping razors, refilling the shampoo bottles and cleaning the windows inside and out, trying his best not to concentrate on the hunger pains in his stomach, his inedible breakfast and his nymphomaniac landlady; certain now that she wanted him not as a lodger but a lover.

At one o'clock, the start of his lunch hour, William walked along Skinnergate so ravenously hungry that, nearing a butcher's shop and seeing a pyramid of hot pork pies in the window, he rushed in, bought a couple and stood unashamedly in a shop doorway to eat them: uncaring of the rich gravy running down his chin, biting hard into the meat and pastry, thinking that he had never tasted anything so good in his life before. At the same time wondering what his mother would say if she could see him now, her precious, well-brought up son wolfing hot pork pies in a shop doorway, breaking every rule of civilised human behaviour.

He could not have cared less. He was young, he was hungry, a stranger in a strange town, so what the hell did it matter? His spirits soared suddenly. This was freedom!

Later that afternoon, a carriage drew to a halt outside the shop, a one-horse vehicle in the charge of a surly looking driver who hopped down from his perch to open the door for his passenger.

The man who came into the shop was tall, thickset, well dressed, abrupt in manner. 'Give me a shave, and be quick about it,' he demanded. 'I haven't got all day!'

'Certainly, sir.'

Wearing an overall borrowed from his employer and several sizes too small for him, William ran the hot water, whipped up a good head of foam in the shaving-mug, stropped the razor and set to work on the man's beard, noticing as he did so his client's heavily veined cheeks and pouched eyelids, the throbbing of a muscle near his left eye and the unmistakable smell of whisky on the man's breath.

Suddenly, Schiller emerged from the adjoining room, a smile of recognition on his lips. 'Ah, Sir Miles,' he said softly, 'it is good to see you again after all this time. I trust that you are well?'

The man in the chair opened his eyes. 'The state of my health is no concern of yours,' he said offensively. 'I came here for a shave, not to fraternise with the enemy, is that clear?'

The old man turned away. William's hand trembled on the razor he was holding close to the man's Adam's apple. 'That's enough!' Sir Miles rose swiftly to his feet. Wiping away the rest of the foam with a hand-towel. 'You, barber, incompetent fool that you are,' he demanded angrily, 'hand me my coat and hat! A child could have shaved me better!'

'Let him go, Wilhelm,' Schiller said sadly, shaking his head.

'But he hasn't paid! I've a good mind to ... The drunken swine! Who does he think he is?'

'His name is Jessington, Sir Miles Jessington.' Schiller's face crumpled. 'He was a client of mine before the war, that so terrible war that turned friends into enemies.'

'Then some good came out of it! That man was never a friend of yours, the arrogant devil!' Filled with a burning sense of injustice on Schiller's behalf, William would have liked nothing better than to

59

speed Jessington on his way with a well aimed kick in the backside.

Snow was beginning to fall quite thickly as Fred Willis emerged from Bank Top Station.

He had packed his samples, strapped his heavy suitcase and left his Newcastle digs at four o'clock that afternoon. His landlady, Mrs Marble, whose Victorian boarding house admitted a constant stream of commercial travellers, had evinced no surprise at his leaving so suddenly. Inured to the ways of her 'gentlemen'. 'Not much doing at this time of year, I expect?' she'd asked, receipting his bill.

'You never said a truer. Selling ladies' lingerie after Christmas is like trying to sell igloos to Eskimos! Never mind, eh? The patent medicine blokes are having a field day. Things will pick up for me come Easter, when the sap begins to rise and you ladies start buying your spring outfits.' He'd grinned amiably. 'Well, toodle-oo. See you next month.'

Snow had been threatening all the way from Newcastle. Thankfully it wasn't far from the station to Maudie's corner shop. Soon he'd be sitting all snug and warm in front of her fire, certain of a warm welcome, a good hot meal. Well, a meal anyway. Maudie wasn't much of a cook, but what did that matter? There were other, more important things than food.

Hurrying down Parker Street, he thought about those more important things—the way Maudie looked getting ready for bed, for instance, her hair about her shoulders, wearing a negligée, driving him mad with impatience as she fiddled about in front of the dressing table, creaming her hands and face. Then, 'For God's sake stop messing about', he'd say to her, and she'd giggle and come to him all warm and yielding. A funny thing, really. The softer the woman the harder the man.

Dreading his return to Maudie Thompson's fireside, William paused for a while on the Skerne Bridge at the lower end of Parker Street. Staring down into the murky water, he saw by flickering gaslight the carcass of a drowned cat washed up on a mudbank at the river's edge alongside a detritus of empty beer-bottles, carelessly flung cigarette packets and a buckled and rusted bicycle frame; all of which served to deepen his present mood of depression.

Now, to make matters worse, it was snowing quite heavily, the rapidly descending flakes driven by a bitter north-east wind and interspersed with sleet so that the snow turned to slush the minute it hit the ground. Frankly, he had never felt so wet, so vulnerable, so miserable in his life before. But then, he had never been relentlessly pursued by a sexually motivated older woman before.

His encounters with the opposite sex had so far amounted to nothing more spectacular than a series of mild flirtations with girls of his own age, a few stolen kisses on their way home from a dance or a party. He had neither the skill nor the inclination to cope with the likes of Mrs Thompson, whose sole aim appeared to be to get him into bed with her.

Deep in thought, he scarcely noticed the girl coming towards him until, 'Hello,' she called out to him. 'Well, fancy meeting you again!'

'I'm sorry, I ...'

'Don't recognise me, do you?' she chirruped. 'I'm Bessie. Bessie Donen, remember?'

'Oh yes. Yes, of course! How are you, Bessie?'

'Fine, just fine! How's yourself?'

'Fine, just fine,' William replied, lying through his teeth.

Bessie stared at him doubtfully from beneath her umbrella and the red crocheted head-shawl covering her fringe of brown frizzy hair. 'You don't look all that fine,' she commented sharply. 'More like you'd lost a bob and found a tanner.'

Not really caring one way or the other, 'So where are you off to in this weather?' William asked her.

'To work, of course, at the Theatre Royal, and I'd best get a move on or I'll be late for the First House!'

'So you're an—actress?' William stared at her bemusedly.

'No, of course not, daft-head!' Bessie laughed, showing her prominent front teeth. 'I'm an usherette! Mind you, I wouldn't mind being an actress, receiving all them flowers an' suchlike, an' with lots of posh fellas queuing up at the stage door wanting to treat me to oyster and champagne suppers.'

Deeply aware of rivulets of snow and sleet sneaking past his upturned coat collar, shivering slightly, 'Well, I mustn't keep you talking any longer,' William responded, 'it was nice meeting you again.'

'No, don't rush away so soon!' Laying a restraining hand on his arm, Bessie continued, 'What say we take a walk together in the park next Sunday afternoon? You could come to tea at our house afterwards, if you like. Meet my family.'

'Your—family?'

'Yes, of course. Why not?'

Why not, indeed? With a modicum of luck, William decided quickly, he might well come face to face with Bessie's sister Lizzie.

'Very well, then,' he said, 'Sunday afternoon it is. What time?'

Scarcely believing her good luck, Bessie laughed delightedly. 'How about three o'clock, outside the main gates of the South Park? You won't forget, will you?'

'No, Bessie, I'll be there, I promise.'

'So long, then, William.'

'So long, Bessie.'

She wasn't such a bad little lass after all, William thought, hurrying back to his lodgings. Besides which, he could now tell Maudie Thompson, if the subject arose, that he was already 'spoken for': that he was deeply attracted to another woman ...

Entering the house by the side door, he heard a familiar bellow of laughter. A laugh he would have known anywhere. Taking the stairs two at a time, he burst into the sitting room to discover Fred and Maudie standing close together in front of the fire.

'Billy Boy!' Crossing the room in a couple of strides, Fred flung a welcoming arm round William's shoulders. 'How are you, old sport? Hey, Maudie, pour the silly young sod a glass of sherry, he's wetter than a duck! Hey, Billy Boy, don't tell me you took a swim in the Skerne on your way home?'

William could have cried with relief. Trust dear old Fred to turn up in the nick of time.

FOUR

The prospect of a twosome had been unbearable. The actuality of a threesome proved even worse. Embarrassing to say the least, with Maudie flirting outrageously with Fred and giving William the cold-shoulder to the extent that even Fred had given up trying to draw him into the conversation.

After supper, Charlie bolted upstairs to his room to play his gramophone records to Maudie's annoyance as strains of 'The Sheikh of Araby' floated down the staircase. 'If I've told him once, I've told him a hundred times not to keep on playing that damn record,' she said angrily.

'Aw, come on, Maudie, live and let live,' Fred laughed, lighting a cheroot. 'What harm is he doing? Everyone's gotta relax once in a while, and that includes you. You too, Billy Boy!'

But 'Billy Boy' couldn't relax. He said,

'If you'll excuse me, I think I'll get a breath of fresh air, then have an early night.'

Fred followed him down to the hall. 'Look here, old son,' he said awkwardly, 'the fact is that Maudie and me have a kind of—understanding. To put it bluntly, we sleep together whenever I'm here. Does that shock you?'

'No, not at all! She *is* a very attractive woman when all's said and done.'

Regarding him shrewdly, 'You haven't quite cottoned on to her though, have you, Billy Boy? Any particular reason why not?'

A loaded question. 'No, not really,' William prevaricated, 'except that I'd rather like to find a place of my own to live. What I mean is—'

'Not to worry, old pal, I know exactly what you mean,' Fred interrupted sagely, 'but that's the way she's made. It happens all the time with women of a certain age. Not that I care tuppence about that. I really love her, you see? And I intend to marry her one of these days. All right? So just you go ahead with your own plans. Find yourself a place to live, and don't worry about telling Maudie you're leaving. She'll take it in her stride, believe me.'

'Thanks Fred, but I haven't anywhere else to go for the time being.'

'Then the sooner you start looking the

better,' Fred advised him. 'You could always stay at the Christian Association's hostel till you find something more permanent. Or have you thought of asking old Schiller?'

'What? Sleep in the shop you mean?' William grinned, heartened by Fred's understanding.

'No, you daft ha'porth, he has plenty of rooms upstairs. The house was requisitioned during the war, so happen it'll be in a bit of a state. The Army was supposed to put it to rights when the war was over, but with him being a Jerry, I don't suppose they was in a hurry. That's why he camps down in the room behind the shop, poor old devil.'

Maudie's voice floated down from the sitting room. 'Fred! What are you doing? What's all the whispering about?' She sounded none too pleased.

Fred rolled his eyes. 'Women, eh? I'd best not keep her waiting. She's in one of her moods. Listen, mate, shall I drop her a hint you're leaving?'

'No, I'll tell her myself when I get something settled.' Putting on his outdoor things from the hallstand, 'How long will you be here, Fred?' William asked.

'Till the end of the week, I reckon.'

'Great!' With Fred in the house, he'd be spared the amorous advances of Mrs

67

Thompson at breakfast tomorrow morning and thereafter, William thought, whistling under his breath as he stepped outside into the cold night air.

The porridge had stiffened to the consistency of wallpaper paste when William went down to breakfast next morning, but at least Maudie was fully booted and spurred this time, and wearing her full complement of rouge and powder.

She said frostily, not beating about the bush. 'It's plain to see that you are not happy here. Frankly, you have thrown kindness in my face. And to think I mistook you for a gentleman!'

'I'm sorry, I don't understand—'

'Then understand this! The high-handed way you demanded a key was not the act of a gentleman in my opinion. You rudely rejected my hospitality. Yesterday, you left the food I had cooked for you at breakfast practically untouched. Besides which, the way you eyed me up and down was nothing short of—disgusting! Oh, I could read your mind like a book! You wished to take advantage of me, didn't you? Well, *didn't* you?'

Sensing an escape route, taking the wind out of his landlady's sails, 'You are perfectly right, of course, Mrs Thompson,' William admitted, getting up from the table, at the same time wondering if the hot meat pie shop would be open this early in the morning. 'I have behaved badly, so now I'd best go upstairs and pack my belongings and, if you'll be kind enough to tell me how much I owe you, I'll pay you on my way out.'

Incensed, Maudie called after him, 'I shall charge you for a full week, make no mistake about that! Huh! You stuck up young prig, you! Well, I shall tell Fred about this! A fine friend of his you've turned out to be!'

Ignoring the tirade, William went up to his room to begin packing, at which point Fred appeared on the landing in his dressing gown and slippers, yawning and scratching his head, wanting to know what the row was about.

'Let's put it this way,' William said, 'I've told Mrs Thompson I'm leaving, not at the end of the week but now ...'

'Oh, God,' Fred commented wearily, 'so where exactly do you intend going?'

William grinned, 'To that butcher's shop in Skinnergate for a couple of hot meat pies,' he said cheerfully.

'You will keep in touch, won't you?' Fred enquired anxiously. 'Tell you what,' *sotto voce*, 'I'll meet you in the King's Head at one o'clock. All right, Billy Boy?'

'All right, Fred,' William agreed.

He'd struck lucky for once. Schiller had been startled when he'd appeared at the shop lumping his suitcase, and with a morsel of pie crust adhering to his lower lip. 'Mein Gott, Wilhelm!' he said in amazement. 'What has happened?'

'I've left home!'

'So it would seem. Come, I have made the coffee. Bring the case with you and tell me how this came about.'

Over a pint of beer in the King's Head, William told Fred that Schiller had offered him temporary accommodation over the shop. Albeit run down, the room was habitable with a bed, a gas-fire, a chair or two, and a table.

Fred sighed deeply, wiping his moustache, feeling guilty that he had been instrumental in persuading William to leave Scarborough in the first place and landing him in his present predicament. It had all seemed so clear-cut and logical at the time. Now he wasn't so sure, and said so. 'I should have kept my nose out of your affairs. You had a comfortable home, a good job. Now look at you! No settled home, with a job not worth mentioning.'

'What about—freedom?' William smiled reflectively. 'If it hadn't been for you, I would never have begun to stand on my own two feet, make my own decisions, my own mistakes. All right, I'll admit things haven't gone smoothly so far, but I have no regrets about leaving home. I like Darlington, it's a great town. Herr Schiller, too! I want to build up his business once more, for his sake, knowing how much that would mean to him; keep everything clean and sparkling; repaint his barber's pole, for instance: smarten things up, show people he's back in business.'

William's enthusiasm was infectious. Fred laughed. 'That's the stuff to give 'em, Billy Boy! Time for another pint, eh? No? Well, never mind. Maudie doesn't know I'm here. I sneaked out when she wasn't looking.'

He paused. 'About Maudie, Billy Boy. I'm no fool, or perhaps I am, feeling the way I do about her? The truth is, there's no rhyme or reason when it comes to falling in love. Either you love someone or you don't. It's as simple as that. And I love Maudie, warts and all! What more can I say?'

Bessie was at the park gates well ahead of time, strung between intense excitement at the prospect of seeing William again and a kind of nervous despair that he might not show up at all. In which case she'd look a right fool, and Dicky and Elsie

71

would make her life a misery. Ma and Pa wouldn't be best pleased either. Who was the man she was meeting? they'd wanted to know. What did he do for a living? And what did she mean, she didn't know? Was he some fly-by-night she'd met at the theatre? This was all Madge's fault, Bessie thought, walking up and down to keep warm, getting herself into trouble the way she had done and leaving other folk to bear the brunt. At least she'd invited her young man to tea, which was more than Madge ever had.

Then, oh glory be, William was crossing the road towards her. Self-consciously, Bessie felt the front of her hair to make sure her fringe hadn't gone flat, and settled her wool tam-o-shanter more securely on her head.

There wasn't much doing in the park at this time of year, nothing much to see either apart from a few patches of snowdrops beneath withered-looking trees. Even the ducks paddling about on the lake looked frozen, and it was far too cold to sit in one of the shelters as Bessie had imagined they might, unless of course William felt like a kiss and a cuddle and suggested a bit of a sit down along the way. But even the romantically-minded Bessie realised the improbability of his suggesting any such thing. He was, after all, a gentleman.

Ebullient by nature, Bessie did most of the talking. Smiling politely, William did the listening, at the same time wondering why he had agreed to this assignation in the first place? Deep down, he knew why—in the hope of meeting Lizzie Imerson later, at the Donens' tea-table.

Feeling guilty, the thought occurred that he was using poor Bessie as a kind of trojan horse. If only she'd stop chattering on and on like a parakeet about the Theatre; stop clinging to his arm so tightly as if he was, somehow, her property. He was nobody's property. He'd had enough of all that for the time being, what with his mother, two sisters, and Maudie Thompson putting a hammer-lock on him when all he wanted was freedom to live his life in his own way. Now, apparently, Bessie Donen had joined the queue of females intent on curtailing his actions in some way. But Bessie was just a kid when all was said and done; a silly young lass as proud as Punch to be seen, walking arm-in-arm, with a member of the opposite sex. Surely he could live with that? William reasoned.

Quitting the park, they walked into town to the High Row, where William paused to admire a statue erected to the memory of Joseph Pease, a town benefactor whose father, Edward Pease, according to the inscription tablets at the base of the statue, had been dubbed 'The Father of Railways', which William found tremendously exciting. Bessie thought hanging about looking up at a silly statue she'd seen a hundred times before profoundly boring. Her thoughts centred on home, a warm fire and a well-filled tea-table.

'Oh, do come on, William,' she said pettishly, tugging at his arm, 'we'll be late for tea if we don't hurry! I don't know about you, but I'm freezing cold, and hungry!'

Emily Donen had set tea in the front parlour, on a starched white tablecloth, and with her best violet-embellished china teaset—a wedding present twenty-five years ago—in honour of Bessie's 'young man'; despite her misgivings that Bessie was far too young and daft to start courting in earnest. But at least she and Jack were being given the chance to run the rule over Bessie's 'intended', to which end Emily had spent the whole of the afternoon in the kitchen baking cakes and sausage rolls, Cornish pasties, making jellies and blancmanges and exhorting Dicky and Elsie to be on their best behaviour when

Bessie brought her young man home to tea.

Polishing his shoes in the kitchen beforehand, 'I can't help feeling sorry for the poor devil!' Dicky Donen remarked, remembering the fiasco of his girlfriend's introduction to the family circle. 'He doesn't know what he's letting himself in for, and that's a fact. In my opinion he can't be quite right in the head choosing Bessie as his intended.'

'That's quite enough!' Emily said tartly. 'We shall find out for ourselves, in due course. So just you stop what you're doing and start mending the front room fire.'

'Yes, Ma. But whatever your opinion of Beulah Cammish may be, I'm giving you fair warning, right here and now, that we intend getting married one day. What I mean is, you were all in favour of Lizzie marrying Tom Imerson, and just look at the mess she's in now! So who are you to judge what's right or wrong?'

William crossed the threshold of the Donens' house with a deep-rooted sense of misgiving, as if he was somehow on trial for his life, though he couldn't think why, unless ...

The realisation that he was here under false pretences as Bessie's 'intended', struck him forcibly as he shook hands with her parents, then her brother and sister before being ushered into the front room. *The condemned man ate a hearty meal,* he thought wryly.

He hadn't the faintest idea how to extricate himself from this dilemma. This tea party had set the seal on what might prove to be a dangerous situation. What Bessie had said to lead her parents to believe they were—courting—he couldn't begin to imagine. Why, he'd only seen the girl three times: once cleaning the front room windows, then near the Skerne Bridge when she was on her way to work, and this afternoon in the park. How could she have possibly imagined that he was even vaguely interested in her romantically?

His mistake had lain in accepting her invitation to tea—to meet her family—he knew that now. His own fault entirely. He should have had the sense to refuse.

To his discredit, he'd seen Bessie as an escape route from Maudie's unwelcome attentions by the simple expedient of telling her he was otherwise engaged. The irony lay in the fact that, had he known Fred Willis had put in an appearance at the corner shop, he need not have lumbered himself with Bessie at all. Yet innate honesty forced him to admit that he had desperately wanted to meet Bessie's sister, Lizzie Imerson, face to face, as a flesh and blood human being, not a mere shadow glimpsed by gaslight. But she wasn't even here.

Seated at the head of the table pouring the tea, Emily Donen said levelly, 'So, Mr Chalmers, you are a newcomer to Darlington?' She smiled, 'What brought you here?'

He said awkwardly, 'The fact is, I felt in need of a change.'

'A change from what?' Jack Donen asked abruptly.

'My old lifestyle, I suppose,' William admitted.

'Why? What was wrong with it?'

'A great deal from my point of view. Otherwise I wouldn't have felt inclined to leave it to make a fresh start elsewhere,' William prevaricated, unwilling to satisfy his host's curiosity.

Emily shot a warning glance at her husband before he upset the applecart, sensing that William resented such direct questioning, and who could blame him? She said, 'What do you think of Darlington, Mr Chalmers?'

'I like what I've seen of it so far. I've never lived in an industrial town before.'

'Were you in the war?' Dicky asked, making inroads into the plate of sausage rolls in front of him, uncertain what to make of this well-spoken stranger with his soft hands and well-tailored suit of clothes.

'Towards the end of it, yes, so I didn't see much action, more's the pity. How about you?'

'Naw. Pa an' me works at The Forge. We weren't called up. Doing work of national importance, the blokes in Whitehall said, so we didn't get a look in.'

'Oh don't start on about the war,' Bessie said pettishly, wanting to be the centre of attention, peeved because William had apparently forgotten her existence. Her sister Elsie snorted derisively. About to say something unpleasant, she changed her mind and kept quiet, catching sight of her mother's 'you do if you dare' expression, which Elsie knew only too well.

'So, Mr Chalmers, what do you do for a living?' Emily enquired pleasantly, handing him a plate of Cornish pasties.

'I'm a barber's assistant,' William admitted. Thinking he might as well tell the truth and shame the devil, he added, 'I was trained as a—ladies' hairdresser. Now, I'm working for a Mr Schiller, in Skinnergate.'

'You mean that German fellah?' Dicky exploded. 'The one who spent the war in an internment camp? That bloody Jerry spy?'

78

Now he'd really put the cat among the pigeons, William realised. With a modicum of luck, the irate Dicky might well frog-march him from the tea-table and chuck him into the street.

At that moment, the door opened and Lizzie Imerson walked into the room. 'I thought I heard voices,' she said quietly, 'is anything the matter?'

'We were on about that German barber in Skinnergate,' Dicky burst forth. 'It seems Bessie's gentleman friend here is working for him.'

Instinctively, William had risen to his feet in the presence of a lady.

Lizzie looked puzzled. 'What's wrong with that? The war's over now. In any case, as far as I can make out, Mr Schiller has lived here in England longer than you've been alive. So why the fuss?'

Emily's face softened. 'Sit down, Lizzie. I'll make some fresh tea.'

'No, I'm not stopping. Tom's not very well and Nan's looking after Emma, so I mustn't be long.'

Bessie wailed dismally, 'You're not leaving already, are you William? You haven't had your tea yet!' She had mistaken his gesture in getting up when Lizzie entered the room as a sign of umbrage on his part, and no wonder with Dicky getting hot under the collar, Elsie snorting

like a pig, Pa firing questions at him and
Ma giving her looks that could kill.

But Lizzie had not mistaken his gesture,
of that he was sure; he could tell by her
eyes. She said, 'Please sit down and finish
your tea, Mr ...?'

'Chalmers,' he said. 'William Chalmers.'
Knowing he would do anything in the
world to please her, the loveliest woman
he had ever set eyes on, and the gentlest;
filled with a kind of spiritual grace which
had little, if anything, to do with mere
physical beauty.

In less than a moment, William knew
beyond a shadow of doubt that he had
fallen deeply in love with Lizzie, another
man's wife and mother of another man's
child; that he would go on loving her till
the end of time, and beyond.

FIVE

Entering her mother-in-law's house, Lizzie
went through to the kitchen where Nan
Imerson was washing the baby's nappies.
Little Emma, soundly asleep in her pram,
resembled a china doll: pink-cheeked, with
a quiff of fine gold hair peeping beneath
the crocheted shawl.

'You shouldn't be doing the washing,' Lizzie said softly. 'You do far too much for me as it is.'

'Oh, get on with you,' Nan went on plumping the nappies up and down in the sink, 'I wasn't about to sit twiddling my thumbs. You look fair worn out, my girl, what with one thing and another. I thought you'd have stayed down yonder for your tea. Why didn't you?'

'I couldn't, not with Tom being the way he is. Besides, Bessie's young man was there, and Dicky was shouting the odds, as usual. Well, you know my brother? A one-man revolution!'

'So Bessie's found herself a gentleman friend, has she? What's he like? Spotty, with an Adam's apple?'

'No, far from. Quite handsome as a matter of fact, with a nice voice and good manners. He actually stood up when I entered the room. Poor Bessie thought he was leaving.'

'Ha!' Nan opined, 'he would have done, given the sense he was born with. Why any man in his right senses would want to lumber himself with that daft ha'porth, beats me. And I must say I'm surprised at Jack and Emily letting her start courting at her age. Especially after what happened to Madge!'

Inured to Nan's outspoken opinions, and

knowing her bark was worse than her bite, 'I don't think it's a matter of courtship just yet,' Lizzie said patiently, 'more a matter of trial by jury. Ma and Pa wanting to make sure that Bessie isn't about to make the same mistakes as Madge.' She sighed deeply, 'I'd best go up and see to Tom.'

Wringing the nappies, 'No, you stay here with Emma,' Nan said, 'I'll see to Tom. After all, he is my son, my responsibility.'

'He's also my husband,' Lizzie reminded her gently.

'I know, lass, and there are times I wish that he wasn't, the trouble he's caused you. You deserved better than this, and I feel I'm to blame, being his mother.'

'That's nonsense, and you know it. I married Tom because I loved him, and if we hadn't married there wouldn't have been an—Emma!'

'And do you still—love him?' Nan asked wistfully.

Lizzie smiled, 'Of course I do. I married him for better or worse, remember? In sickness and in health, till death do us part.'

In the end it was Nan who went upstairs to see to Tom. Lizzie did not argue the toss, knowing Nan did not want her to see him in the state he was in, a grown man as helpless as a baby. Truth to tell,

Nan could scarcely bear to look at him either, sprawled on the spare room bed, face flushed, saliva dribbling from the corners of his mouth, snoring deeply, smelling of drink; oblivious to the world beyond these four walls, uncaring of wife and baby daughter.

Sitting on the edge of the bed, Nan remembered her son as he used to be: a handsome, alert, bright-eyed lad who had lied about his age to get into the army, so keen was he to get into uniform—for a 'bit of a lark', as he put it, and this was the result.

He and Lizzie had been childhood sweethearts, Nan recalled, but there'd always been a bit of a wild streak in him, a desire to see some action before settling down. Not that he'd doubted he and Lizzie would get married eventually, as they had done. But Nan had known even then that Tom was a changed man, no longer bright-eyed and charged with the energy of youth, but old before his time; had known the reason why this was so. He'd seen a pal of his shot for desertion, a lad of his own age tied to a post, his head in a bag, crying out for his mother as the firing squad took aim. Tom had been a member of that firing squad.

Getting up from the bed, bending down, Nan wiped her son's mouth and kissed his forehead before going downstairs to hang the baby's nappies on a clothes' horse near the kitchen fire.

'Is Tom all right?' Lizzie asked in a low voice, setting the table for a meal that neither of them wanted. Anxiously, 'He hasn't been sick again?'

'No, he's fast asleep and snoring. He'll sleep till morning, I shouldn't wonder!' Nan spoke cheerfully for Lizzie's sake. Lizzie smiled, for Nan's sake. All they could do was draw strength from one another from day to day, at the same time dreading what tomorrow might bring.

'What did you make of Bessie's young man?' Emily Donen asked her husband at bedtime.

Jack grunted. 'He seemed a bit prissy to my way of thinking. Not Bessie's cup of tea at all. For the life of me I can't think what he sees in her. What's he after, that's what I'd like to know?'

'Not Bessie, that's for certain,' Emily said sagely. 'My belief is that Bessie has her eye on him and he doesn't know what to do about it.'

'Then he needs his brains testing! If he isn't interested in her he should say so and let well enough alone.'

'Perhaps he has a kind heart and is too much of a gentleman to do that,' Emily said thoughtfully. 'I thought he handled himself well on the whole, in the circumstances.'

'What—circumstances?' Jack thumped his pillow into submission.

'You and Dicky behaving like bears with sore heads, for one thing,' Emily reminded him. 'Not to mention Elsie snorting like a pig and Bessie wailing like a banshee. He must have wondered what he was letting himself in for.'

'That's the whole point,' Jack muttered grumpily. 'Why let himself in for anything at all if he doesn't want to?'

'Perhaps Bessie isn't prepared to let go of him and he doesn't want to hurt her feelings?'

'Oh, I don't know. What's more I don't care,' Jack grumbled.

'Well, if you don't care about our daughter's happiness, *I* do,' Emily said sharply. 'She's obviously taken a shine to this young man, and I don't want to see her hurt and humiliated. The whole thing will die a natural death, I daresay, given time, when someone else catches her eye.'

She paused, then, 'Jack, love, please don't let what happened to Madge harden your heart. I told you once that you were the kindest man I'd ever known, part of the reason why I married you. I don't want to lose that, to see you become embittered and angry as you are these days. I'm sorry, but it's true, and I can't bear it!'

Jack groaned, 'Come here, my lass,' he said hoarsely, drawing her into his arms. 'Everything you've said is true, only I hadn't the sense to see it. I know we've lost Madge, but I couldn't bear the thought of losing you, too. I love you far too much for that. I always have and I always will.'

Eventually, Jack fell asleep in his wife's arms, his head cradled on her shoulder whilst Emily, still wide awake, stared up at the bedroom ceiling lit up by the effulgent glow from a gas-lamp in the street below, thinking of the family that she and Jack had created together.

First of all Lizzie, her lovely gentle Lizzie, denied the blessing of a happy marriage through no fault of her own, and worried about a baby whose father was fast losing his grip on life. What would the outcome be? Thank God that Lizzie had Nan Imerson to rely on, but what would life be like for little Emma growing up in so unhappy a household?

She thought of her son, Dicky, and his girlfriend Beulah Cammish. Every mother, she imagined, would have fault to find with a prospective daughter-in-law, but had any mother the God-given right to inhibit her son's choice of a wife in the way that she had done? Was she running the risk of losing or damaging in some way the precious bond between herself and her son? How could she have been so blind, so stupid?

If forced into making a choice between herself and Beulah Cammish, Emily realised her son would choose the girl he loved, and rightly so. An old adage sprang to mind, *'A son's a son till he takes a wife. A daughter's a daughter all the days of her life'*. Letting go of someone she loved as much as her one and only son would be a hard burden to bear, Emily thought, but, ironically, only by letting go of him would she stand a chance of retaining at least a small portion of his love; the corner of his heart reserved for herself alone, and no-one else in the world.

Strangely enough, Emily harboured none of the deep feelings for her two younger daughters, Elsie and Bessie, that she had for Madge, their wayward girl, with her wild rose beauty, masses of shining red-gold hair, hazel-green eyes and smiling red lips.

Elsie, a cross fretful baby, was fast growing into a cross fretful young woman, lacking Lizzie's tenderness, Dicky's enthusiasm for life, and Madge's beauty. Why this was so, Emily had no idea. She had cared for Elsie the same as the others but the child had not responded in the same way, as if she'd been born awkward, or perhaps she'd felt jealous of her siblings?

Not that Emily had treated her differently from the rest. At least she'd tried hard not to. There hadn't been time for one thing with all the cooking, cleaning, washing and ironing to see to, and with another baby on the way—the fifth and the last, she'd warned Jack—they couldn't afford to have any more given the size of the house, and his wages.

Funny things families, Emily thought, the way children grew up so fast, developing their own traits and characteristics, often at odds with those of their parents. As a young woman she had fondly imagined that her children, sprung from the same source, would all be alike, reasonably contented and happy, given a secure home, plenty of good nourishing food and lots of love. Above all, love. How wrong she had been.

Nothing remained static, she knew that now, not even mother love. It worried her to think that she had never come close to understanding and loving Elsie as she had done Lizzie, Dicky and Madge; that so often nowadays Bessie's sheer silliness irritated her past bearing. Of course she loved *all* her children, Emily persuaded herself. But not all in the same way. There were, after all, degrees of loving ...

At last, William's hard work on his employer's behalf was starting to reap results. The newly painted barber's pole, clean windows and interior of the shop had begun attracting customers; a trickle at first then more and more as word got around.

Schiller was over the moon, unable to do enough for him by way of expressing his gratitude for the fresh influx of business. He wanted to make his assistant's living quarters more habitable, an offer which William felt unable to accept. This, after all, was temporary accommodation, until he found somewhere more permanent to live.

One day the old man asked shrewdly, 'Tell me, Wilhelm, are you in love? Thinking of marrying and settling down, perhaps? I have noticed, you see, a certain young lady making sheep's eyes at you, standing outside the shop at one o'clock, awaiting the pleasure of your company during your lunch hour. I am not mistaken, am I, in believing that this so delightful young fraulein has to do with the light of love in your eyes nowadays?'

Startled, 'I'm afraid you *are* wrong. Entirely wrong, if that's what you think,' William burst forth. Then, less aggressively, ashamed of his outburst, 'I am in love, yes, but not with her. The truth is, she's taken a fancy to me and I don't know how to get rid of her!'

Schiller pondered the situation, frowning slightly. 'Then why not be honest with the poor child?' he suggested. 'Take her aside and tell her plainly and simply that you are in love with someone else?'

'I wish I could. But you see, Herr Schiller, it is not quite as plain and simple as you imagine. The woman I love happens to be her sister.'

In the mood for confession, 'To make matters worse,' William continued, 'the woman I'm in love with is married, with a baby, so she will never know the way I feel about her. So far as she is concerned, I am supposedly courting her sister Bessie, and if I stop courting Bessie, I might never see Lizzie again. That's it in a nutshell.'

Two months had passed since William's introduction to the Donen family, but Bessie still continued to pester him, chattering inconsequentially of this and that, driving him half mad with her naïve assumption that he somehow belonged to her; waiting outside the shop for him, clinging to his arm as avidly as a shipwrecked mariner to a lifeboat, forever drawing him towards jewellers' shop windows to look at the cards of engagement rings on display—when all he really cared about was news of Lizzie. His lovely, sad, unhappy Lizzie with her pale careworn face, those violet shadows like bruises beneath her luminous grey-blue eyes.

And yet the mere fact of knowing he was in love with her imbued his life with a sense of purpose and happiness hitherto unknown. He woke up thinking about her, fell asleep thinking about her; thought about her every minute of every day, heartened by the simple fact that they were alive together in the same world, that the rain that fell on his head, fell on Lizzie's also; the sun that shone, shone for Lizzie, too, so that he experienced an ever deepening natural bond between himself and the woman he loved: to do with rain, sunshine, moonlight and star-shine. All the natural, lovely things of life that somehow embodied the natural sweetness and charm of his beloved Lizzie.

But dreams of her were the best of all, when they would walk together hand-in-hand upon the meadowlands of space, with nothing save love between them until the dawning of a new day without her.

One afternoon in May, crossing the Skerne

91

Bridge from the market square where she had been shopping, wheeling Emma in her pram, suddenly Lizzie experienced a sense of foreboding akin to a dark cloud blotting out the sunlight.

Walking along the lower end of Parker Street, she noticed groups of slatternly women were gathered together on the pavement outside the Ox public house, staring after her as she passed by. Then one of them called out to her, 'You'd best hurry up, love, there's trouble in store for you!'

Not stopping to ask questions, Lizzie hastened her footsteps, passing other women as she did so, friends and neighbours standing on their doorsteps arms folded, as silent as statues, until at last nearing home, Emily stepped forward, her face wet with tears, to take hold of the pram. 'You'd best go in alone,' she said in a low voice, 'I'll take care of Emma. Oh Lizzie, my dear, you must be very brave, very strong now, for Nan's sake.'

Without a word, Lizzie hurried along the street to her mother-in-law's house. Nan was in the narrow hallway, her face the colour of putty, surrounded by four or five bareheaded men, dangling their caps in their hands as they filed solemnly from the front parlour.

'Nan, what is it? What's happened?' Lizzie asked fearfully. 'Where's Tom? Has he been taken ill again? What are these men doing here?'

'They brought Tom home.' Nan's face crumpled but she didn't cry.

'Home from *where?* What happened? Has he had an accident?'

Nan squared her shoulders. 'Worse than that, Lizzie, love, Tom's dead. They found him in the yard of the North Eastern Hotel. He'd been taken ill, you see, and ...' Her voice faltered, she trembled violently from head to foot; reached out a hand to steady herself. Lizzie caught hold of her hand and held it tightly, too shocked to speak.

One of the men said, 'Come on, Mrs Imerson, you'd best sit down. Come through to the kitchen. Bert, you put the kettle on, make some tea. The doctor will be here in a minute, I daresay.'

'No,' Nan demurred. 'I must stay near my son.'

But the man insisted, speaking gently, 'Nay, missus, best come away and sit down. There's nowt you can do till the doctor's been. You too, lass. It's just a matter of waiting.'

Finding her voice, Lizzie said brokenly, 'You don't understand. I must see my husband! I *must!* He may still be alive!'

The man shook his head. 'Nay, lass, he's not. I was in the war, and I knew he was gone the minute I set eyes on him. He was just lying there in the pub yard.'

He paused, 'Me mates an' me and Tom were having a game of cards, a glass or two of ale, when all of a sudden Tom got up, saying he felt queer and needed a bit of fresh air. Well, we thought nowt of it at first—not until he'd been gone for some time, when me an' Bert went to look for him.'

'Go on, please,' Lizzie whispered, 'I want to know what happened. Had he fallen, hit his head?'

'Aye, he'd fallen right enough, and cut his head, poor lad, but that weren't what killed him. You see, lass, he'd taken summat. The bottle was still in his hand.'

'Taken something?' Lizzie stared at the man in horror. 'I don't understand. What had he—taken?'

'That's not for me to say, lass.' The man, grey-haired, roughly spoken yet kind of heart, turned his head away, unable to face the suffering he saw in Lizzie's eyes.

'Some kind of poison, you mean?'

'Well yes, lass. Leastways, that's what it seemed like to me.'

SIX

The worst thing was not knowing why Tom had committed suicide. Had she made him so unhappy that he could not bear to go on living with her? Lizzie wondered.

The inquest shed some light on why Tom had ended his life. A money-lender was called on to give evidence and it turned out Tom had been borrowing sums of money over a period of time, getting deeper into debt as a result, with no prospect of reducing the loans or the rapidly mounting interest. The present sum owing amounted to one hundred and fifty pounds.

On the day of his death, Tom Imerson had been to his shop with a view to increasing the loan. The money-lender, Samuel Lowry, had turned down his request. He was, after all, a businessman not a philanthropist, he'd said smoothly, hands outspread showing the palms, and with a dismissive shrug of his narrow shoulders.

At that moment, with a burning sense of hatred towards the man who had led

Tom down the broad path to destruction, Lizzie vowed that she would somehow repay every penny, no matter how long it took.

After the inquest and its verdict of suicide whilst of unsound mind, Nan told Lizzie about the firing squad incident. 'I begged him to tell you,' she said gently, 'but he wouldn't. He was afraid you'd think him a coward, decide not to marry him after all. He made me swear not to tell you. I promised, and I kept my promise. Now, well, what difference does it make?'

'All the difference in the world to me,' Lizzie said, 'now I know what was really troubling him. I'd got it into my head that his feelings towards me had changed, that he didn't want to marry me after all. It has been at the back of my mind all the time, and especially at the christening when he went off the way he did. I thought he didn't care for our baby, either.' She covered her face with her hands.

'You must never think that,' Nan said compassionately. 'Tom adored you and little Emma, he told me so himself. He was simply not strong enough physically or mentally to shoulder his responsibilities when he started drinking. But I knew nothing of his involvement with that money-lender.'

'I am going to pay off that debt,' Lizzie said, 'for Tom's sake. I'll not have his memory dishonoured. With your help, Nan, I can do it. If you'll take care of Emma for me, I'll go out to work; save every penny I can. I'll work my fingers to the bone, every hour that God sends, if necessary.'

'You can count on me,' Nan said grimly. 'And I'll work, too. Take in washing and ironing. It wouldn't be the first time, not by a long chalk!'

The two women clasped hands across the kitchen table, coming to terms with the future. What they could not face so readily was the present, the awesome presence of Tom's coffin in the front parlour, awaiting tomorrow's funeral rites: his burial in the Carmel Road Cemetery, preceded by a short service in St Cuthbert's Church where Tom had once served as an altar-boy.

William received news of Tom Imerson's death from a distraught Bessie in complete and utter silence. Not that he could have got a word in edgewise had he wished to do so.

Stunned, deeply shocked, he simply listened as a man in a dream, his mind centred solely on the woman he loved, wanting to be by her side, to hold her in his arms, to comfort and sustain her in her hour of need.

'Oh, you can't think how awful it's been,' Bessie wailed, 'with everything in such an uproar, an' Tom taking his own life the way he did, the poor bloke. Not that I ever liked him very much anyway for the way he treated poor Lizzie. What I mean is, what she ever saw in him, beats me. Now Ma is having to take care of the baby, an' we can scarcely move for wet nappies drying near the kitchen fire. An' I'm dreading the day of the funeral, so please come with me, William, to take care of me. Promise you will?'

'Yes, of course I'll come with you,' William promised, knowing he would have gone anyway, to be near Lizzie.

'Oh, that's all right then!' Bessie sighed blissfully, clawing his arm as they walked together along Skinnergate, 'I'll wear my best navy blue costume and trim my hat with black veiling, as a mark of respect. I should look rather fetching, don't you think?'

Never had William felt more inclined to tell Bessie how much he loathed her than he had done then; this silly, empty-headed little fool he was lumbered with because of Lizzie.

One day soon, William realised, he

must in all fairness put paid to his so-called courtship of Bessie Donen. But not now, with Tom Imerson's funeral about to take place the day after tomorrow, when he must appear by Bessie's side as her 'intended'. Otherwise, what possible excuse could he proffer for being there at all? Most importantly, how else could he get close enough to Lizzie to offer his heartfelt condolences on the death of her husband?

In some ways, William was proving to be an unsatisfactory gentleman friend, Bessie thought. Too much of a gentleman perhaps? Not that she would have admitted as much to anyone else, especially not her catty sister Elsie. Frankly, Bessie thought that William and her would have reached the kissing and cuddling stage by now, but William seemed slow in that department to her great disappointment, lacking in natural affection, as though he were in a dream half the time.

On the day of the funeral, he refused to walk down the aisle with her after Tom's coffin, saying it wouldn't be fitting to join members of the family, electing instead to sit alone at the back of the church.

It was a sad procession. William's heart went out to Lizzie, all in black, her face as pale as moonlight, holding her father's arm, staring straight ahead of her at the coffin.

Before the service ended, he slipped silently from the church and walked quickly to the cemetery to await the arrival of the cortège. A long walk, and yet he'd been glad of it, the warm air on his face, the burgeoning trees along the way; May blossoms, lilacs and laburnums, near the iron gates of the cemetery.

The carriages drove in through the gates, people dismounted and began walking along the paths to the graveyard, following the pall-bearers and the white-surpliced vicar who had conducted the church service.

Catching sight of William, Bessie uttered a cry and hurried towards him. Weeping copiously, she leaned her head against his shoulder, 'I thought you'd gone,' she sobbed.

'Hush, Bessie. People are looking.'

'I don't care! Let them look!' She swayed against him. At a loss, he put his arm about her to steady her. Lizzie turned her head at that moment, distracted by her sister's outcry, to see what appeared to be a tender moment between Bessie and her young man. There was nothing to be done about it except to support his burden to the graveside, an uncomfortable procedure with Bessie leaning her full, not inconsiderable weight against him and sobbing hysterically as if to deliberately draw attention to herself. As if she had really cared for the man they were burying—unlike Lizzie whose air of quiet composure in the face of her overwhelming grief was far more moving than her sister's crocodile tears.

The burial over, Bessie begged William to squeeze into the carriage beside her for the return journey to Parker Street for the funeral tea; an invitation that William felt unable to accept.

'Why not?' Bessie wailed.

Helping her into the carriage, William smiled and shook his head, knowing he could not face the squeezed confines of the Donens' front room, being lumbered with Bessie and catching fleeting glimpses of Lizzie in a room full of strangers. Witnessing her silent suffering at a time when, above all things, what she needed most was rest and quiet to come to terms with her grief, not a—wake. A bloody tea-party!

Ignoring Bessie, he walked back the way he had come, his brain in turmoil, wishing he'd possessed enough courage to stand by Lizzie at the graveside when her husband's coffin was lowered into the ground, hoping against hope that his presence might somehow convey to her that she was not alone after all.

Of course he had done no such thing. An impossibility in any case with Bessie clinging to him like a limpet to a rock. Well, he'd had all he could take of Bessie's histrionics. The time had come to finish the so called 'affair'. He couldn't care less if he never set eyes on her again. He would break the news to her the next time she waited for him outside the shop.

He might have known it would not be that simple. Nothing ever was, in his experience. His own nature was at fault, he imagined: his dislike of deliberately hurting another human being, especially a simple-minded soul like Bessie who obviously adored the ground he walked on. Besides which, only through Bessie could he hope to glean further news of Lizzie.

'Would you believe it?' she said one day, a week or so after the funeral, 'Lizzie's taken a job as a dairymaid to a milkman in Victoria Road; driving his milk float of all things! Starting her round at five o'clock in the morning, then going on to another job as a nursemaid to some rich man's kids to give them their breakfasts and see them safely to school. I can't think what's got into her, really I can't. What I mean is, can you imagine Lizzie driving a milk

102

float? Why, she wouldn't know one end of a horse from the other, unless one end of it bit her!'

Maintaining a discreet silence but smiling inwardly, William could easily imagine Lizzie driving a team of wild horses if called upon to do so. She was that kind of girl. Proud and fearless in the face of adversity.

At the inquest he had known instinctively that Lizzie would not rest until she had paid back, in full, the money Tom Imerson had borrowed from Samuel Lowry. He just hoped that Lizzie, in her present frail state of health, had not bitten off more than she could chew.

One day in June, Maurice Schiller called him through to his private sanctum. 'I have news for you, Wilhelm,' the old man said. 'Good for me, not so for you, I fear.' He paused. 'The idea has been at the back of my mind for some time now. It has to do with a boyhood friend of mine in Germany.'

William waited expectantly, not speaking, dreading what he was about to hear. Schiller continued, 'This friend of mine, Emile Schmidt, and I kept in touch until the war—then nothing. That so dreadful war!' He shuddered slightly. 'I had no way of knowing what had become of him, whether he was alive or dead. Then, to my joy, I had a letter from him in the new year. He had, *danke Gott,* survived. Can you imagine, Wilhelm, how much that meant to me?'

'Yes, of course I can,' William responded warmly, 'though I can't see quite what you are driving at.'

'Simply this,' Schiller said quietly, 'I am going home, back to Germany where I belong, to live out the rest of my days with my dear boyhood companion.'

'I see,' William said slowly, 'but is that possible?'

'But of course,' the old man said proudly, 'I am still a German national by birth, the holder of a German passport, otherwise I should not have spent the war years in that soul-destroying internment camp.'

'Yes, but this is a big step you're taking,' William reminded him, deeply concerned for Schiller's welfare and realising how fond he'd become of his employer. 'How can you be certain it's a step in the right direction?'

The old man smiled wistfully. 'How can anyone be certain of anything these days? Except, perhaps, the dictates of the human heart in search of a resting place, a place to call home with a person one loves? My friend Emile has an apartment in Munchen he wishes to share with me, so I shall have a roof over my head. Much more besides: someone with whom to share memories of the past.'

'But what about all this? This house? The shop?'

Schiller sighed deeply, 'That is what I meant by the bad news for you, Wilhelm; the loss of your employment. You see, my friend, I had no choice other than to sell the property to raise money. Soon it will be taken over by a firm of estate agents who will, no doubt, close the shop and turn it into an office.' He shrugged his shoulders sadly. 'I am sorry, Wilhelm, after all you have done to help this old German.'

What to do now? William pondered the situation. All he knew was hairdressing. Common sense told him that it would be foolish to turn his back on work for which he was fully qualified to try something new.

When Bessie asked him what was on his mind, saying he looked as if he'd lost sixpence and found a farthing, he told her reluctantly, uncertain of her reaction and unwilling to discuss Herr Schiller's private affairs.

'Oh, is that all?' she said airily. 'Well, the job weren't much cop anyway, were it?' William flinched, Bessie continued, 'Elsie was saying the other day that the hairdressers on the High Row is wanting an assistant. She saw the notice in the window. Why not give it a try? I would if I was you. It's a real posh shop with ladies' heads in the window.'

'Huh?' William looked stricken.

'Oh, not real 'uns, daft head. I meant dummies wi' wigs on, an' lots of diamond combs and ta-raras. Mind you, the woman what owns it is a bit on the stiff side, Elsie says, but I 'spect she has to be with all them posh customers of hers arriving in carriages and such like, Elsie says, an' she should know seeing as how the shop where she works is next door but one from Madame Marcia's, an' them kind wants to try on every hat in the shop, then like as not walk out without buying one ...' Bessie paused for breath, then. 'Well, what do you think? You did say you was trained as a ladies' hairdresser, didn't you?'

William knew the set-up all too well. Madame Marcia's establishment sounded very similar to that of his mother's diamanté-studded back-combs, paste tiaras and all. He said, 'I'll give the matter some thought.'

'Well, don't think about it too long,' Bessie advised him, wishing he had a bit more 'go' about him, 'otherwise the job'll be gone, an' the accommodation that goes with it.'

106

'Accommodation?' William's interest quickened. 'What—accommodation?'

'A room or somesuch above the shop,' Bessie said impatiently. 'It's all in the advert. Why not go and see for yourself?'

Why not, indeed?

Madame Marcia's name was Hunter. William had written to her requesting an interview which took place one evening in her private treatment room behind the salon.

Crossing the threshold, his nostrils had been assailed by the familiar smell of green soft soap, violet oil and other immutably mingled perfumes peculiar to women's hairdressing which William, to his surprise, found strangely comforting; imparting a feeling of being on familiar ground. Not that he entertained any real hope of landing the job, despite his qualifications.

Mrs Hunter, a tall dark-haired woman in her late forties, conducted the interview in a straightforward manner. When they were seated in a room marked Strictly Private containing a couch and various items of beauty treatment equipment, she said briskly, 'Tell me, Mr Chalmers, are you familiar with boardwork?'

'Yes, indeed.' William recalled the struggle he'd had to master the intricacies of clamps, weaving sticks, hackle and

107

threads when it came to making hairpieces and pincurls. He added truthfully, 'Not that it is my favourite occupation.'

'Then what is?' Madame regarded him shrewdly.

'I enjoy Marcel waving, and tinting. I have a proficiency certificate from the Inecto School in London.'

'And are you *au fait* with the latest day and evening styles? You see, Mr Chalmers, we are often called upon to attend weekend house parties to dress the women's hair before dinner and during the day if requested. I might add that my clients are wealthy, discerning women used to the best that money can buy; often demanding as a result. Do you feel yourself capable of pleasing such women?'

'I think so. You see, Madame, I received my training in a first-class establishment not dissimilar to your own: Madame Clara's, of Scarborough, a Court Hairdresser's. I once accompanied Madame Clara to London when she was called upon to dress ladies' hair in readiness for being presented to their Majesties at the Queen Charlotte's Debutantes' Ball.'

Marcia Hunter raised her eyebrows. Thinking it best not to sail under false colours, 'I should explain,' he said quietly, 'that Madame Clara is my mother.'

'Is she indeed? Then may I ask what you are doing here in Darlington?'

Unwilling to divulge his personal reasons for leaving Scarborough he said, 'I felt in need of a change after the war.' He smiled disarmingly, 'Ours is a family business in which my two older sisters are also involved. I felt myself to be—expendable. One man in a family of women.'

'I see.' Mrs Hunter nodded sagely, liking William's honesty allied to his discretion, his quiet cultured way of speaking, his charm of manner, not to mention his startling good looks, of which he seemed totally unaware. Most handsome young men, in her experience, were inclined to ogle members of the opposite gender, especially older women such as herself, taking full advantage of their looks to gain their own ends.

'Are you familiar with beauty culture, Mr Chalmers?'

'I'm afraid not,' he admitted ruefully. 'I was never allowed into my mother's inner sanctum. Most ladies wish to be seen at their best, I imagine, and not with their faces smothered in mudpacks. I think they would feel highly embarrassed by a male presence in what has to be a strictly female preserve.'

Well satisfied by his response, Marcia rose to her feet, 'Now, if you'd care to follow me, I'll show you the accommodation on offer. Are you a married man, by the way? No? Just as well, perhaps. It is rather high up in the world. An attic flat as a matter of fact, but quite self contained, with a private staircase.'

Leading the way, she explained that since the death of her husband during the war, she and her thirteen-year-old daughter occupied the rest of the house while her fifteen-year-old son was away at a boarding-school in York.

At last, 'Well, here we are,' she said, panting slightly, unlocking a door on the top landing. 'As you can see, it is nicely furnished, and with a panoramic view of Darlington from the sitting-room window.'

William saw with pleasure the neatly planned room with a divan bed beneath a dormer window, two chintz-covered armchairs drawn up near a narrow fireplace with a gas-fire; a table, two dining chairs, a scattering of rugs on the floor, pictures on the walls; a small dressing table and wardrobe near an arched partition leading through to the kitchen beyond.

'The cooking arrangements are somewhat limited, I'm afraid,' Mrs Hunter explained. 'Just a couple of gas-rings, but at least there's a sink for washing up, plenty of cupboard space, and a full complement of pots and pans and so on.

The—er—usual offices are through here by the way, though the bath and washbasin are a bit on the small side.'

She paused momentarily, bemused by the expression of absolute joy on William's face, as if he had been handed the world on a platter, then said as matter-of-factly as she could, 'The job I'm offering is yours, if you want it, Mr Chalmers? Of course you'll need time to think about it, I daresay ...?'

William said eagerly, 'I have thought about it, and the answer is yes: But first, with your permission, I must work a week's notice for my present employer, Herr Schiller. You see, Madame, I couldn't possibly leave him in the lurch.'

At that moment Marcia knew beyond a shadow of doubt that she had chosen well. From a long list of applicants, none could have held a candle to William Chalmers.

SEVEN

The dairyman, Mr Simons, had broken his leg. Fortunately his house and office formed part of the mews where his horse was stabled, where the milk churns were scoured by two young apprentices, and

111

where Mrs Simons hung out her washing to dry on Monday mornings.

Lizzie had applied for the job of driving the milk float because of the hours involved: from five o'clock till seven in the morning and because the dairy was near home. She had been given the job because women cost less to hire than men. In any case the horse knew the round as well as it knew its own tail, and as Mr Simons told Lizzie on her first morning, it was a pity it hadn't got hands instead of hooves as it would probably measure out the milk as well.

Bob Simons explained that his son-in-law had arranged to come in to harness the horse and hoist the churns on board on his way to work. She could either lead the horse or drive it from the back step. She'd soon get the hang of it, but she'd have to keep her wits about her and not give folk more than a fair measure—exactly as much as they asked for an' no more—and see they gave her the right money. No listening to hard luck stories.

Bob Simons wasn't a bad sort of chap, Lizzie knew; a bit rough and ready but he had a living to make, and although the job was temporary and not entirely to her liking, her wages would go towards paying Tom's debt.

There were bound to be snags. The

weather for one, getting soaked to the skin on wet mornings; the physical energy entailed in getting in and out of the float. Some women came out of their houses, muslin-covered milk jugs at the ready. Other folk left their jugs on the back step or in the wash-house in the yard, which meant finding her way down ginnels and back lanes where all the gates looked alike.

Moreover, most of the women who came to the float with their milk jugs were prone to a bit of a 'crack on', but Lizzie hadn't time to gossip even if she'd wanted to, with another job awaiting her when she'd finished her round.

Not that she cared much for that job either. The three children she had to get ready for school were badly behaved, cheeky and disobedient. Not to be wondered at since their mother, heavily pregnant with a fourth child and with a mysteriously absent husband, had given up attempting to cope with her unruly offspring. She preferred to remain in bed whilst Lizzie did battle with them and cooked breakfast which, oftener than not, they refused to eat saying they didn't like it or they wanted something else.

Nor did they want to put on their clothes or go to school. Arms refused to go into sleeves, legs into knickers, feet into

113

shoes. Spat out food stuck to the kitchen floor, bread bloated in spilt milk. Then, when the children had finally been dressed and sent off to school with a neighbour's brood, Lizzie would begin the mopping up operations, cleaning up the mess from the floor, clearing the table and starting on the washing up. Invariably, a voice would float down from Mrs Marchbank's bedroom demanding tea, toast and marmalade, and Lizzie would have to take up a tray to her flaccid employer, draw back the curtains, fold her discarded clothing from the day before, plump up her pillows and listen to a long diatribe of complaints. The selfishness of men in general and her husband in particular were frequently dwelt on.

'I told Harold I didn't want another child. But would he listen? No, not he, the selfish brute! All men care about is their own pleasure. Now look at me, the size of an elephant and with another two months left to go. I can't bear it, I really can't!'

Going back to the kitchen to finish clearing up, Lizzie felt that she couldn't bear it either. She must look for something more permanent, less stressful. Secretly, her sympathy lay entirely with the errant Harold Marchbank. The poor devil must dread the thought of ever returning to his

114

feckless wife and three unruly children.

The following Friday morning Lizzie handed in her notice to Mrs Marchbank, who called her a selfish bitch. A bitter pill to swallow, but at least she had a few more shillings in her purse to give to the money-lender.

Moreover, she had spied in the *Darlington & Stockton Times,* an advertisement for a part-time housekeeper to a single, elderly, respectable business gentleman. Hours to suit. Under a box number.

'What do you think?' Lizzie asked her mother-in-law, in need of advice.

'I should answer it if I were you,' Nan Imerson said directly. 'After all, what have you got to lose? An elderly respectable gentleman sounds more your cup of tea than the Marchbanks' menagerie!'

She wondered at first if she had come to the right address. The name of the bookshop was 'Attica' with a narrow façade of Georgian design, three steps leading to an open door; the interior filled with ceiling-high shelves of secondhand books.

Frowning slightly, Lizzie took out the reply to her letter of application, written on good quality paper and signed, '*Yours faithfully, Lewis Gilbert*'. And yes, this was certainly the right address, 3 Tubwell Row, and so presumably Mr Gilbert was an antiquarian bookseller by profession? Nothing wrong with that.

Settling her hat more firmly on her head, she walked up the steps and into the shop, wondering what an antiquarian bookseller would look like? Old, frail and bent, she imagined, with straggling grey hair and half-moon spectacles perched on the end of his nose. The man who came forward to meet her was nothing of the kind. Grey-haired, yes, but tall and thin, in his mid-fifties, Lizzie reckoned. Certainly not old.

He said, 'I am Lewis Gilbert. Are you Mrs Imerson?'

'Yes, I am. H-how do you do, Mr Gilbert?'

'Moderately well on the whole, Mrs Imerson. And you?'

'I'm quite well, thank you.'

She didn't look well, Lewis thought, noticing the paleness of her skin, shadows beneath her eyes, her tightly clenched fingers on the handbag she was holding, the abject thinness of her body accentuated by the plain black costume she was wearing. And yet there was something about her that belied her looks—a kind of inner strength in the way she held her head, the proud uplifting of her chin and the directness of her gaze as she looked up at him.

He said, 'I live above the shop. If you

would care to come up to my sitting room, we can talk better there. If you'll excuse me, I'll close the door, this being my lunch hour.'

'Yes, of course.' Lizzie knew instinctively that here was a man she could trust not to take advantage of her. Cautiously, she allowed herself to relax a little.

His sitting room was comfortable but crowded with piles of books everywhere. There were some exquisite pieces of antique furniture, mainly Georgian she imagined, including two magnificent brocade wing chairs flanking the fireplace; a corner cupboard filled with tarnished Georgian silverware, and a long delicately curved sideboard against the wall opposite the fireplace.

When they were seated, Lewis said ruefully, 'Now you can see for yourself why I need a housekeeper to restore the house to some semblance of order. The fact is, since my wife's death I've simply let things go, myself included. She would be horrified if she saw the state of the place nowadays. She was so houseproud, you see? So insistent on my eating properly. Now I can scarcely be bothered to eat at all, so I thought ... Well, you know what I thought since you took the trouble to answer my advertisement in the local paper.'

'Yes, I understand,' Lizzie said simply. 'The fact is, I—that is—my husband died recently.' She added reflectively, 'It isn't easy to carry on afterwards, is it? Once the mainspring of life has been broken?'

This young woman expresses herself well, he thought, and she is obviously still in mourning for her husband. A memory stirred at the back of his mind. Imerson? He recalled a recent tragic death, the newspaper report of an inquest on a young man who had taken his own life.

'What I need is someone to keep the house tidy and cook for me. Plain cooking, nothing fancy. Food I could warm up myself when I close the shop in the evening. Someone to shop for me. Nothing too arduous. No rough work—floor scrubbing, washing, that kind of thing.'

'That isn't very practical, Mr Gilbert, if you don't mind my saying so. There's nothing wrong with washing clothes and scrubbing floors; taking a pride in one's work. I'd think myself a pretty poor housekeeper not to do the job properly. As for the cooking, you'd be better off sitting down to a decent midday meal, not warmed up food in the evenings which you might forget to eat anyway if you were tired and didn't feel like it.'

'Please go on, Mrs Imerson. I value your opinion.' Lewis said encouragingly.

'You are right, of course. I've fallen into lazy habits these days. What do you think I should do about it?'

'It's not up to me to say, but a good hot midday meal would be a step in the right direction; the kitchen left tidy afterwards, the washing up done. Then, in the evening, you could have something cold from the pantry—a kind of high tea—a slice or two of cold ham, perhaps; bread and cheese, or whatever the housekeeper had left ready for you. Plenty of fatty-cakes or a cut-and-come-again cake.' Lizzie smiled. 'That way you wouldn't go to bed hungry.'

'I see. Well that sounds like good advice to me,' Lewis replied quietly. 'The question is, what hours would suit you, and how soon could you begin?'

Lizzie said disbelievingly, 'You mean you're offering me the job?'

'I'm sorry, I should have asked you first if you wanted it. You haven't seen the rest of the house yet. It would be unfair of me to expect you to make up your mind without showing you round; telling you a bit more about myself.'

Leading the way along a passage to the kitchen at the back of the house, 'It is really too big for one person,' he said, 'but I'm fond of it. Besides which, living above the shop has its advantages and I'm not ready to retire just yet.'

119

Glancing round the kitchen, 'Oh, this is nice,' Lizzie said. 'Plenty of cupboard space, and a good big table to bake on.'

'There's a dining room through that door over there,' Lewis said. 'A repository for more books, I'm afraid. I haven't felt in need of a dining room since my wife died. Not that we did much entertaining apart from a few close friends now and again.'

'Have you no—family? No children?'

'I'm afraid not. Alice, my wife, lost her parents at an early age and went to live with an aunt of hers whose death occurred shortly after our marriage. As for myself, my only brother married an American and left England with her before the war. They are now living in New York, running a successful antiques' shop in Greenwich Village, I believe. They have three children, two boys and a girl. Perhaps I'll visit them when I retire. Who knows?

'Alice and I never had children of our own, I'm afraid. A pity really. I'm fond of children. Have you any, Mrs Imerson?'

'Just one, a baby daughter, Emma.'

'I see. Then, forgive me for asking, but—'

'I know what you're thinking,' Lizzie said quietly, 'and now seems a good time to tell you more about myself. The plain fact is, I need as much work as I can get right now. My husband died owing money, every penny of which I'll repay sooner or later, with my mother-in-law's help. For her son's sake, Emma's and mine, she has willingly agreed to take care of our child until that debt is paid off in full. That's the kind of woman she is.'

Gilbert smiled wistfully, 'If you decide to accept this job, do you think once in a while you could be persuaded to bring Emma to work with you to keep your eye on her?'

Lizzie's eyes filled with tears, knowing he really meant what he said, feeling suddenly more safe, more secure than she had done for many a long day. She said, with an upsurge of happiness, 'I could start on Monday morning if you like at, say, ten o'clock? Go round to the market to do your shopping first of all, then set about the cooking and cleaning. That window over the sink could do with a good clean for a start—'

Lewis Gilbert laughed, feeling suddenly more at ease than *he* had done for a very long time. 'I'm in your hands entirely from now on, Mrs Imerson,' he said.

William left Skinnergate and moved into his apartment above Mrs Hunter's shop. Maurice Schiller had been touchingly pleased by his assistant's success in finding a new job so quickly and sad to lose him, but events were moving rapidly now. The premises had been sold. Soon workmen would start to dismantle the shop and clear the house in readiness for alteration. His passage to Germany had been arranged and his friend in Munich was making preparations for his arrival.

'You will write to me? Let me know how you are getting on?' William asked.

'Yes, of course I shall,' the old man promised. 'I will never forget you, Wilhelm, and perhaps we'll meet again some day?'

'Perhaps. Who knows?' Certainly he would never forget Herr Schiller's influence on his early days in a strange town and the many lessons he had taught him.

Bessie continued to plague him. Now she had taken to hanging about Madame Marcia's establishment at lunchtime, to Marcia's annoyance. 'Who *is* that girl?' she demanded sharply. 'A friend? Then kindly arrange to meet her elsewhere in future.'

Bessie was advised to stand inside the market hall—if stand she must, at which suggestion she turned decidedly huffy. 'Oh, I suppose I'm not good enough to be seen with you now you've found your feet? And you've never even asked me to look at your rooms.'

'That's out of the question. I'm sorry,

Bessie, but it is.' His mind boggled at the thought of finding himself alone with Bessie in a room with a bed.

'But I hardly ever see you! I wouldn't see you at all if I didn't wait for you at dinnertime! A fine courtship that is, I must say. Now I'm supposed to stand in that draughty old market.'

Guiltily, William realised that he was being unfair to the girl. The time was fast approaching when he must put an end to this worrying situation for his own sake as well as hers. If only he knew how.

He had written to Fred Willis telling him about his new job, Schiller's recent departure to Germany, and that he was supposed to be courting a girl he had no intention of marrying—a letter in the nature of a *cri-de-coeur* to an old friend and confidant whose help and advice would come as a godsend in his present dilemma.

Fred wrote back immediately saying he'd be in Darlington on business the next weekend and suggesting a meeting in the King's Head on Saturday night at eight o'clock; intimating that he too was having problems of a personal nature which he wanted to get off his chest.

At the appointed time and place, the two met up in the cosy atmosphere of the bar where they began drowning their sorrows in the time-honoured fashion.

After the third pint, wiping his moustache with the back of his hand, 'Women,' Fred said despondently. 'Damned if I can begin to understand 'em! Maudie's like a bear with a sore head at the moment. That's basically why I'm here, if you must know. Damned if I'm prepared to put up with her shenanigans when I try my best to please her in every way. Well, you know what I mean? It's a bit rough on a bloke to be treated like dirt when he's done nowt to deserve it.'

He sighed deeply, 'I reckon it has to do with Charlie. He's getting on her nerves, that's the truth of the matter. Forever playing that damned gramophone of his. I don't know what to do about it and that's a fact. There's something seriously wrong with that lad, that's for sure. Whatever, it's playing hell with my love life. But enough of my troubles. How about yours? So you're courting a girl you're not in love with? Frankly, Billy Boy, I can't quite see the problem. How did you get stuck with her in the first place? And if you don't want her, why not tell her so and have done with it?'

The words, *'Because I'm in love with her sister'*, stuck in William's throat. Suddenly the thought of admitting the truth across a table in a bar, even to his best friend, seemed inimical to him. His feelings for

Lizze Imerson ran far too deep for that.

He said, 'Thanks for your advice, Fred. It's just that I don't want to hurt the girl's feelings.'

Fred peered at him, slurring his words slightly. 'So whaddayou gonna do? Wait till you're up in front of a parson, saying "I do. With this ring I thee wed" an' all that crap? It'll be too late then to tell the poor cow you don't love her. Next thing you'll know she'll have a bun in the oven an' you'll be hooked for life. Get rid of her now, mate, before it's too late to change your mind.'

Two hours later, William felt it expedient to escort Fred to Parker Street considering the state he was in. But Fred, unwilling to face Maudie in one of her moods, insisted on one for the road in the Ox near the Skerne bridge. William's protestations that he'd already had far more beer than was good for him were to no avail. Fred forged his way into the pub and up to the counter to smile foolishly at the barmaid ... Lizzie Imerson.

Never till his dying day would William forget that moment of shocked horror when he saw the woman he loved standing behind the bar of a seedy, run-down public house, serving drink to the residents of Lower Parker Street; men whose lewd eyes were riveted on her breasts, her thick brown hair, her pale heart-shaped face, as if licking their lips in anticipation of how it would feel to bed so lovely a woman.

'Lizzie,' William said tautly, 'what the hell are you doing here?'

'What does it look like?' she uttered, blushing to the roots of her hair. 'Earning a living, if it's any of your business.'

'I'm making it my business. Get your things and come with me. I'm taking you home.'

'You'll do no such thing. Who are you to give me orders?'

'This is no place for you, and you know it. Earning a living's one thing, selling your pride for money's something else entirely!'

'Here, what's going on?' The landlord, a burly brutish looking man, emerged from the back room. 'What's your game, Mr bloody lah-di-dah? My place not good enough for you, eh? Well that's soon settled. See if you like the pavement any better.'

'That's right, Sid. You show 'im. Chuck 'im out. Comin' in 'ere givin' orders to the barmaid. Well don't just stand there, Liz, pull me that pint I ordered an' be sharp about it!'

William stood his ground, ignoring the crowd of men near the bar, and the

126

landlord behind it, 'I told you to get your things, Lizzie,' he said. 'I'm taking you home.'

'Why? Fancy yer chances, do yer?' the landlord leered, leaning across the counter, his face within inches of William's, 'Well I give the orders here, an' I'm ordering *you* out. I'll give you to the count of three. One, two—right, you've asked for it, now you're gonna get it!'

'Eh? Wassamatter? Wha's up?' Fred looked round bemusedly as the crowd parted to let the landlord through the bar-flap, cheering him on, looking forward to seeing the stranger flat on his back in the street.

'Go on, Sid, teach the bastard a lesson he'll not forget in a hurry!'

'No! Please don't!' Lizzie cried out in terror, knowing the landlord's temper, afraid that William might be seriously injured by the fall he was about to take.

The man lumbered towards William like a bull, even snorting like one, hands outspread to grab his shoulders. The women near the far wall started screaming. Two climbed up on a table for a better view.

The sheer size of Sid Belcher would flatten any man on contact, William realised, adroitly side-stepping out of the landlord's way at the last second, before

127

the man could lay hands on him. A deft movement which sent Belcher staggering towards the open door where he clung momentarily to the jambs for support, shaking his head to clear his brain, uncertain what had happened. His victim had been within his grasp one second, gone the next.

Turning slowly, menacingly, he saw William standing near the bar looking cool and unruffled. Well, he'd soon put paid to that. Now he'd give the bugger the thrashing he deserved for having made a fool of him.

Clenching his hands into fists, smiling grimly, he aimed a blow at William's chin. Next thing he knew, William's right fist landed squarely in his face and he was staggering backward into the far wall, his nostrils spurting blood.

'Why, you ...' regaining his balance, wiping away the blood with the back of his hand, Belcher sprang forward like a tiger, swinging wildly with his fists, eyes narrowed, teeth bared, hell bent on revenge.

William's second blow landed on the point of Belcher's outthrust jaw. Groaning, the man staggered backward once more to land flat on his back amid a welter of broken chairs and an overturned table, where he remained—out for the count.

Shocked to sobriety, 'Let's get out of here, the quicker the better,' Fred urged William.

'I'm not leaving without Lizzie,' William said stubbornly.

'If you mean the barmaid, she's already left,' Fred told him. Still partially bemused, 'Hey, wait for me.'

But William was already out of the pub, running up Parker Street like a deer to catch up with Lizzie just ahead of him; calling to her to stop, desperate to talk to her—to say what, exactly? He scarcely knew.

She had reached the door of the Donen house before he caught up with her. She was panting, obviously distressed, as she turned to face him. 'Haven't you done enough damage for one evening?' she said angrily. 'By what right did you order me out of the pub?'

The die was cast. The time was now or never. 'Because I love you,' William said simply.

'*What?* Are you out of your mind? You must be, either that or too drunk to know what you're saying!'

'I'm neither mad nor drunk,' William said levelly, 'and I know exactly what I'm saying. I've loved you since the first moment I saw you pushing Emma down Parker Street in her pram. I was looking out of the window of the corner shop at the time. You didn't see me; didn't even know I was there.'

'I—I don't understand! What about Bessie? I understood that you and she were courting? That day in the cemetery, at Tom's funeral, you had your arms about her. So what are you really saying? That being in love, so called, with one woman, you paid court to another? How low can any man stoop?'

At that moment, about to leave the house to meet Bessie from work, Dicky Donen heard every word of the conversation between Lizzie and William. Not eavesdropping intentionally, but incensed with rage on his sisters' behalf, Dicky flung open the door. Collaring William, he burst forth, 'Why, you rotten little swine! I've a good mind to smash your face in, the trouble you've caused poor Bessie in particular. What the hell the poor kid saw in you in the first place, I'll never know. If you didn't want her, you should have said so and had done with it, instead of stringing her along making a damn fool of her!

'Well, I'm telling you right here and now, Mr Bloody Chalmers, if ever I catch you bothering either of my sisters again, I'll beat the living daylights out of you. Now hop it while you're still in one piece!'

Later that night, lying in bed unable to sleep, Lizzie remembered the way William's fists had gone into action on her behalf, acknowledged his concern for her welfare and knew he was right in saying the Ox was no fit place for her. She wondered if he really meant what he'd said when he told her he loved her?

Equally wide awake, William deeply regretted the mess he had made of things. Above all, losing Lizzie the way he had done. Of course she hadn't believed him when he told her he loved her. Why should she? As for poor Bessie, she would no longer be waiting for him every dinnertime in the covered market, he suspected.

He hoped and prayed that Dicky possessed the common decency not to divulge the identity of the 'other woman' in his life. He could not bear the thought of a rift between Bessie and Lizzie on his account.

Sobbing herself to sleep, her fringe in curl-rags, Bessie had perforce swallowed her brother's story that William wanted nothing more to do with her on account of his having another lady-friend in tow—which explained a lot of things to the unfortunate Bessie. For instance,

131

the reason he had never wanted to kiss and cuddle her nor to look at those pads of engagement rings in the jewellers' shop windows. His excuses for not wanting to walk out with her on Sunday afternoons, or come to the house for tea. The way he'd refused to ride in the carriage with her after Tom's funeral, as if he was ashamed to be seen with her.

Well, he'd made a right fool of her, and she wanted nowt more to do with him, not now nor ever again. There were as good fish in the sea as ever came out of it. The trouble was, she was still in love with him; could not envisage a future without him. But if she ever came across him and his lady-friend, she'd tell him exactly what she thought of him!

Meanwhile, Fred Willis had decided to pack up and leave Darlington by the first available train and head back to Newcastle the following morning. Back to his lodgings at Mrs Marble's establishment where at least he'd be certain of a welcome, well-cooked food and some cheery company. There were times when a succulent steak and kidney pudding outweighed the pleasure of sharing a bed with any woman—especially Maudie Thompson in one of her moods.

EIGHT

Work was to prove a blessing in disguise. Marcia's was a busy salon and William was up against a certain amount of prejudice to begin with as a new member of staff—and a man into the bargain.

His mother's clients had long been inured to a male presence in a traditionally female preserve, and the fact that he was Madame Clara's son had smoothed his path. Things were different now. He had to prove his worth by the quality of his work and to overcome prejudice by the simple expedient of keeping his mouth closed and his hands dextrous, particularly with clients who regarded him as suspiciously as they would a rooster in a hen-run.

'Don't worry. They'll soon get used to you.' Marcia advised him, well pleased with her new assistant. And what she said was true. Soon he had begun to build up a coterie of clients captivated by his painstaking attention to his work, his expertise with the waving irons, his quiet manner and amazing good looks.

He'd proved popular with the rest of the staff from the word go: five young women who flirted with him outrageously in the hopes of an evening out and who constantly vied for his attention: gifts of fat cream buns, for instance, for his mid-afternoon tea-break; an occasional bunch of flowers placed at the foot of the stairs to his apartment with a 'Guess who From?' message attached.

Innocent fun so far as William was concerned when the only woman on his mind day and night was Lizzie, whose scathingly uttered words: *'How low can any man stoop?'* still rang in his ears.

Pretty low, he reckoned. Had he ventured to tell her the truth that Bessie, not he, had done the pursuing from the word go, it would only have seemed worse.

The fact remained that the burden of guilt lay on his shoulders, and he knew it. He had treated poor Bessie shabbily. If only he knew how to put things right.

One day a tall, dark, flashily dressed woman entered the salon, whom William recognised vaguely as one of Marcia's beauty treatment clients. Not that he knew her name or anything about her until on this occasion, almost bumping into her as he emerged from a cubicle, he heard her say in a hectoring tone of voice, 'What do you mean, Madame Marcia's engaged at the moment? Tell her at once that Lady

Jessington is here for her eleven o'clock appointment, and be quick about it. I warn you, my girl, I am not accustomed to being kept waiting!'

Sorry for the girl, a newcomer to the salon, who looked as if she was about to burst into tears, William stepped into the breach. Smiling disarmingly, 'Please do take a seat, your ladyship. I'm certain you'll not be kept waiting more than a few minutes, knowing Madame Marcia's reputation for punctuality. Actually, ma'am,' consulting his pocket watch, 'the time is 10.57 precisely, in which case may I congratulate you on being early rather than late for your appointment? Now, if you'll excuse me, I have a customer waiting for me.'

So saying, he turned his attention to an elderly lady whose hair he had just finished shampooing and Marcel waving, to her obvious satisfaction, whom he referred to, surprisingly, as 'Your Grace'.

Later that day, Marcia informed William that he was to attend a weekend house-party at Jessington Hall as hairdresser in residence to Lady Myra's female guests. Jessington, he thought, the name ringing a bell in his mind, vaguely at first until he remembered the man; Sir Miles Jessington, whose face he had shaved last February in Maurice Schiller's barber shop.

An insensitive brute if ever there was one, aptly married he presumed to an equally insensitive woman whose dressing down had brought tears to the eyes of fourteen-year-old Polly Parkin. Poor girl, who stood as much chance of becoming a fully qualified hairdresser as he, William, stood of becoming Emperor of Japan.

The girls pulled faces and commiserated with him when they knew what he was in for. His predecessor, Miss Bartlett, had hated it. 'The lord of the manor took a fancy to her and tried to have his wicked way with her,' one of them said; the rest chorused assent.

William laughed, 'I don't suppose I'll run that risk.'

'Not from *him*, but watch out for her, my lad. Why do you imagine she put in a special request for you? Cor, you ain't half naïve, Billy Boy. She'll be down to the basement when all's quiet, an' you'll never know what's hit you!'

'The—*basement?*' William's heart sank. 'Why the basement?'

' 'Cos that's where the women come to have their hair titivated, daft-head, in a special little boudoir with a single bed an' a private entrance from the garden wing, so called. A thumping great conservatory her ladyship had built onto the house, according to Freda Bartlett. Ever so creepy, she said it were, with all them potted palms for his lordship to hide behind on his way down to her room.'

'Thanks for the warning. I'll keep the door locked.' William assured them.

'You do, an' her ladyship will tell Madame M your work was unsatisfactory, then you'll be in real trouble. Lose your job, like as not. Ain't that so, girls?'

'But that's tantamount to blackmail!'

'It's also tanta, what you said, to adultery,' Monica reminded him, 'but them gentry folk don't care nowt about the likes of us, as long as they get what they want. Not that they're real gentry. Rumour has it she was an actress in one of them "repeating" companies when he married her, an' he weren't a Sir then neither. Huh, a fine pair I must say, but they have pots of money, an' that's what really counts, ain't it?'

She lowered her voice confidentially, 'They do say he fathered a child on a bit of a lass who was sent off to America to get over the shame of it, but I'll bet any money *he* didn't pay the fare!'

William's heart lurched suddenly, 'Do you know the name of the girl?' he asked hoarsely.

'No. Why?' Monica and the rest of the girls looked at him curiously. 'Don't tell

137

me she was your kid sister?'

'No, of course not! It's just that I'm not looking forward to the weekend, that's all, after all you've told me.' A lame excuse, but the best he could think up at the time. Beulah Cammish, the barmaid at the King's Head Hotel, he recalled; had mentioned Lizzie's sister Madge who had got herself into trouble with a married man and gone to America. Too great a coincidence to his way of thinking, especially having met and loathed on sight the high and mighty Sir Miles Jessington, not to mention his equally high-flown wife, Lady Myra.

But above and beyond all that, William regretted the loss of freedom he'd envisaged when he first came to Darlington. Now, here he was, linked indivisibly with the Donen family: in love with Lizzie, at loggerheads with her brother Dicky, at odds with her sister Bessie, tied hand and foot by circumstances brought about by his own stupidity. Faced now with a weekend visit to Jessington Hall and the likelihood of losing his job and living quarters if he failed to respond to the overtures of a sex-starved woman old enough to be his mother. So what was the answer? Or was there an answer? Damned if he knew. Even so, forewarned was forearmed. He'd far sooner sweep streets for a living than betray the woman he loved.

Not that she would either know or care about his trials. Lizzie had her own life to live, and through his own stupidity he had no part to play in it.

She had fallen into a routine of shopping, cooking and cleaning for Lewis Gilbert which kept her busy and fulfilled. Lizzie was a born homemaker, taking after her mother from whom she had garnered housewifely skills from an early age: how to bake cakes and make good nourishing meals for next to nothing.

As a child, she had liked nothing better than going to market with Emily, holding on to her siblings' pram with one hand, carrying a shopping bag in the other, gazing in fascination at the market stalls piled high with produce: mounds of rosy-cheeked apples, green cabbages and heads of lettuce with garden soil adhering to their stems. In season, greenhouse tomatoes, radishes and green and cream striped marrows.

Not that her mother could afford such luxuries, Lizzie knew, as Emily made for the cheaper produce: carrots, turnips, swedes, onions and potatoes, although once her mother had bought a marrow for her to take to a harvest festival service in St Cuthbert's Church. Lizzie remembered she had refused to hand it over to the parson at the last minute, unable to bear the thought of parting with it, and nothing that anyone could say or do had made her change her mind. She had clung on to that marrow like grim death, and returned to the pew holding it fiercely to her chest to her mother's secret amusement, although she had shaken her head gravely at the time.

Later, several pots of marrow jam had appeared on the pantry shelves, a rare treat in the Donen household, which Lizzie had lathered onto thick slices of bread and margarine with careless abandon, having sacrificed her vegetable to a higher cause than a mere harvest festival service. Even at the tender age of five, Emily's usually compliant daughter had betrayed signs of a rugged sense of independence which would stand her in good stead and without which she might run the risk of being too soft, too compliant for her own good.

The wages paid to her by Lewis Gilbert were sufficient to ensure a weekly sum set aside to reduce the debt owing to Samuel Lowry.

Now that the dairyman's broken leg had mended satisfactorily, Lizzie had given up her early morning milk round to concentrate on taking care of her antiquarian bookseller, deriving infinite pleasure from restoring his house to order. Dusting and polishing his furniture, cleaning his windows, sweeping his carpets and providing him with a good hot midday meal which she served to him in the now neat and well-scrubbed kitchen; delighting in his appreciation of the food she had cooked for him and his 'filling out' as a result of her ministrations.

To Lizzie's way of thinking, the poor man seemed starved not only of food but affection. Here was a man born to be a father, as she discovered the first time she took little Emma to work with her. She would always remember the way his face lit up when the child handed him her favourite teddy bear to admire, the gentle way he spoke to her, his amusement at her antics; the picture book of nursery-rhyme characters he had given her.

At first Lizzie had been reluctant to share the food she cooked for him, making do with a cup of tea and a slice of bread when he had gone back to the shop, not wanting to impose on his kindness and because she didn't want to break the ritual of an evening meal shared with Nan.

A sensitive man, Lewis made no attempt to persuade Lizzie to sit with him at the kitchen table. Instead, he suggested taking home with her the food she was entitled to as his housekeeper—fish, meat, vegetables and eggs—a compromise which Lizzie accepted in time, for Nan and Emma's sake.

Despite her new job and Nan's efforts, money was still tight in the Imerson household. Taking in washing was no easy option, and Lizzie worried that her mother-in-law had bitten off more than she could chew, up to her eyes in steam all day long, and with Emma to take care of.

As time went by, Lizzie told Lewis more about her family background, just snippets here and there: the marrow incident, which made him laugh; about her sister Madge's disappearance, Bessie's job at the theatre, building up a picture of a closely integrated family whose lives had been overshadowed by the disappearance of one member and the tragic death of another. Not that Lizzie had mentioned the death of her husband since the day she arrived, but reading between the lines Lewis guessed her anguish that the father of their child would never share the joy of seeing her grow up.

It was then he suggested that Lizzie should bring the baby to work with her every day, not just occasionally. 'But mightn't she be in your way?' was Lizzie's immediate reaction. 'She's into everything now she's started crawling, and I wouldn't want her to be a nuisance to you.'

Lewis laughed, 'My dear Mrs Imerson, that child of yours comes as a breath of springtime to a crusty old devil such as myself. In any case, how could she be in my way? I'm in the shop most of the time.'

Lizzie looked at him askance. 'Is that the way you see yourself?' she asked softly, 'As a crusty old devil? Why, you're not even old, and you're certainly not—crusty.' She hadn't intended to say it, but she meant what she said, and he knew it.

In time to come, Lewis Gilbert would realise that was the moment he fell in love with Lizzie Imerson.

Filled with a deep sense of foreboding, William entered Jessington Hall carrying his hairdressing equipment in an attaché case, to be met by a pert parlourmaid who showed him down to his makeshift basement salon. Lady Myra was upstairs titivating herself in readiness for her influx of weekend guests, the girl said.

She added, *sotto voce*, 'The uproar these weekend house parties cause, you wouldn't believe. Cook's already threatened to give notice, and what's it all in aid of? I'm sure I don't know. Well, here's your room, an' when you've finished unpacking, Cook says you're to come along to the kitchen for a cuppa and a buttered teacake. My name's

Ethel, by the way. What's yours?'

'Billy.'

'Oh, short an' sweet, like a donkey's gallop,' Ethel remarked. 'Well, a word of warning, Billy, her ladyship's received word her hubby ain't coming tonight as expected, so just you watch out. She'll be on the rampage around midnight, I daresay!'

She added, pityingly, 'Frankly, Billy, I wouldn't want your job for all the tea in China, having to deal with a load of old hens wanting to look like spring chickens. It won't be no picnic, believe me.'

William believed her, hating the set-up more with every minute he spent in this strange house, a once lovely Georgian mansion ruined by ill-considered attempts at modernisation. A huge, blatant conservatory had been tacked onto one end of it, not to mention an entrance hall chock-a-block with Victoriana totally out of character, so that one scarcely noticed the beauty of the delicately spindled staircase curving to the upper landings. The welter of gilt-framed mirrors and oil-paintings, brass plant-holders and side tables crammed with objets d'art, bespoke the wealth but certainly not the good taste of the present incumbents of Jessington Hall.

He had caught a horse-drawn bus from

the High Row to Cockerton, as befitted his station in life, arriving at the Hall at a quarter past five. The house party guests would start appearing from six o'clock onward, Ethel told William. Dinner would be served at eight, so the women would be wanting his services beforehand, as soon as they'd changed into their evening finery—and rather him than her. He wished she'd stop saying that.

The kitchen was in the charge of a stout, rosy faced woman shouting orders to her helpers: ' 'Ere, watch that pan of milk before it boils over! Mind how you peel them potatoes! There'll be nowt left of them the rate you're going!' Turning her attention to the newcomers, 'You, Ethel, make the tea an' butter the teacakes. An' you, young man, come through here for your dinner when the gong's sounded an' the soup's gone up to the dining room, an' a hand with the washing up wouldn't come amiss!'

William grinned amiably, feeling more at home in this warm, steamy hive of industry than his 'salon' with its Victorian dressing table and stool, and with a curtained-off alcove containing a single bed, a bentwood chair and a row of pegs with dangling coathangers. 'An' think on,' Cook reminded him, 'them women will be down like a pack of

145

hounds to have their hair redressed before breakfast, so you'd best be up an' doing in good time to remove all those fakey hair ornaments an' false curls from the night before.'

'Thanks, Cook. I'll remember your advice.'

'Yes, well, I'd rather have my job than yours any day of the week,' she replied. 'Not that mine's a picnic by a long shot, specially not when her ladyship's in one of her moods. But I told her straight, I did. I said to her, "I'm a good plain cook, your ladyship, not a magician! If it's cold soup—consummate—you're wanting, roast pheasant with fried breadcrumbs an' Pear Bells Helen for pudd'n, you'll have to get someone else to do it. Otherwise, I'm off!" '

The woman bridled importantly, 'I mean to say, what's wrong with good hot soup, roast beef an' Yorkshire pudd'n an' a good steamed ginger pudd'n an' custard to foller?'

'Good for you, Cook,' William said admiringly, wishing he possessed half her spirit in the face of adversity, inwardly dreading his coming incarceration and being called upon to cater to the needs of a gaggle of rich, middle-aged matrons to enhance their appearance at the dinner table.

His spirits sank further with the realisation that he would be called upon not just tonight, but tomorrow, Saturday, and most of Sunday, or until the party ended and the guests went back to wherever they belonged. *A consummation devoutly to be wished* ... Just as long as Lady Myra Jessington had no thoughts concerning a consummation with a hapless hairdresser in her employ. But no, surely not, he convinced himself—akin to whistling in the dark—scarcely likely the lady of the house would stoop so low?

On the whole, events passed off far better than William expected, inasmuch as he dressed the women guests' hair to their complete satisfaction before dinner.

Afterwards, when the gong sounded upstairs, he went through to the kitchen to tuck into a generous helping of roast beef and Yorkshire pudding, following which he rolled back his sleeves and helped with the washing up.

So far he had not so much as set eyes on the mistress of the house which seemed to him a negation of the flights of fancy of Monica and her cronies in the back room of Madame Marcia's salon. He might have known, might have guessed that they were taking the rise out of him, teasing him unmercifully, wanting to gauge his reaction. And yet, one thing they'd told him had rung all too true: that Sir Miles Jessington had fathered a child with a girl who had fled to America.

The name of that girl, in William's considered opinion, must have been Madge Donen. Who else? It was too strong a coincidence. Sir Miles Jessington was obviously incapable of gentleness or sensitivity —a pig of a man with pouched eyelids, red-veined cheeks, and the smell of whisky on his breath.

If ever they came face to face again, William determined, he would do to him what he had done to the brutish landlord of the Ox—for Lizzie's sake—and to hell with pussyfooting about under the fellow's roof, dressing silly women's hair for a living.

Approaching midnight, he returned to his room to undress and crawl into bed, following a deeply satisfying session of mirth and merriment with Cook and her staff in the kitchen quarters of Jessington Hall. When the clock in the hall had sounded the witching hour they had all bade one another a fond, albeit slightly tipsy farewell until breakfast-time.

At one o'clock, William aroused from sleep to the sound of a light yet insistent tapping on the door of his room. Bemused and with no idea of the time, he got out of bed clad only in his nightshirt and opened the door a crack to discover Lady Jessington standing in the hall beyond, seductively clad in a sheer white-lawn nightgown and matching negligée, holding a bottle of champagne in one hand, glasses in the other.

Pushing past him, smiling, setting down the champagne and the glasses on the dressing table, she said throatily. 'Well here we are at last, William, alone together. A cause for celebration, wouldn't you say?'

Faced with the reality of the situation, William had no more idea how to handle it than he had done his brief encounter with Maudie Thompson. He certainly couldn't run out of the house wearing a nightshirt.

Myra laughed, 'What's wrong with you? Don't tell me you're surprised to see me? I could tell you fancied me in the salon the other day, and I certainly fancied you. That masterful way you have with women. That's why you're here, to prove just how masterful you are.'

She had obviously been drinking. Her face was flushed, eyes sparkling, hair loose about her shoulders. Turning abruptly, he went through to his alcove and put on his trousers. Mistaking his purpose Myra followed him, thinking to find him in bed awaiting her with open arms. Instead,

149

there he was stuffing his nightshirt into his waistband.

'What the hell ...?' She stared at him in amazement. 'Is this some kind of joke?'

'I hoped it might be, your ladyship, for your sake. I have no wish to take advantage of your er—generosity: a woman in your position, of your reputation.' He was speaking at random, saying the first thing that came into his head, anything to get her out of his room.

'Are you mad, or is this your usual approach to lovemaking? If so, it's peculiarly effective, quite refreshing as a matter of fact. Most men can't wait to take their clothes off in my company. You couldn't wait to put yours on!' She burst into peals of laughter. 'I really am impressed by your technique. Now, open the champagne. Well don't just stand there! Now what's wrong? Don't tell me you don't know how?'

'I don't. I've never opened a bottle of champagne in my life.'

'You must have led a damned sheltered life then.' Myra had stopped laughing, the charade was beginning to bore her.

'Yes, I have.' Desperately, 'My parents were Quakers, strict teetotallers.'

'How bloody boring for them. And are you a Quaker?'

'Not now, your ladyship.' Inspired,

150

William said, 'I'm a Methodist.'

'You'll be telling me next that Jesus wants you for a sunbeam,' Myra said coldly. Picking up the bottle and the glasses, she headed towards the door, opened it and disappeared without a backward glance.

Leaning against the door with relief William wiped the sweat from his forehead with the back of his hand. The last thing he'd envisaged would have been getting rid of predatory Myra Jessington by the simple expedient of putting on his trousers and admitting that he didn't know how to open a bottle of champagne.

Pressed further, he would also probably have admitted that he had never made love to a woman in his life either, and had no desire to engage in experimental sexual intercourse with a woman of her, Myra Jessington's calibre. Then the fat really would have been in the fire.

NINE

At a loose end throughout that long hot summer, William had taken to walking the streets of Darlington on Sundays and after work to soak up the atmosphere of the town, inevitably on the lookout for a familiar, well-loved face. Hoping against hope that he might one day bump into Lizzie in the market hall where he did his weekend shopping, or in the square near St Cuthbert's Church where the stalls were set out with all manner of goods: new and secondhand clothing, Victorian jewellery, household items, and where 'medicine men' sold homemade remedies guaranteed to cure everything from coughs to scurvy.

There were soapbox orators, too, spouting their political beliefs, alongside doom and gloom merchants prophesying the end of the world in the year ahead. Not that anyone took a blind bit of notice of them now the war was over and things were beginning to get back to normal. Darlington, sprawling and prosperous, had fared better than most during the war, with its great steelworks, engineering workshops and munitions factories as well as its indivisible links with George Stephenson, inventor of the first locomotive; founder of the Stockton to Darlington Railway which continued to bring wealth and kudos to the town.

There was something about Darlington's raw vitality which struck a chord in William's heart. An uplifting quality offering hope for the future despite his present loneliness of spirit. He refused to concede the possibility of never seeing Lizzie again, and one Saturday afternoon he did catch sight of her in the open market wheeling the pram, but the woman he recognised as her mother-in-law was with her. In any case he lost sight of her in the crowd on the far side of the square before he could get to her.

Thankfully, Lady Jessington had not uttered a word of complaint regarding William's brief sojourn at Jessington Hall, for the simple reason, he imagined, that her ladyship had no underlying cause for complaint—apart from the fact that her resident hairdresser had bored her half to death when she had gone down to his room in the early hours of the morning; in the face of which she had left in a huff, of her own accord.

All that Madame Marcia said afterwards, with a slight lifting of the eyebrows and a ghost of a smile was, 'I must congratulate you, William, on your handling of a delicate situation. Lady Myra explained that she had offered you the gift of a bottle of champagne which you, according to the strictures of your religious upbringing, felt unable to accept. All very right and proper, I must say. But I thought you were Church of England, not a Methodist with Quaker connections?'

153

'Ah well, needs must when the devil drives,' was all he would say on the subject.

His living quarters were a source of pleasure and much needed privacy. He enjoyed keeping the place in order, shopping and cooking for himself, using his ingenuity to produce a variety of meals on the gas-rings at his disposal. Stews were easily prepared, he'd discovered, from cheap cuts of meat from the covered market, plus plenty of vegetables—all cooked in the same pan, which saved washing up; and a good panful of stew lasted two days.

He'd taken to eating fruit for afters and porridge for breakfast, though his favourite food remained those hot pork pies from the butcher's shop in Skinnergate which he visited on a regular basis. Although they never tasted quite as good, eaten cold at suppertime, as they had done that day eaten hot in a shop doorway, and he never passed Maurice Schiller's old premises without experiencing a tug of regret that the old man had died shortly after his return to Germany; that he had not lived long enough to enjoy his homecoming.

The thing he loved most about his top-floor eyrie was the view from the sitting-room window: the myriad twinkling lights when darkness fell, the rosy glow of the distant steelworks, his sense of belonging. Because of Lizzie.

If only he knew for certain how she was faring, whether or not she was beginning to come to terms with the death of her husband; if she was still driving that milk float Bessie had mentioned?

Bessie, the girl he mistreated so badly ...

Truth to tell, Bessie was fast growing sick and tired of her job at the theatre. Showing folk to their seats without a word of thanks, gawping up at the stage once the performance had begun, envying all those toffee-nosed actresses in their fine clothes whose dressing rooms were filled with flowers and supper invitations galore, who then lined up on stage to take their bows to a storm of applause when the performance ended, not caring tuppence for the likes of herself with nothing to look forward to other than a walk home with her Pa or Dicky, a slice or two of brawn and a cup of cocoa before bedtime.

All very well for those actresses to get all the applause, they were just making believe at being unhappy. Unlike herself—she really *was* unhappy. Not that she got a ha'porth of sympathy from Elsie or her mother either, come to that. Emily had told her kindly but firmly to stop acting

155

like a tragedy queen. A broken romance at her age wasn't the end of the world, and William was too old for her anyway.

Elsie had simply crowed and said it served her right for giving herself airs and graces and being so stuck up, rubbing it in that she saw him quite often on the High Row during his dinner hour if she happened to be looking out of the hat shop window at the time, to which the irate Bessie responded sharply that it was a pity she had nowt better to do than stand there gawping.

Irritated past bearing by the silliness of her two youngest offspring, Emily said it was a pity that neither of them had anything better to do than squabble over a man when they could be giving her a hand with the housework. Emily knew the truth of the matter: that it was Lizzie William was in love with, because Dicky had told her. A nugget of information she kept to herself and begged her son not to divulge either, realising the trouble it might cause.

'I want your solemn promise, son,' she'd said, 'that you will not tell anyone else what you've just told me?'

'Not even Pa?'

'Not even your father. I'll tell him myself if I see fit. All I want is to keep the peace. We've had more than our fair share of

156

trouble lately, what with Madge going off the way she did and poor Tom committing suicide. The last thing I want is ill-feeling between Lizzie and Bessie. If Bessie found out it was Lizzie her young man had fallen in love with ... well, in my view, least said soonest mended.'

'All right, Ma. You have my promise, I won't say a word.' He'd added hopefully, 'By the way, I've saved up enough money for an engagement ring—'

Drawing in a deep breath, suddenly bone weary, she said, 'Fair enough, son. Now you'd better start saving up enough money for a house and furniture.'

Surprisingly, William missed Bessie to some extent. He'd become accustomed to her prattling presence in his life, not that he harboured the faintest desire to invite any of the girls he worked with to Sunday afternoon walks in the park or an evening out at the theatre. He realised the danger in creating a precedent in that direction, a misunderstanding of his motives. They could easily get it into their heads he was after a romantic liaison, not just an hour or two of lighthearted conversation; someone to talk to, the way he used to talk to Fred Willis. But he hadn't clapped eyes on Fred since the night of the brawl in the Ox.

Wondering how Fred was faring, his

doorbell rang one night and there was Fred on the pavement looking sheepish. 'Fancy a drink, Billy Boy?' he asked without preamble. 'Sorry I ain't been around lately. I'll be across the road at the King's Head if you fancy a noggin. Say in half an hour?'

'Why not come in and wait? It won't take me long to change.'

'Naw, best not. I'll get the drinks in. You nip across when you're ready.'

Walking across to the King's Head twenty minutes later, William wondered what he was in for; Fred's subdued demeanour was totally at odds with his usual hail-fellow-well-met outlook on life.

Entering the bar, he found Fred propped up against it, deep in conversation with Beulah Cammish, who, frowning slightly, said, 'Oh, I remember you. Billy's the name, isn't it? You left without finishing your drink.'

'Not in my company, he didn't,' Fred butted in. 'We were in here a couple of months ago, only you weren't on duty at the time. I'd have remembered if you had been—a bonny lass like you!' Hiccupping, saying, 'Beg pardon, I'm sure,' Fred continued, 'What a night that turned out to be, eh Billy Boy? With you thumping that landlord the way you did, an' running up Parker Street after the barmaid as if the devil was after you.'

Beulah's interest quickened, having heard about a fracas in the Ox a while back. Dicky's sister Lizzie had been working behind the bar at the time. Knocked out cold, the landlord had been, by some posh-spoken gent who'd had his eye on Lizzie, according to rumour. Well, this was a turn-up for the book and no mistake. But why Lizzie? She'd gained the impression it was Bessie Donen that Billy was walking out with. Well, now that she and Dicky were about to become officially engaged, she'd winkle the truth out of him in two seconds flat.

Seated at a corner table, their drinks in front of them, 'I wish you hadn't mentioned that night at the Ox.' William said irritably.

Eyebrows raised, 'Why ever not?' Fred enquired in all innocence. 'I don't get it, Billy Boy. Why the mystery? You can tell me.'

But William knew that he couldn't confide to Fred the way he used to. He also knew that Fred had been drinking quite heavily before he'd turned up on his doorstep. 'It isn't important. I was—courting,' the word almost stuck in his throat, 'the barmaid's sister, at the time. The girl I told you about, remember?'

'Yeah, sure,' Fred responded hazily, 'the

one you'd got lumbered with and wanted rid of because you were in love with someone else? So what happened?'

'Nothing. Nothing at all worth mentioning.' Hurriedly changing the subject, 'But never mind about me. How are you and Maudie getting along these days?'

'Since you ask, Billy Boy, not well. Not well at all,' Fred admitted despondently, 'and I don't know what to do about it. I'm still in love with her, you see, but she won't sleep with me any more. She's stuck me up in the spare room with that bloody scripture over the wash-stand as a punishment for walking out on her the way I did last time.'

'Well, what the devil else was a man supposed to do? I told you she'd been treating me like dirt, God alone knows why, after I'd tried my damndest to please her. I mean to say, that underwear I gave her last Christmas—those stays, brassieres, bloomers an' that pink peignoir—cost me a week's wages. Then summat went wrong all of a sudden; like she'd got her eye on someone else an' couldn't be bothered with me any more.'

The truth emerged at last. 'I think that someone was *you,* Billy Boy,' Fred said hoarsely. 'I'm not daft, you know. I cottoned on that it was you she really wanted from the word go. Oh, I'm not blaming you entirely. I knew you didn't want *her*, and that's when the trouble started. She couldn't bear the thought of making a fool of herself the way she did. Then, to make matters worse, Charlie started acting up because you went away so suddenly without saying goodbye to him, poor little sod.'

Fred laughed mirthlessly, 'Funny, ain't it? Poor Charlie apparently thought the sun shone out of your backside and you didn't even bother to say goodbye to him!'

'I'm sorry about that. It all happened in a bit of a hurry, if you recall? Maudie as good as told me to clear off, which I'd decided to do anyway. Just one thing, Fred, I never laid a finger on Mrs Thompson, nor had I any intention of doing so.'

'I know that. So does she—that's what's upsetting her. You'd have done better to have buttered her up a bit, told her you admired her looks, anything to keep her sweet.'

'*What?*' William looked shocked. 'And risk ending up in bed with her? What the hell do you take me for? I'm sorry, pal, but enough's enough. I'm off home.'

'No, don't go! Sorry, Billy Boy. No offence. I'm not thinking too clearly at the moment.'

'So I gathered, and that stuff won't help.' William liked a pint as well as

161

the next man, but Fred had downed his like a man dying of thirst, and there was no telling how many pints he'd drunk beforehand.

'I know. I know. It's just a question of Dutch courage, getting up the nerve to ask Maudie to—to marry me.'

William sat down abruptly. '*Marry* you? But I thought you said—'

'I know what I said, but dammit, Billy, I'm in love with the woman, an' I thought, well ... What I mean is, I think being married would make a difference; make her feel more secure like. Being appreciated an' all. Anyway, my mind's made up. I'm gonna ask her tonight, an' if she says no, well that'll be the end of it. She'll not see hide nor hair of me again. I'll clear out of her life for good and all!' He was speaking jerkily, emotionally, obviously deeply distressed.

William said, 'Come on, Fred, you're coming home with me. No way can you face Maudie the state you're in now. What you need is some strong coffee, a wash and brush up, a clean collar, a bit of shut eye, otherwise you won't stand a cat in hell's chance of success.'

Fred's eyes filled with tears. 'I knew I could trust you not to let me down,' he said, rising unsteadily to his feet. Turning in the doorway, 'Goo'night, Miss,' he called out to the barmaid.

Frowning, staring after Fred and his pal Billy, Beulah wondered what the hell was going on. Once again, Billy's pint of beer had been left half finished. So why not simply order half a pint of the stuff and have done with it? Men! She'd never get the hang of them if she lived to be a hundred. But why worry? She was going to her fiancé's house to tea tomorrow afternoon by way of celebrating their engagement, when she would wear the ring he'd bought her for the first time. Not that she was exactly looking forward to tea in the Donens' front room, having been there before. Not a barrel of laughs exactly, with Mrs Donen looking daggers at her, Dicky's pa as grumpy as hell, his sisters as daft as two-bob watches—except Lizzie, who had more sense than the other two lumped together.

William brewed up a pan of hot strong coffee the way Maurice Schiller had taught him, sent Fred to the bathroom to swill his face and hands, then pumped coffee into him until Fred protested he'd be sick if he drank any more of the stuff. 'That's the idea,' William said grimly as Fred hurried back to the bathroom. 'Feeling better now?'

'Not much. Have a heart, Billy Boy. No

more coffee, for Gawd's sake!' Leaning his head back, he fell asleep in his chair, waking an hour later by which time William had found him a clean shirt and collar.

'Now how do you feel?'

'Not bad at all, considering. How do I look?'

'A damn sight better than you did an hour ago.' William paused, 'Look, Fred, are you sure you're doing the right thing, asking Mrs Thompson to marry you?'

'It's the only thing I *can* do. I need to know where I stand.'

'What if she says no?'

'Then I'll trek back to Newcastle. Things are picking up now in my line of business, with the Christmas stock coming into the warehouse.'

'But we're only just into September?'

'I know, but the shopkeepers will want to place their orders well in advance, so I'll have plenty to keep my mind occupied if ... You don't really think she'll say no, do you? Gawd's truth, it don't bear thinking about.' Getting up, he took off the crumpled shirt he'd been wearing and put on the clean one. 'Only one way to find out, I suppose. Just tell me one thing, and be honest about it. Does my breath smell?'

'No more than usual.' William grinned, pleased by the old feeling of comradeship between them. 'Let me know how you get on?'

'Yeah, sure thing, and thanks, Billy. Any message for Maudie, by the way?'

'No, but if you see Charlie, give him my regards. Tell him I'm sorry I left without saying goodbye.'

TEN

One day towards the end of October, Lizzie made her weekly pilgrimage to Samuel Lowry's shop in Northgate to pay another instalment. Feeling as she always did on these occasions, unclean somehow, she entered the premises of a man she loathed and detested deeply conscious of the pawnbroker's sign above the doorway and the plethora of unredeemed pledges in the window. Pathetic reminders of ordinary people such as herself in dire financial straits who had found it necessary to part with precious personal objects—rings, watches, brooches and the like—often with no hope of redemption.

She hated the smell of the shop almost as much as its owner. The odour of fried food, floating down from the living quarters upstairs, had got trapped in the narrow confines of a shop crammed with secondhand furniture, and seemed also to have permeated the hair and clothing of the man himself. A spider of a man in the centre of a web spun from other people's misfortunes.

'Ah, if it isn't Mrs Imerson?' Lowry said smoothly as she laid a ten-shilling note on the counter. 'My word, things must be looking up for you at last. Working hard, are we, in aid of the dear departed? Still, quite a long way to go yet, haven't we?'

Refusing to bandy words with the man, hanging on to her dignity, 'If you wouldn't mind giving me a receipt?' Lizzie said quietly, physically repelled by the sight and smell of him leering at her across the counter. Deeply distressed by his reference to Tom as 'the dear departed', so objectionally uttered—a snide reference to the manner in which her husband had met his death; a kind of slur on his memory.

'Ah yes, of course, the receipt,' Lowry said mockingly, 'without which you would have no proof whatever that you had paid me anything at all. Well, that's true, isn't it? Think about it, Mrs Imerson. Your word against mine? On the other hand, I might be persuaded to cancel the debt outright if you were not so standoffish. A little kiss or two to begin with, perhaps?'

Suddenly seizing her wrists, pulling her

forward, breathing heavily, he attempted to kiss her on the mouth. Struggling to free herself, crying out, turning her head this way and that to avoid his lips on hers, sickened by the sight of his decaying teeth, the foul smell of his breath near her nostrils, in desperation she sank her teeth into the fleshy part of his right hand between finger and thumb drawing blood, causing him to loosen his grip on her wrists, to curse and swear as the blood welled from the wound she had inflicted on him, calling her a bloody bitch, and worse.

Not that Lizzie cared what he called her now that she was free of his grip, the obscene presence of the man, the sickening sight and smell of him. Turning, she ran blindly out of the shop into the fresh air and all the way to Tubwell Row, heart hammering against her ribs; scarcely able to breathe let alone run, in a near state of collapse, her legs like jelly. One thought drove her on: to seek refuge in the kitchen of Attica, knowing that Nan had taken Emma to South Park this afternoon to feed the ducks, and they wouldn't be back yet.

How she managed the stairs, she scarcely knew. She was in the kitchen sobbing her heart out when Lewis Gilbert entered the room wanting to know what had happened,

167

what was wrong, speaking to her gently, alarmed by the state she was in.

When she told him, albeit disjointedly, he made her some tea, told her to rest awhile on the sitting-room sofa, and went downstairs. Later, she heard what sounded like the closing of the shop door, but she couldn't be certain. Tired out, she fell asleep almost immediately beneath the rug Lewis had tucked about her feet and legs, her cheek on the soft cushion he had placed beneath her head.

How long she slept she had no idea. The room had been light when she fell asleep, now it was shadowy and she was not alone. Lewis was in a chair near the fireplace, deep in thought. Sitting up, 'What time is it?' she asked anxiously.

'Please listen, Lizzie,'—the first time he had called her that—'I have something to tell you. You may be angry with me, but I did what I thought was in your best interests.'

'What have you done?' Lizzie looked at him apprehensively.

'I've been to see Lowry to tell him to keep his filthy suggestions to himself in future. Not that you'll be troubled by him again. You see, I've paid off the money you owed him.'

Getting up, still shaking slightly from her ordeal, 'You've done *what?*' she said hoarsely. 'By what right do you meddle in my affairs without even asking my permission? It was *my* business, not yours to pay off that debt. Poor I may be, but I'm not a charity case yet.' Rounding on him fiercely, 'Paying off that money for Tom's sake was my way of honouring his memory in the only way I knew how, the only way left to me.'

'Charity doesn't enter into it,' Lewis said quietly. Standing up to face her, 'At least not in the way you mean. The money involved seemed of little importance compared with the treatment you received at the hands of that brute. Did you really imagine I would stand by without doing all in my power to spare you the humiliation of ever entering that shop again? No man worth his salt would stand for seeing the woman he loves beholden to a man not worthy so much as to clean her shoes!'

He hadn't meant to tell her he loved her, knowing it was far too soon—a woman still in mourning for her husband. Turning slowly, he said softly, 'I'm sorry, Lizzie, I shouldn't have said what I did, but it happens to be true. I do love you, and I believe I always will.' Drawing in a deep breath, 'You have become a part of my life, you and Emma. It would break my heart to lose you now, through my own stupidity.'

Anger forgotten, and in any case anger allied to foolish pride, Lizzie realised the depth of the man's suffering at her hands, 'Who said anything about losing me?' she said gently. 'Unless you're thinking of sacking me, and I wouldn't blame you if you did. The trouble is, you have become a part of our lives, too. Mine and Emma's.' The room was almost dark now. 'You'd better light the gas, hadn't you?'

'Yes. Yes, of course.' Dipping a spill into the embers of the fire, he lit the gas mantles flanking the fireplace one by one, dispelling the shadows between them as Lizzie smoothed back her hair, pinned on her hat and put on her jacket.

'I'll walk home with you,' Lewis said.

'No, I'll be quite all right, thank you. I've caused you enough trouble for one day.'

'As you wish.' He left it at that, knowing there was nothing more to be said for the time being. It was up to Lizzie to decide. His future happiness lay in her hands now, and he would count every day she remained with him as a blessing, whether or not she ever loved him in return.

Crossing the Skerne bridge past the Ox, Lizzie remembered the fight that had taken place there; the way William Chalmers' fists had gone into action on her behalf.

William. Strange how often she recalled that episode and thought about him since that night. He had told her he loved her, not that she'd believed him. Now another man had told her the same thing, but there was a world of difference between them. William was young, impulsive; Lewis Gilbert a man of maturity, kind and thoughtful.

She trusted Lewis implicitly. William, on the other hand, had treated her sister badly. And yet she had known all along that he was not in love with Bessie; had said as much to Nan the day of that Sunday afternoon tea-party. She also knew Bessie's penchant for running after men, and it wasn't surprising she'd taken a shine to the well-spoken, handsome William Chalmers. It would be hard, almost impossible for anyone not to like him.

Deep in thought, she remembered the way he'd stood up when she entered the room that Sunday afternoon; the frisson of pleasure she'd experienced when he smiled at her. As if they had met before somewhere, a long time ago, only she couldn't remember where or when.

She wished now, too late, that she had not reacted so angrily when he told her he loved her, accusing him of being either drunk or mad instead of listening to what he had to say. Maybe interceding on his

171

behalf when Dicky rushed out of the house like a raging bull threatening to beat the living daylights out of him if he showed his face in Parker Street again?

It had lain within her power that night to diffuse a difficult situation. Dicky would have listened to her had she explained that William had fought a battle of honour on her behalf in the bar of the Ox, had she possessed the grace to admit that he was right in saying she should never have taken so demeaning a job to the detriment of her self-respect.

Was there, she wondered, some flaw in her character, some lack of humility which prevented her accepting kindness? Had she grown too proud, too stubbornly independent since the death of her husband, to admit gratitude?

Today, for instance, she had turned on Lewis Gilbert in a fury over the repayment of her debt to Samuel Lowry. But why? For what reason? Like William Chalmers, Lewis Gilbert had acted unselfishly on her behalf, their actions motivated by—love.

Halfway home, Lizzie pondered the meaning of the word. Love, as she knew it, sprung from her earliest memories of childhood: the ceaseless, untiring, undemanding love of her parents. Later had come a different kind of love with her childhood playmate, Tom Imerson, which had blossomed in time to a boy and girl relationship of a few stolen kisses on her doorstep when they'd said goodnight to one another.

Even now, she remembered the fast beating of her heart when Tom's lips met hers, and yet she had known even then that kisses were merely a part of, not the whole of loving; had wondered what the whole of loving entailed? Seeking her mother's advice, albeit nervously, blushing to the roots of her hair as she did so. Emily had told her, quietly and practically, the facts of life—about the deeper physical aspects of love to do with marriage and the procreation of children born of an intimate physical relationship between man and wife.

This was by far the most wonderful relationship in life, Emily had told her daughter, and nothing to be afraid of. And yet Lizzie had been afraid, on the eve of her wedding to Tom Imerson, that she was about to marry not the boy she had been in love with since they'd chalked hopscotch squares together on the Parker Street pavements, but a total stranger.

Yet, blessedly, her brief marriage to Tom had bequeathed to her the gift of Emma. Now she was beginning to realise, as Emily had done, that mother love bore no resemblance to any other kind of loving.

Reaching home, she thought given the chance she would tell William Chalmers she was sorry she had behaved badly towards him. Not that there was much likelihood of that happening. Time had moved on since the Ox incident. Passing St Cuthbert's Church, she had noticed that the trees in the churchyard were beginning to shed their leaves.

When Emma had been put to bed, Lizzie told Nan about her visit to the pawnbrokers. Deeply shocked, 'That's it, then!' she said angrily, 'You're not to go there again, do you hear? *I'll* go in future. Happen he'll not fancy kissing me when I've given him a piece of my mind. The very idea! Taking advantage of a young widow.'

It was then Lizzie told her mother-in-law that Lewis Gilbert had paid off the debt; speaking hesitantly, uncertain how Nan would react to the news—a woman as fiercely proud and independent as herself.

To her surprise and relief, Nan's face softened. She said, 'He must think the world of you to have done such a thing, Lizzie love.'

'Well yes, Nan. As a matter of fact—'

'No need to tell me,' the older woman interrupted gently, 'it's as plain as the nose on your face, the man's in love with you?'

'Yes, but—'

'But what? You're a lovely young woman in the prime of life, and this Lewis Gilbert's heart is obviously in the right place. I'd have been surprised if he hadn't fallen in love with you, the way you've looked after him.'

'He's looked after me, too, and Emma,' Lizzie replied wistfully, 'but I can't help wishing he hadn't told me he loved me. It's far too soon, after Tom.'

'From your point of view perhaps,' Nan conceded thoughtfully. 'But Tom, God rest him, would have been the last person to stand in the way of your future happiness.' Her face puckered talking of her son, remembering all that he had meant to her and Lizzie during his lifetime. 'All I'm saying is: don't turn your back on happiness from a sense of duty towards Tom. The chance of happiness, real happiness, seldom comes twice.'

Nan concluded, setting the kitchen table in readiness for their evening meal, 'If Lewis Gilbert is in love with you, happen he'll ask you to marry him one of these days. If so, take my advice, Lizzie. Find a resting place in your heart for Tom, then put the past behind you and make a new life for yourself and Emma.'

'All well and good,' Lizzie retorted, prodding a panful of potatoes bubbling

175

on the kitchen range, with a skewer, 'presupposing that I would want to marry Mr Gilbert even if he asked me.' She added, replacing the lid on the potatoes, 'You see, Nan, I'm not in love with him. Oh, I like and respect him enormously. He's one of the nicest, kindest people I've ever met, but I'm not in love with him. The—magic is missing somehow. You know? The magic of being in love?'

She was thinking of William Chalmers at the time. Nan looked at her quizzically. 'I don't, as it happens,' she said matter of factly. 'Tom's dad wasn't the romantic type and neither was I. I went into the butcher's shop where he worked one day. He asked me to walk out with him, I said yes, and that was that. Mind you, he wasn't bad looking and he had a good steady job. I felt—comfortable with him. There was nowt magical about it, we just paired off like most young couples did in those days. Started saving for a house—this house—and when we'd saved enough, we got married, as simple as that.'

Nan laughed, 'We did our courting in the front parlour of my folks' house in Victoria Road, sitting side by side on the sofa. Him at one end of it, me at the other, with my ma poking her head round the door every five minutes to make sure we hadn't moved. Truth to tell, on our wedding night we didn't know what to say to each other, we felt that embarrassed. But he was a good man, a good husband and father, and that's what mattered.'

Lizzie knew what she was trying to say, that there was more to marriage than falling in love—security for one thing, mutual respect for another; kindness and consideration. And perhaps Nan was right.

She had, after all, had her taste of springtime romance with the boy of her choice, her childhood sweetheart, Tom Imerson. The magic of springtime could never be reprised; that awareness of the beauty of the world by night, of stars, shadows and moonlight. War had ended that springtime magic.

'Those potatoes should be done now,' Nan said, breaking in on her reverie. 'No, you sit down, Lizzie, I'll see to them. You've had a shock, so you're bound to feel a bit up in the air.'

'I'm worried about tomorrow,' Lizzie confessed. 'Things might be awkward between me and Mr Gilbert after—well, you know.'

'I wouldn't worry about that, if I were you,' Nan advised cheerfully. 'These things have a way of working out all right in the end. Take that night when Bessie's young man made a fool of himself. You did right to give that young idiot his marching orders. Your ma wasn't sorry to see the back of him neither. She said he was too old for Bessie anyway. Not that she disliked what's his name?'

'William,' Lizzie reminded her.

'Yes, that was it. Well, as your ma said, he was quietly spoken, well mannered, good looking, but not right for Bessie. So that worked out all right in the end, didn't it?'

Lizzie made no reply. She wasn't quite sure what to say. Things certainly hadn't worked out all right for Bessie, or herself come to think of it, since she still held herself responsible for the abrupt ending of her sister's happiness.

ELEVEN

The awkwardness Lizzie feared between herself and Lewis Gilbert did not arise thanks to Emma, whose gurgled delight at seeing him again made them both laugh. In any event, Lewis had not seemed ill at ease; quite the opposite—more buoyant than usual!, imbued with a new sense of purpose. As though taking positive action on her behalf and telling her he loved her had added to his stature.

Recalling her conversation with Nan the night before, Lizzie realised what she'd said was true, that the chance of happiness seldom comes twice in a lifetime. Food for thought. And Lewis Gilbert was a fine man: a decent, upright man—albeit much older than herself—but still attractive to look at, possessed of a keen sense of humour, well-read and intelligent. Above all, kind. A man of shining integrity deserving of his share of love and happiness and children of his own to care for.

With these thoughts in mind, Lizzie knew deep down that the day would come when Lewis Gilbert would ask her to marry him. In the meanwhile, she was happy in her work. Dicky and Beulah were engaged and saving up to get married, and Bessie had found herself a new gentleman friend, so Emily had told her when Lizzie called to see her mother on her way to work. 'Which means another Sunday afternoon tea-party,' Emily said with a martyred air. 'Let's hope it turns out better than the last.'

She added, 'Why not ask Mr Gilbert to tea one Sunday? Dad and I would like to meet him, and he might enjoy a bit of company seeing he's alone on Sundays?'

'All right, Mum, I'll ask him, but he's a little on the shy side,' Lizzie responded, not entirely happy with the idea.

179

The tea-party took place a fortnight later. In a state of nerves, though she couldn't think why, Lizzie helped Emily with the cooking, baking and setting the front room table, wondering what Lewis—as she now called him—would make of her family environment. Doubly uncertain what her family would make of him.

Thankfully, her outspoken brother would be having tea at his fiancée's house, but Bessie and her new boyfriend, her sister Elsie, Nan and little Emma would be present; quite a gathering for a shy man to contend with. Lizzie hoped that Lewis would not gain the impression he was being vetted as a possible suitor. Her blood ran cold at the thought, recalling William Chalmers' grilling in that very room as a suitor for Bessie, and the trouble it had caused in the long run.

The witching hour in this case was not midnight but five o'clock on a murky November afternoon. At a quarter to, Bessie and her boyfriend, a slender youth called Jimmy Blaney who was a stagehand at the theatre, appeared looking nithered after a walk in the park. Bessie's face suspiciously red from close contact with Jimmy's embryo moustache. As if, Lizzie thought, he wished to prove himself capable of growing hair on his face at his age.

Minutes later, Nan entered by the back door with Emma in her arms, warmly wrapped in a shawl. Then Elsie came downstairs, her face as long as a fiddle, at odds with the world as usual and tea-parties in particular; deeply resentful of Bessie's success with the opposite gender whilst no man had ever given her so much as a second glance. She wished William Chalmers would. That would be one in the eye for Bessie, Elsie thought darkly. William was a proper man, not a skinny bit of a lad who couldn't be bothered to shave his top lip.

She still didn't know what had gone wrong between Bessie and William because it had been hushed up for some reason. Dicky, Ma and Lizzie knew, but they weren't letting on. Now some old bloke Lizzie worked for was coming to tea, and what this was in aid of God only knew, with Tom Imerson scarcely cold in his grave.

At five o'clock precisely the door knocker rat-tatted and Lizzie hurried along the passage to find Lewis on the pavement holding a bunch of flowers. 'Oh, how pretty,' Lizzie said. 'Please come in, you must be frozen. It's so cold out.' It seemed odd somehow, a complete role reversal, inviting Lewis Gilbert into her home instead of vice versa; seeing him in his outdoor things instead of his usual informal clothing worn at the shop: corduroy trousers, soft-collared shirts, pullovers or cardigans.

Today he wore a grey suit and a starched collar in honour of the occasion. Introducing him to her family and young Blaney, Lizzie wished this had never happened—this formal tea-party with everyone in their best bib and tucker. Once again, Emma broke the ice, holding out her chubby fists to him, crowing her delight, wriggling in Nan's arms and wanting to be held by him.

Emily laughed. 'She certainly likes you, Mr Gilbert.'

Lewis smiled, 'Yes, Emma and I are old friends.'

Elsie thought he wasn't bad looking for an old man. Bessie was too wrapped up in Blaney to care tuppence about anyone else. At least Jimmy had a bit of go about him in the kissing and cuddling department, though she wished his tash would grow a bit faster. It was at the rag, tag and bobtail stage at the moment and playing havoc with her complexion.

Jack Donen had reservations about Lewis Gilbert's appearance for Sunday afternoon tea in the front parlour. He much preferred having his tea in the kitchen, shirt-sleeves rolled up to his elbows, braces showing, and not having to wear a suit, collar and tie on his day of rest. A fortnight ago he'd been required to dress up to meet Bessie's latest gentleman friend whom he'd disliked intensely the minute he'd clapped eyes on him—a fakey young fellah in his opinion, with that face-fungus of his.

He greeted Gilbert perfunctorily with a brief nod, leaving the smiling and handshaking to his wife and Nan Imerson. Uncertain of Emily's motives in providing a slap-up meal for the man in the first place unless ... but no, surely not?

Glancing at Lizzie, her cheeks seemed pinker than usual, Jack thought, but then so did Bessie's, and he could guess why. Well, he'd have a word or two to say about that later, when this blasted tea-party was over. Lizzie's colour, however, may have derived from all the baking she'd done earlier in a warm kitchen. Certainly not from a courting session in a shelter in the South Park on a cold winter afternoon, as Bessie's did.

All in all, the party passed off quite successfully, to Lizzie's relief; mainly due to Emma's presence at the table in her highchair, banging her spoon in anticipation of jelly and custard.

At a quarter to six, 'I'd best be taking

her back home now,' Nan said, lifting her grandchild from the highchair as she rose to her feet, at which point Lewis stood up also—a mark of respect in the presence of a lady about to leave the room. William Chalmers had once risen to his feet, Lizzie remembered, when she entered it.

'She's half asleep already,' Nan said, cradling the child's head against her shoulder, 'so I'll pop her into her pram for the time being, shall I? It seems a pity to disturb her.'

'Of course, Nan. I'll be along soon to bath and change her,' Lizzie said, as Lewis quietly moved away from the table to open the door for them.

Looking up at him, 'It has been a real pleasure meeting you, Mr Gilbert,' Nan said warmly. 'I hope we'll meet again one day.'

'I hope so too, Mrs Imerson,' Lewis responded, liking the woman immensely, praying inwardly that his tentative plans for the future would one day come to fruition. Knowing those plans depended entirely on Lizzie's reaction when he asked her to marry him.

'I still can't understand why you invited Gilbert to tea,' Jack said later, getting ready for bed. 'Is there something I don't know about? I notice you and Nan have

184

had your heads together a lot lately.'

'No more than usual,' Emily said, braiding her hair. 'You know I pop in most afternoons for a cup of tea. Good gracious, we've been friends a long time now.' She paused. 'What did you think of Lewis Gilbert?'

'He's all right,' Jack conceded, 'but what's he up to, that's what I'd like to know? I couldn't help noticing the way he looked at Lizzie.'

'Well, why not? She's worth looking at, isn't she?' Emily got into bed.

'Of course she is. That's not the point. I don't want him getting too fond of her, a man of his age.'

'Look, love, there's something I haven't told you. Two things, as a matter of fact.'

Jack groaned, 'Now what?' Fearing the worst. 'He hasn't—?'

'No, of course not! Oh for heaven's sake get into bed, man, before you catch your death of cold. How can I talk to you standing there in your nightshirt? That's better, now just listen to what I have to say. It's about the money Tom Imerson borrowed from that pawnbroker ...'

Listening intently, Jack heard the story from beginning to end, the way Gilbert had fettled Samuel Lowry on Lizzie's behalf and paid off the debt owing to him to spare her the necessity of ever having to enter his shop again. Then Emily told him about the night at the Ox when young William Chalmers had told Lizzie he loved her, and when their son, overhearing the conversation, had threatened William with physical violence if he ever showed his face in Parker Street again.

'So what are you really saying?' Jack asked bemusedly when his wife had finished speaking.

'Simply this,' Emily explained, 'that Lizzie needs a good man to take care of her and a secure future for herself and Emma. Lewis Gilbert *is* a good man who really cares about her and our granddaughter, so if he asks her to marry him, and if she wants to, let's not stand in the way of her happiness, shall we?'

Jack said unexpectedly, 'I suppose not, if you really think Lizzie would be happy with a man she's not in love with.'

Emily said quietly, 'There are different degrees of loving.'

But Jack couldn't make head nor tail of that point of view. To his way of thinking, no woman in her right senses would want to marry a man she wasn't in love with. Physical intimacy between a man and his wife depended, in his view, on a mutual depth of feeling for one another, without which the act of love would amount to nothing more than a meaningless charade.

Knowing exactly what he felt, yet lacking Emily's superior facility with words, all he said was, 'Why all the rush? Lizzie's still young, with her life before her. In any case she's still in mourning for Tom Imerson.'

Snuggling down to get warm, it struck Emily as odd that Lizzie's husband was usually referred to as Tom Imerson, seldom by his christian name alone, as if he had never really been an intrinsic part of their lives. Harking back, she remembered saying, 'Lizzie's out playing with young Tom Imerson'. Later, 'Lizzie and Tom Imerson have gone for a walk in the park'. Later still, 'Tom Imerson's been posted to France'.

Somehow he'd never seemed quite right for Lizzie, just a boy she'd grown up with who had taken it for granted that they would get married one day. Lizzie had done all the loving and giving, and it had worried Emily that she entered a one-sided marriage with a man prepared to give little or nothing in return. Affection, perhaps. Certainly not love. Which was why Emily now wanted Lizzie to marry someone who loved her as she deserved to be loved; to provide the security, warmth and happiness so sadly lacking in her marriage to Tom Imerson.

Strangely enough, Emily had discovered, Nan Imerson felt the same way—that Lizzie deserved a secure future with a man capable of dispelling the shadow of the tragedy which had befallen her so early on in life. Lewis Gilbert ...

The first week in December, Lewis asked Lizzie to marry him. She stared at him, dumbstruck at first, across the kitchen table on which she had just placed a steaming Lancashire hot-pot.

Then, finding her voice, 'But it's far too soon,' she said huskily, 'I'm still in mourning for Tom.' She added, 'Besides, this is scarcely the time or the place. I mean with me in my pinafore and you about to tuck into a plate of stew.'

'On the other hand,' Lewis said gently, 'I felt it appropriate to ask the woman I love to marry me in familiar surroundings. You see, Lizzie, all I own, this house, this kitchen, myself included, might well cease to exist without you.

'Oh, I'm not conceited enough to believe that I could ever take the place of Tom Imerson in your heart. I wouldn't even try. And I'm not asking you to marry me on any given date in the future. All I'm asking is that you will think over my proposal and decide whether or not to accept it.'

He paused, 'Need I add that if you say

yes, I will do everything within my power to make you happy? You and Emma. I love you both so much.'

At this dramatic turning point in her life, Lizzie knew the time had come to get the future into perspective for her child's sake as well as her own. The past years had taken their toll; war years of doubt and uncertainty, heartbreak and bereavement from which no-one had emerged unscathed either emotionally or physically.

She had been luckier than most inasmuch as Tom had come home apparently in one piece. Other girls of her generation—in Parker Street alone—had been less fortunate; laughing companions of her schooldays whose husbands had died on the battlefields of France, whose young lives had also been touched by tragedy.

Now, given the chance to put the past behind her, to make a fresh start, had she the right to deny Emma the right to a better, more hopeful future in a world at peace? And yet ...

Lizzie said softly, sitting down at the table, 'I'm sorry, Lewis, I couldn't leave Nan after all she's been through.'

'I wouldn't want you to,' Lewis said, covering her hands with his. 'She'd be welcome to live here with us. This is a big house, my love, with far too many empty rooms.'

A sweet feeling of relief flooded through Lizzie; the awareness of a richer, more mature love than she had ever known. She loved this house above the bookshop, and the shop itself with its towering shelves, library ladders, musky scent of leather bindings; the little partitioned-off cubicle where Lewis kept his account books, the wall near the office hung with prints of old Darlington—one of which, depicting a flock of geese on their way to market at the turn of the century, was Emma's favourite.

Looking across the kitchen table at Lewis, feeling the warmth of his hands on hers, Lizzie knew he had been right to ask her to marry him in this setting with Emma playing happily with a rag doll Nan Imerson had made for her. Most importantly, she knew that she loved him, not as she had loved Tom but that this was as it should be.

How wise Nan had been, how understanding in advising her to find a resting place in her heart for Tom then to put the past behind her and make a new life for herself and Emma.

Smiling at Lewis, reaching her decision, 'I'll do my best to make you a good wife,' Lizzie said softly.

Closing his eyes momentarily, Lewis thanked God in his heart for Lizzie's reply. Then, rising to his feet, drawing her towards him and holding her gently in his arms, he kissed her.

It was a time of quiet celebration.

She and Lewis would marry in St Cuthbert's Church early in the new year, Lizzie told her parents and Nan, without undue fuss or bother. It would be a simple family affair followed by a buffet lunch in her new home.

The bride, like her mother before her, would wear a plain grey costume and carry a prayer book instead of flowers. There would be no honeymoon as such. She and her husband would spend the rest of the weekend after the wedding ceremony at home alone with Emma, though they might well go for a walk in the park on the Sunday afternoon with a bag of bread for the ducks. Emma would love that. Feeding the ducks on the South Park lake had always been a favourite pastime of hers.

With Christmas fast approaching and with Lizzie's wedding in the offing, Emily Donen scarcely knew if she was on her head or her heels with all the extra cooking, cleaning and shopping to see to. Nan would make Lizzie's wedding cake, and Emily had already bought the material for her daughter's wedding outfit

191

from a department store on the High Row—fine woollen material in a pretty shade of dove grey.

Seldom had Emily felt happier than she did then, planning the family Christmas, buying presents: slippers and socks for Jack, embroidered hankies for Elsie, a bottle of eau-de-cologne for Bessie, chocolates for Beulah, a jack-in-the box for Emma, lavender water for Nan, a tie for Dicky, a new prayer book for Lizzie, initialled linen handkerchiefs for Lewis.

She ran out of ideas when it came to Jimmy Blaney, but supposed she must give him something since he and Bessie were now 'going strong'— Wickedly, she thought of a moustache-cup. But no, better not she thought, settling for a tie-pin.

Her only regret was that Madge would not be present at the dinner table on Christmas Day.

TWELVE

William's meeting with Bessie came about by chance one Saturday afternoon on the High Row. The salon closed at one o'clock on Saturdays, after which he usually did his weekend shopping. Today, however,

192

he had Christmas presents and cards to buy along with what appeared to be half the population of Darlington.

The High Row was a seething mass of humanity beneath the early-lit gas lamps, people jostling in and out of the shops, carrying parcels, oblivious to the keen December wind and the pattering of hailstones on the pavements.

About to enter a stationer's to buy greeting cards for his mother, sisters and the girls at the salon, he came face to face with Bessie Donen unexpectedly, the first time he had set eyes on her since the unfortunate showdown with Dicky.

Bearing the girl no ill will, rather blaming himself for the abrupt ending of their ill-fated 'courtship', 'Hello, Bessie,' he said.

'Huh!' she burst forth, 'You can keep your hellos for them that wants 'em. I'm sure *I* don't, you nasty little snake in the grass!' Cheeks reddened by the wind, eyes watering, 'Stringing me along the way you did and carrying on with someone else behind my back at the same time. Well, where is she, that other woman of yours? Or have you given her the brush off the same as you did me?'

'You've got it all wrong, Bessie,' he said, miserably aware of the hailstones sneaking past his overcoat collar, the way they had done the night he'd bumped into her on her way to work, he recalled. 'There is no "other woman", there never was. At least, not in the way you mean. I certainly wasn't "carrying on" behind your back.' Aware of entering deep water, knowing he could never explain to her satisfaction the reason why he had given her the brush off, he said simply, 'I'm sorry, Bessie, I never meant to hurt you so much. Please say you forgive me?'

'Why? Conscience bothering you, is it? Well I don't give a toss about your conscience, nor you neither. So put that in your pipe and smoke it! I've got a proper gentleman friend now, if you must know. An' so has Lizzie, so happen there'll be three weddings in the family next year now Dicky an' Beulah Cammish have got engaged an' with me an' Jimmy going strong. So now you know!'

They were standing in close proximity to one another, crowded together near the stationer's doorway by people pushing to get past them. Deeply shocked, William said hoarsely, 'Lizzie's getting married? But that's not possible!'

'Oh? And why not, I should like to know? If it's any of your business, she's getting married in January. It's all arranged. Ma's making her wedding dress an' me an' Elsie are gonna be bridesmaids.'

Bessie's moment of triumph, derived

from rubbing in the fact that she and her new gentleman friend might well be altar-bound in the foreseeable future, seemed infinitely more rewarding when William, white-faced and obviously upset, excused himself abruptly, pushed his way through the throng of people surrounding them and disappeared among the even thicker crowds hurrying along the High Row.

Forgetting his shopping spree, the cards and presents he had meant to buy that afternoon, alone in his apartment above the salon, William buried his face in his hands. What Bessie told him could not possibly be true, he thought dully, feeling the warm seepage of tears between his fingers. And yet he knew that it was, that he had lost Lizzie, the love of his life, beyond recall. But why? For what reason?

He knew why. Because, in his immaturity he had failed to understand that a woman of Lizzie's calibre and independence of spirit could never be taken by force. He knew now that the Ox incident had been a mistake from start to finish. All he had done that night was humiliate her in front of a roomful of onlookers. Now he was paying the full price of his folly.

Alone in his despair, he became gradually aware of a cessation of noise from the street below. All the frantic afternoon shoppers

195

had gone home to their own firesides and the shops had closed their doors for the night.

Getting up, he stared out of the window at the panorama of rooftops and chimneys adumbrated against the reddish glow from the steelworks' furnaces, and knew that he no longer wanted to stay in that town which had once seemed so exciting and filled with promise for the future.

He thought then of his former life, of his mother and sisters making preparations for Christmas, of Scarborough with the sea on its doorstep; of all he turned his back on so carelessly in his abortive quest for independence, freedom, in the mistaken belief that with personal liberty would come a much-needed feeling of maturity. Nothing of the kind had happened—apart from his love for Lizzie.

He saw it all clearly now, in retrospect. Knowing he loved her, he should have ended his relationship with Bessie as kindly as possible before the so-called affair got out of hand. Herr Schiller had given him good advice which he had chosen to ignore. Then, lumbered with Bessie, he had lacked the courage to tell her the truth: that it was Lizzie not her he was in love with.

And what if he had? Would that have made any difference in the long run?

Probably not, but at least his conscience would have been clear. Free from the burden of guilt caused by his own weakness and shabby treatment of Bessie.

He'd heard nothing from Fred Willis since the night he'd set off to propose marriage to Maudie Thompson. Maurice Schiller was dead and gone, Bessie hadn't had a kind word to say to him—and as for Lizzie ... Filled with an overwhelming sense of misery, he thought about the man she was going to marry. Who was he? What was he? Was she in love with him? Would he make her happy? Questions to which he would never know the answer.

His mind made up, he would hand in his notice to Marcia Hunter, work until the salon closed on Christmas Eve, then catch a train home to Scarborough.

Christmas, William thought, turning away from the window of his lonely eyrie, was a time when families should be together; a time of reconciliation. He knew that his mother would welcome his return home despite what she considered to be his naughtiness in leaving it in the first place; witness her many hastily-penned letters to him on the subject during the past months of his defection, all ending with the P.S. *'Nell and Louisa send you their love'*.

Devastated by his decision to leave her employ on Christmas Eve, 'But *why*, William?' Marcia Hunter wanted to know. 'Haven't you been happy here? Oh, I realise you disliked your visit to Jessington Hall intensely, and I can see why, believe me. On the other hand, you have begun to build up your own clientele. Besides which,' she added cannily, 'the girls think the world of you.'

The girls were equally devastated when they knew he was leaving. But nothing they could say or do could persuade him to change his mind. And so, on the eve of his departure, they gave him a set of rolled-gold cufflinks, a Christmas card bearing all their signatures, to wish him luck and to kiss him goodbye.

With a final look round his apartment, the final fastening of his suitcase, William walked resolutely towards the Bank Top Station, from which he had emerged one winter afternoon, almost a year ago.

Taking the quickest route, he walked across the open market place, past St Cuthbert's Church, across the Skerne bridge into Parker Street. Memories of his brief sojourn in Darlington flooded back bringing tears to his eyes, as if he were seeing the town for the first time, not the last.

Passing the corner shop, he glanced up at the lighted front room window and wondered if Maudie Thompson's fire was burning as brightly now as it had been the first time he'd entered that room; whether Fred was spending Christmas with her; and whether poor Charlie was still playing his favourite gramophone record or if his mother had carried out her threat to smash it to smithereens.

As he anticipated, the light was on in the Donens' front parlour. He imagined Mrs Donen making last-minute preparations in readiness for tomorrow; placing sprigs of holly behind the picture frames, perhaps? Doubtless she would have been to the market that afternoon to buy a goose, a bundle of holly, sprigs of mistletoe and a small Christmas tree. If only he had enough courage to knock on the door, to wish the Donens a merry Christmas, to leave a message for Lizzie saying he was leaving town. But what would be the use? In any case, he had a stiff hill to climb to the Bank Top Station, and he must not miss the last train home.

Home, he thought wearily. If the old adage, 'Home is where the heart is', was true, then it was here he belonged, with Lizzie.

Reaching the station, he bought a one-way ticket to Scarborough. Setting down his suitcase on the platform near George Stephenson's engine, which was mounted on a stone plinth near the buffet, he wondered if he had time for a cup of tea and ham sandwich before his train arrived. A man was standing near the old railway engine, apparently waiting for someone. That someone—a young girl, poorly dressed yet pretty—emerged from the buffet and tripped lightly towards him, smiling in anticipation of a warm welcome from her admirer; calling out to him, 'Sorry I'm late, Miles, I've only just got off duty.'

Suddenly William knew who the man was and why he was there, lurking in the shadows like a rat in a sewer, intent on seduction and the ruination of yet another girl's life.

Filled with a burning sense of anger, not stopping to think twice, he strode forward to confront Sir Miles Jessington.

Taking the man by surprise, grabbing hold of his lapels, forcing him back against the plinth. 'You won't remember me, I daresay,' William hissed, 'but I haven't forgotten *you*, you arrogant bastard!'

'What the hell?' Jessington blustered, 'I warn you, I'll send for the police if you don't let go of me!'

200

William smiled grimly, 'I very much doubt that, Sir Miles. No, this is just between the two of us.'

'If it's money you're after—'

'Oh no,' William assured him coldly, contemptuously, 'it isn't your money I'm after. The exact opposite, as a matter of fact. I'm here to repay you, in full, for the treatment you meted out to Maurice Schiller and a girl called Madge Donen.'

Jessington sank to his knees, groaning from the blow to his solar-plexus delivered by William's bunched up right-hand fist. Then, staggering to his feet, clutching his hands to his midriff, he lurched unsteadily towards the exit and his carriage, by which time his latest conquest, the pretty young buffet assistant, had quit the scene as fast as her legs could carry her.

Having settled his score with Jessington, William paced the platform impatiently, awaiting the arrival of the last train to Scarborough. Suddenly, unexpectedly, he came across the hunched figure of Charlie Thompson near the platform's end: a picture of misery, head bowed, inadequately dressed against the bitter wind blowing along the platform, a bundle beside him.

'Charlie, what on earth are you doing here?' William cried out in alarm, squatting down beside him, placing a comforting arm about the boy's shoulders.

'I've left home,' Charlie said, teeth chattering. 'I couldn't stand it no longer.' The boy's eyes filled with tears. 'Ma has a new lodger now—an' he hit me!'

Glancing along the platform, William caught sight of the plume of smoke signalling the arrival of the train. Making up his mind in an instant, 'Get up, lad,' he said firmly, 'you're coming home with me. I'll take care of you.'

Bravely spoken words, but just how he would take care of Charlie, William had no precise idea at that moment.

All he knew was that he could not, in all conscience, have left Charlie, cold and alone on a station platform, on Christmas Eve. The poor kid needed a decent meal inside him and a good night's sleep; someone to watch over him.

He said lightheartedly as the train slid away from the platform, 'What have you got in that bundle of yours, by the way?'

' "The Sheikh of Araby",' said Charlie.

THIRTEEN

'Who on earth is *that?*' Madame Clara stared at her son in disbelief. Having stuffed the fatted goose in his honour, made up his bed and decided upon a dignified, not over-effusive approach to his reappearance at this late hour on Christmas Eve, she had scarcely expected him to arrive with a strange looking lad in tow. A gangling, spotty-faced youth wearing a flat cap and carrying a bundle.

'His name's Charlie Thompson,' William explained, 'and he's going to spend Christmas with us.'

'*Is* he indeed?' Clara plumped up her shoulders in the manner of a hen ruffling its feathers. A sure sign of displeasure, William remembered, feeling as he always did in his mother's presence, like a naughty schoolboy caught in the act of blowing cigarette smoke up his bedroom chimney.

Remembering that he was no longer a schoolboy but a responsible adult, he said levelly, worried about Charlie and the state he was in: cold, hungry and alone in the world, 'I'm sorry, Mother, if my bringing Charlie here doesn't meet with your approval. The fact remains that he needs food and shelter, someone to look after him and a good night's sleep.'

Smiling at Charlie, 'Come on, son,' he said gently, 'you can sleep in the spare room. I'll show you the way. Just get into bed and I'll bring you something to eat.'

'Now see here, William,' Clara protested angrily, 'How dare you bring a complete stranger into my home without my permission? Offer him food and shelter beneath *my* roof. Just who *is he,* anyway?'

'He's my friend, Mother,' William said quietly. 'Now, isn't it about time you were getting ready for church?'

When William went up to the spare room later, carrying a tray of thickly cut ham sandwiches and a mug of tea, Charlie was already fast asleep. Sitting beside him, William tried to come to terms with the past, and to consider the future.

Common sense told him that he must contact Maudie Thompson as soon as possible to set her mind at rest concerning her son. On the other hand, how could he in all conscience return poor Charlie to Parker Street to receive physical abuse at the hands of Maudie's latest lover? He couldn't. For the time being, he reckoned, it was up to him to do the best he could for the lad.

Obviously, Fred Willis's proposal of marriage to Maudie had fallen on stony ground, which explained his recent lack of communication, William supposed. But where was Fred now? If only he knew for certain, just as he wished he knew what was happening in the Donen household at that moment ...

Entering the kitchen of 23 Parker Street, bustling importantly, Elsie Donen saw her mother and Lizzie busily engaged in their preparations for Christmas Day, 'Would you believe it? That William what's his name? Oh yes, Chalmers, has handed in his notice to Madame Marcia and gone back to Scarborough to live. Well, good riddance to bad rubbish is all I can say!'

White-faced, Lizzie paused in the process of making mince pies, 'Oh, surely not! What I mean is, I thought he was settled here?'

'Well you thought wrong then, didn't you?' Elsie delighted in imparting news of this kind to make people take notice of her. She was just sorry that Bessie was upstairs in their room getting ready for work. She'd enjoy telling her upstart sibling that her former gentleman friend had left town. But she'd leave that till Bessie came home from the theatre with her new light of love.

205

Emily said sharply, 'Well don't just stand there, Elsie. There's a pile of pots in the sink that need washing.'

'But I've been run off my feet all day in the shop,' Elsie complained, eyeing the sink with distaste and feeling herself hard done by.

'You're not the only one,' her mother reminded her. 'Lizzie and I have been baking all afternoon, and your Dad and Dicky will be in soon wanting their supper, so just make yourself useful, young lady. I want those pots washed, this table cleared and scrubbed and set within the next half hour, is that understood?'

'I'll scrub the table,' Lizzie said, 'when I've put this last batch of mince pies in the oven.'

'You'll do no such thing! Elsie can help me with the tidying up,' Emily said firmly, thinking how tired Lizzie looked; how upset she'd seemed when Elsie had burst in with news of William Chalmer's departure. A natural enough reaction, she supposed, considering the trouble he'd caused her one way and another.

Emily herself felt tired with all the extra housework, cooking and planning the festive season entailed; the emotional stress involved in trying to keep the family cart on its wheels. No easy task with Bessie and Elsie at loggerheads with one another most of the time and Jack still sick at heart over Madge. Watching and waiting constantly for news of her: a card or a letter which never came, and probably never would after all this time, Emily realised, sharing her husband's grief yet trying her best to keep strong for his sake.

She wished suddenly that tomorrow was over and done with: the forced gaiety of Christmas Day with so many mouths to feed. Her own all important role to play as the hostess, mother and provider of sustenance from morning to night. The linchpin around which her family revolved.

When Dicky and Jack came home from work, the washing up was done, the table scrubbed and set in readiness for their supper, the pantry shelves filled with tins of cakes and pastries, bowls of jellies and blancmanges, plum puddings, and a goose stuffed in readiness for tomorrow's Christmas dinner.

'Summat smells good, Ma,' Dicky declared, sniffing the air. 'What's for supper? I'm starving!'

Jack said nothing. He simply crossed to his chair near the fire, sat down, and stared into the flames.

Emily said despairingly, 'Your food's in the oven. You'd best help yourselves for once in your life. I'm going out!'

'Huh?' Dicky's mouth sagged open in surprise. 'What do you mean—you're going out? Where to?' Then, anxiously, 'When will you be back?'

'When I feel like it, not before,' she threw back at him. 'Perhaps when your father begins to treat me as a human being, not a servant! Your sister Madge was *my* child, too, remember?'

'Please, Ma, don't go!' Dicky called after her, but she was already halfway down Parker Street, heading towards the Skerne bridge, eyes streaming from the cold wind blowing in her face as she crossed the bridge and hurried towards St Cuthbert's Church.

Suddenly she heard pounding footsteps behind her, a voice calling her name, 'Emily,' over and over again. Then her husband's arms were about her, holding her tightly, and he was begging her to come home; telling her how much he loved her.

Then, because this was Christmas Eve, the night of the Star and the Stable, a time of forgiveness, she walked back with him to their own front door. The familiar trap of home, Emily thought, from which, apparently, there was no escape. And yet, how deeply she had savoured her momentary taste of independence.

The last thing William wanted was a row with his mother—especially on Christmas Eve. Understandably, she was displeased that he had brought Charlie home with him, but Clara was not about to let matters rest there. Soon she brought up the subject of his defection from home earlier on that year, and the distress it had caused her and his sisters, which he did not believe for one moment.

'Oh come now, Ma,' he said lightly, 'we were getting on each other's nerves. You know that as well as I do. They were glad to see the back of me. Especially Nell, and Louisa couldn't have cared less one way or the other. Where are they, by the way?'

'At a Christmas Eve dance on the Spa, if you must know. They'll be in late, but that's beside the point—'

'What exactly *is* the point, Mother? I thought you'd be pleased to see me. Apparently I was wrong, as usual.'

'The point is, I thought you'd have had more regard for my feelings than to bring with you that—hobbledehoy. You should have taken him to the nearest police station. Well, I'm not having him at my dining table, and that's final.'

'Very well, Ma, we'll eat in the kitchen. And don't worry, I'll pay you for his board and lodging.' Sick at heart, William realised the full extent of his mother's snobbery and meanness of spirit.

'Don't be so ridiculous! The boy can eat in the kitchen. You will dine with your sisters and me. Furthermore, I want your assurance that you will send him back to where he belongs as soon as possible. How you became entangled with such a creature in the first place is beyond my comprehension.'

William kept his temper in check until his mother referred to Charlie as a 'creature'. He said heatedly, 'That *creature*, so-called, happens to be a sensitive human being, not an animal. And as for your comprehension—you have none! You are blinkered, Mother. Your outlook is governed by the narrowness of your mind; it always has been!'

'How dare you speak to me in such a fashion?' Clara demanded. 'I *am* your mother, remember.'

Nell and Louisa entered the room at that moment, flushed with dancing and drinking, dressed to the nines in their evening regalia. Louisa, the plumper of the two, stood in the doorway as if transfixed. Nell, on the other hand, swept into the room like a whirlwind. 'What the hell's going on?' she asked in a high-pitched voice, 'Or need I ask? Good to see you're back, brother dear, causing trouble, as usual.' Shrugging off her cloak which she threw carelessly over the arm of the settee. 'Well, what's the row about this time? Don't tell me you've got some wretched servant girl into trouble and left her in the lurch? The reason you came running home so suddenly, I daresay?'

'No need for vulgarity,' Clara said reprovingly, mouth trembling, feeling for a hanky. Then, sharply, 'Oh for God's sake, Louisa, don't just stand there with your mouth open. Sit down, girl, for heaven's sake!'

'Yes, Ma,' Louisa said nervously, adding to Clara's distress at finding herself lumbered with three such inadequate offspring. They had never even begun to understand or appreciate all she had done for them to smooth their paths in life, at the cost of her own well-being and peace of mind.

Realising that he was not outnumbered, as he had so often been before, by the female population of his life, William said quietly, 'I'm off to bed now, if you'll excuse me. As for Charlie, I meant what I said, Ma. We'll eat in the kitchen together if needs be. In fact, I think that Charlie would prefer it that way, and, quite frankly, so shall I.'

Looking in on Charlie on his way upstairs, William discovered the boy wide awake sitting bolt upright in bed, trembling like a leaf.

'What's the matter, lad? I thought you'd be asleep. Are you still hungry?' He noticed the sandwiches had gone.

Charlie shook his head, 'Naw, it's just that you should've left me where I was. I'd've been all right. Now I've got you into trouble. I know the lady don't want me here.'

'Never mind about that. *I* want you here. Come on now, lie down and stop worrying. Tell you what, first thing in the morning I'll find you something to wear, a shirt and a pair of flannels, one of my old school blazers. You'll have a good hot bath, a shave and a haircut. You'll feel a lot better then. Afterwards, I'll cook you a proper breakfast, eggs and bacon, sausages and fried bread. Then we'll go for a walk along the seafront to blow away the cobwebs. How does that strike you?'

'It's morning now, ain't it?'

'So it is.' William smiled. 'Christmas morning. In which case, Merry Christmas, Charlie.' A thought struck him. 'Wait just a sec, I have something for you.'

Hurrying to his room along the landing, William returned carrying a wind-up gramophone which he set down on Charlie's bedside table. 'There, that's for you—and "The Sheikh of Araby",' he said.

'Thanks, Mister.' Charlie's face lit up. 'Ma's lodger smashed my old 'un.'

Clara came into the kitchen when William was cooking breakfast, and looked hard at Charlie, now respectably dressed in grey flannels, white shirt and a navy blue blazer. He flushed to the roots of his hair and got up from the table when she entered the room—more from a sense of fear than good manners. A gesture which nevertheless impressed Clara who had spent a restless night regretting the quarrel with her son; fearful that he might decide to return to Darlington after Christmas when she needed him here with her.

'I had no idea you were so domesticated, William.'

He grinned, 'I've learned how to look after myself recently.'

'Hmm, so I see.' Making the effort, 'And you, young man, did you sleep well?'

'Dunno,' Charlie said awkwardly, shuffling his feet, 'I can't remember.'

Taking the initiative, 'Charlie slept just fine,' William said, 'under the circumstances. He's had a pretty rough time of it lately. That's why I brought him home with me. He's a good lad, is Charlie.' William felt proud of his protégé with his smart new haircut and neatly knotted tie. 'What I'd really like is to find him

213

a job and a decent place to live, for the time being at any rate, until his future is decided to my satisfaction.'

'But surely he must have a family of his own to take care of him?' Clara responded sharply. 'It's really not up to you, William, to take charge of his future without their consent, is it?'

Charlie broke in suddenly, fearfully, 'Oh please, Mister, don't send me back home! My Ma don't want me, she never has, an' I'm frightened of—*him!* The man who hit me!'

'It's true, Mother,' William said quietly, 'and Charlie's decision to leave home in the face of all the verbal and physical abuse he has suffered recently, was a brave one in my opinion.'

'I see,' Clara said hesitantly. 'Very well, then, the boy is welcome to spend Christmas with us, but more than that I am not prepared to say at the moment.'

Nell and Louisa regarded Charlie as they might have done a cuckoo in a bird's nest; especially Nell, when she saw that the strange houseguest was wearing her brother's cast-off school clothes. 'Who the hell's *he*, and what's he doing here?' she demanded fiercely of Clara, *sotto voce*.

'Don't ask *me*, ask William,' Clara muttered defensively.

'Don't worry, I *shall!*' Nell, who had drunk too much wine the night before, was suffering the effects of a hangover. 'Trust William to cause trouble.'

Louisa, the more compliant of the two sisters, said anxiously, 'Then why stir up more? I'm glad Will's home. I've missed him. I hope he'll stay.'

'Of course he'll stay,' Clara said sharply, determined that he would if she had any say in the matter. Trade had fallen off since William had left home, and she knew why. William was a born hairdresser, and the customers doted on him. Neither Nell nor Louisa possessed his skill with the waving irons, his charm and patience when it came to handling her more difficult clients. Nell was far too acid-tongued and outspoken to pour oil on troubled water. Louisa too slow when it came to getting a move on during the rush periods. Besides which, Clara reflected, what William really needed was to settle down after his brief escapade in Darlington. A wife, a home of his own, and children to care for. Moreover, she already had in mind the perfect candidate ...

Charlie ate his Christmas dinner hungrily, taking care at the same time not to splash the tablecloth with gravy, wanting to make a good impression for William's sake. Trying hard not to mind that the hard-faced one called Nell was watching him like a hawk, as if willing him to send a sprout rolling across the table onto her lap, lick his knife or help himself to more potatoes without asking.

Aware of Charlie's discomfiture and Nell's hostility, William decided to break the tension, quietly, with malice aforethought. He allowed his own knife to slide across his plate, sending a sizeable chunk of goose, plus gravy, shooting onto the tablecloth. His ploy worked.

'Really, William,' Clara said, looking shocked, 'that was extremely careless of you!'

'Yes, it was, Mother. I apologise. But accidents do happen in the best of circles. Do you remember, Nell? That dinner party when you tilted your soup bowl too far and the contents ran down the table-leg onto the carpet? Tomato soup, as I recall.'

Louisa giggled. Nell looked daggers at her sister: William winked at Charlie across the table. The lad smiled suddenly, and that smile lit up his face making him appear almost handsome, William thought. Or he would be once he got rid of his spots and learned how to shave himself properly.

Later that day, when Charlie had gone

up to his room to play 'The Sheikh of Araby' on his new gramophone, Nell found William alone in the sitting room and launched a fierce attack on her brother.

'You really enjoyed making me look small at the dinner table, didn't you?' she demanded heatedly. 'All that funny business with the goose didn't fool me for an instant. You slid it off your plate deliberately. I saw you! But *why?* That's what I want to know!'

'Because you were hell-bent on making a fool out of Charlie,' William said levelly. 'A poor scrap of a lad down on his luck.'

'Damn it, William,' Nell uttered self-righteously, 'I never said a word to him.'

'You didn't need to,' William reminded her. 'Your attitude towards him spoke louder than words. Think about it, Nell. Just a smile, a friendly word, would have made all the difference in the world to him.'

Nell pulled a face. 'Spare me the lecture. Just who *is* he, anyway? And why have you appointed yourself guardian angel? It all seems a bit rum to me. What did you get up to in Darlington? I thought you were enjoying life there. Next thing we knew, you'd quit your job and wrote saying you were coming home. Now here you are with a strange youth in tow, upsetting

Ma and chucking your food about into the bargain.'

'It's a long story.' William paused, 'Have you seen anything of Fred Willis lately? I need to get in touch with him.'

'Oh, for God's sake don't bring *him* here unless you want Ma to have a breakdown. I haven't any idea where he is. I thought you'd be sure to know. I wish I knew what was going on, that's all. Has he anything to do with the mysterious Charlie Thompson?'

'Indirectly, yes.' William would say no more. He'd made up his mind to walk down to the seafront where Fred lived, taking Charlie with him for a breath of fresh air.

PART TWO

PART TWO

FOURTEEN

The tall, broad-shouldered young fisherman, face tanned with salt air and
sea-wind, wearing navy trousers and a
thick-knit jersey, swung jauntily along
the foreshore to the harbour whistling
his favourite tune, his mop of fair curly
hair ruffled by the breeze blowing inland
from the vast expanse of foam-flecked water
beyond the harbour mouth. A handsome,
happy, fulfilled individual with a good
breakfast inside him, bright-eyed and
clear-skinned, and with a day's fishing
to look forward to aboard the trawler *The
Pride of Scarborough* which he regarded as
his second home ever since the day he set
foot on her five years ago as a deck-hand
cum cabin-boy; the butt of teasing remarks
from the crew.

Not that he'd cared tuppence. Not even
during bouts of seasickness; the teasing of
his rough and ready male companions as
he'd hung over the deck-rail 'feeding the
fish', as they'd put it. Just as long as he
could remain aboard the boat, savouring
his newfound feeling of freedom in the
rush of the tide beneath its keel, the

221

taste of salt spray on his lips, a limitless horizon ahead of him. A revelation after the confines of his mother's corner shop in Parker Street.

Every day of his life, come hail, rain or shine, Charlie Thompson thanked God for William Chalmers, who had rescued him from a cold station platform one Christmas Eve and Fred Willis who had offered him a roof over his head.

Charlie still remembered the gist of their conversation that day: Fred saying forcefully, 'Leave Maudie to me to deal with, Billy Boy. She never wanted the poor kid in the first place, so he'd best stay here where he's safe for the time being at any rate. And if she kicks up a fuss ... Well, like I said, just leave her to me to deal with—her an' that new lodger of hers. I'll fettle the pair of them right enough!' He smiled grimly, 'And I'll enjoy doing it, believe me.'

And so Charlie had moved into Fred's two-up, two-down cottage on the seafront, taking with him his only possessions: a record and a wind-up gramophone—a bewildered fourteen-year-old boy, uncertain of his future.

After the holidays, Fred had gone on a day excursion to Darlington to see Maudie and returned bringing with him a case containing some of Charlie's clothes. 'Your

Ma said you might need these,' Fred said gruffly, 'an' you can stay on here if you want to.'

He didn't tell the kid that his mother didn't want him back and had said so in no uncertain terms, calling him a selfish, ungrateful, useless little runt who had caused her nothing but trouble since the day he was born.

The new lodger, a stockily built bloke, handsome in a florid kind of way, thick-lipped, with more than his fair share of teeth, had been present at the confrontation. Chipping into the conversation, adding fuel to the bonfire, saying the boy needed a damn good hiding, until Fred, incensed, told him to shut his mouth if he wished to hang on to his molars, otherwise he'd end up spitting them onto the carpet.

'That's intimidation,' the man snarled. 'I could have you for that. There's such a thing as the law, you know!'

'I'm glad you mentioned that.' Bunching his fists. 'Don't tempt me! Intimidating a helpless fourteen-year-old kid not half your size is just about your hammer, I reckon. But it didn't stop at that, did it? Proud of yourself, were you, when you hit him and smashed his gramophone? Gladdened your heart, did it, when he ran away from home because he was scared stiff of you?

223

'As for you, Maudie, you should think shame on yourself standing by doing nothing when this fat swine laid into your son. What kind of mother are you anyway? Don't bother to tell me, I know! Faugh, you make me sick, the pair of you. All I can say is you're well suited. Two fat porkers for the price of one!'

The following summer, Fred encouraged the lad to help a pal of his look after the troupe of beach donkeys who came down to the sands every day to give the children donkey rides. And when he was away from home, William would sleep at the cottage to take care of the boy, to make sure he had a proper breakfast and evening meal. Charlie adored the animals in his charge, and now that he was free at last of his mother's overbearing influence over him, long days spent on the sands in the sunshine and fresh air cleared his skin as if by magic. William and Fred had marvelled at the change in their protégé. But summertime could not last forever, and when the donkeys had been farmed out to their various winter quarters come the end of September, the lad would need another job. But what?

When asked, Charlie said unerringly, 'I'd like to be a fisherman, to work aboard one of them trawlers in the harbour, setting off at sunrise, heading out to sea. I'd really like that, Mister,' he said wistfully, 'I dunno why, but I would.'

William had instinctively known why. Because Charlie, having tasted freedom for the first time in his life, could never return to work as—a grocer's assistant, for instance, standing all day long behind a shop counter as he had done in his Parker Street days.

And so Fred Willis, a long-time habitué of the many pubs adjacent to his house near the harbour, experienced little trouble in persuading the skipper of *The Pride of Scarborough*, to take aboard his vessel a likely lad called Charlie Thompson ...

Madame Clara had not been best pleased by her son's occasional overnight visits to Fred Willis's cottage to play nursemaid to Charlie, especially in view of her carefully formulated plan to introduce William to the daughter of a wealthy client of hers, a Mrs Rachel Courteney, whose daughter Gwendoline would make William a perfect wife—if only he would show some interest in her.

Gwendoline was a lovely girl, dark-haired, slender, intelligent, who had come to Scarborough to live with her mother, last November, following the death of her father. Mrs Courteney had quickly decided to sell the family home and her late husband's chain of grocers' shops in the milieu of Huddersfield, Leeds and Bradford, and move to the seaside. Her capital safely invested, she had settled on Scarborough as her future home; bought a house on Cliff Bridge Terrace overlooking the South Bay and thanked her lucky stars that her elderly husband had passed away leaving her well provided for yet still young enough to create a new lifestyle for herself and Gwendoline ...

St Cuthbert's Church seemed very cold, very still, on that wintry January morning when Lizzie walked down the aisle on her father's arm towards the tall figure of Lewis Gilbert.

The altar vases contained sprays of golden winter-flowering jasmine and white chrysanthemums. The organist played 'Jesu, Joy of Man's Desiring' as Lizzie walked towards her bridegroom, followed by her two bridesmaids whose footsteps could be clearly heard clattering on the stone flags of the aisle.

There were few people present to witness the wedding ceremony. Merely a handful of the bride's family and friends occupying the front pew; even fewer on the bridegroom's side of the aisle, the organist nodded, feeling sorry for the man—until he caught sight of the bride's face beneath the wide-brimmed hat she was wearing. A pale, heart-shaped face illuminated with grey-blue eyes—a beautiful face framed with upswept wings of light brown hair, and a gently smiling mouth. At which point he stopped feeling sorry for the bridegroom. But was this really a love match? he wondered, a lovely young woman marrying a man old enough to be her father?

After the wedding, the congregation repaired to Attica to partake of the food Lizzie had prepared for them the day before, whilst Lewis set the dining room table with a pristine white cloth, cutlery and china, according to her instructions, in readiness for the wedding breakfast.

The last thing they wanted was the starchiness of a formal wedding reception. Emily and Nan would bring the food to the table, Beulah and Bessie would make the tea after Dicky, Lewis's best man, raised a toast to the future health and happiness of the bride and groom, although he would have preferred to drink to their future happiness from a tankard of ale rather than a glass of sherry. But what the heck? Soon, his own best man would be proposing a toast to the bride and groom when he and Beulah tied the knot. But they'd be having a proper wedding reception at the King's

Head Hotel; a proper honeymoon too, in Blackpool, after which they'd move into Nan Imerson's house when she left Parker Street to live with Lizzie and Lewis and little Emma.

Truth to tell, he felt a bit sorry for Lizzie, starting married life in a readymade home with an elderly husband and her mother-in-law from her former marriage. But Lizzie seemed happy enough. Even so, he couldn't help wishing she'd married a younger man.

Clara decided a fancy dress party would be an ideal means of bringing William and Gwendoline into closer contact with one another. There was a sizeable stockroom to the rear of the salon which would make an excellent venue. A room which, when the premises were built in the mid-eighties, must have been the owners' dining room. Big enough to accommodate a table of banqueting dimensions with parquet flooring and several gilt-framed mirrors still in situ, which Clara would decorate with boughs of greenery threaded with scarlet ribbons to create a romantic atmosphere.

She would hire a firm of caterers to provide food for the occasion, and a trio of musicians to play the latest dance tunes. At which point, Nell said succinctly that what she really needed was a gramophone and a stack of records. Who the hell would want to dance to a trio? She for one wasn't interested in dancing the minuet to the sawing of a couple of violins and a cello. Nor was she prepared to appear at the party as Little Bo-Peep or a Dresden shepherdess.

'I'll come as a gaucho,' Nell declared mischievously.

'A—*what?*'

'A South American cowboy. Dressed all in black, with a sombrero and a black moustachio!'

'You dare, and I'll never speak to you again.' Clara was not amused.

William laughed, 'She's having you on, Ma.'

'Is she? Well, I'm not too sure about that. I can't think what's come over her lately.'

Nell said impatiently, 'The world's changing, Ma, in case you hadn't noticed. Fashions are changing. Women are changing.'

'Huh! Not for the better, if you ask me.'

'You're just old-fashioned,' Nell said in that uncompromising way of hers. 'Things are a damn sight better now than they've ever been before. What I'd give for a date with Valentino, dancing the tango with him in a Paris nightclub wearing one of those new length evening dresses. Better still, a night in his tent in the desert wearing next to nothing at all.'

'Really, Nell! I just hope you'll have the sense not to express such outrageous thoughts to the customers.'

'Why not? Old fogies they may be—well most of them anyway. But I'm not one of them, thank God. I'm still young enough to want a bit of excitement in my life. And if you really want to know what's come over me lately, the truth is I'm bored stiff with hairdressing; standing day long in a stuffy cubicle listening to the moaning and groaning of a lot of silly old women who've forgotten what it's like to be young—if they ever were. Or perhaps they were born old?'

'That's enough, Nell,' William said equably, pouring oil on troubled water. 'Let's make a compromise, shall we? I'll wear the gaucho costume, you come as a Spanish señorita complete with a black lace mantilla and a rose between your teeth. How does that strike you?'

Nell chuckled. 'Better still, why don't you come as Rudolf Valentino in *The Sheikh?* Myself as a member of your harem?' She frowned suddenly, 'Well, what's so funny about that?'

'Nothing really.' He was thinking of poor Charlie and his 'Sheikh of Araby' record, of

Nell dressed in bangles and beads, himself in one of his mother's whitecotton sheets. He wondered why she'd decided to throw a party in the first place?

He asked Nell that question later, 'It's in your honour,' she told him. 'The wanderer's return and all that jazz!'

'Talk sense, Nell. I've been back almost six months now.'

'You can't be all that naïve, surely?' Nell laughed. 'There's a girl Ma wants you to meet.'

'*Girl?* What—girl?' William's heart sank.

'Mrs Courteney's daughter, Gwendoline.' Revelling in her brother's discomfiture, 'Don't tell me you haven't noticed her?'

'Noticed her? I've scarcely *heard* of her, or her mother! Just who is Mrs Courteney?'

'A bosom pal of Ma's since she came to live here last November. Louisa and I call her The Merry Widow—not to her face, of course. You get the picture? Oceans of money, well preserved for her age. Looks good in black? Anxious to make new friends, with a marriageable daughter in tow whom, one imagines, she wishes to get rid of as quickly as possible in order to maintain her youthful appearance. After all, brother dear, it can't be much fun for a woman crowding fifty to be lumbered with an unmarried daughter more than half her

231

age, and far better looking than herself. So now you know how *you* fit into the picture, don't you?'

'No, I'm damned if I do,' William protested vehemently. 'If Mother thinks for one moment that she can fob me off with this—Gwendoline Courteney, she has another think coming.'

'All right. No need to get hot under the collar,' Nell remarked coolly. 'But I feel it my duty to tell you that there has been some gossip about that all male *ménage à trois* of yours on the Foreshore. Yourself, Charlie what's his name, and Fred Willis gathered so cosily together under one roof. Think about it, Will, for Ma's sake, if not your own.'

'If you're saying what I think you're saying, it simply isn't true,' William uttered defiantly. 'The fact is, I happen to be in love, very much in love, with a girl I met in Darlington.'

'Really? So what happened? Why didn't you marry her?' Nell asked, eyebrows raised in surprise.

'I'd rather not talk about it,' William said wearily, wishing he'd kept his mouth shut.

'So that's the reason you came home in such a hurry?' Nell persisted. But William had said all he was prepared to say on the subject. The very thought of Lizzie married to someone else haunted him day and night, leaving room for little else in his mind. He had simply been glad of Charlie's presence in his life to ease the pain of losing the woman he loved.

Lizzie had not realised, until the wedding guests had departed, how strange she would feel in her new home, like a fish out of water. As if, when the time came she would set the kitchen table with Lewis's supper things and go home to Parker Street, calling out to him, 'See you in the morning'.

Even little Emma had seemed puzzled when, at bedtime, she had been taken upstairs to sleep in an unfamiliar room in an unfamiliar cot. 'Nannan,' she wailed. 'Nannan,' over and over again, and Lizzie understood the depth of the child's misery at finding herself separated, for the first time in her life, from her Grandma Imerson.

Glancing at Lewis who was standing on the threshold of the nursery he had created especially for the little girl, 'I don't think she's going to settle down just yet,' Lizzie said quietly. He'd then suggested taking Emma downstairs again to play with her toys for a while longer, until sleep overcame her.

Downstairs, near the living-room fire, looking across at Lizzie in the chair opposite, holding her child in her arms, he said, 'This can't be an easy situation for you either, my dear. Finding yourself alone in a strange house, with a strange man, on your wedding night.' He added gently, 'It's true, isn't it?'

'Yes, I suppose so,' she admitted reluctantly. 'But I love this house, and—I love you too, Lewis. It's just that I hadn't really thought of it as *home* before, or you as my—husband.'

He said wistfully, 'I love you too, Lizzie, more than I have ever loved anyone in my life before. All I can possibly say is, you are free to leave here if you want to. I'll never ask more of you than you are prepared to give of your own free will, except that you'll always remain a part of my life, if at all possible.' He covered his face with his hands.

Laying her sleeping child gently on the sofa in front of the fire, crossing swiftly towards Lewis, she knelt at his feet, taking his hands in hers. Uncovering his face, Lizzie said close to tears, 'I am your wife now, not your housekeeper, remember?'

Then, smiling through her tears, 'Well that too, I suppose, from now on. A pretty safe job, I'd say, since you couldn't very well sack me. That's the trouble with wives. They can't be got rid of as easily as housekeepers.

'Now I think that Emma is ready for sleep, and so am I. How about you? We're all worn out. This, after all, has been a long, tiring day one way and another.'

Gratefully, Lewis realised that Lizzie was telling him as subtly as possible, that she would not expect him to make love to her that night. A deep feeling of relief swept through him that he would not be called upon to prove, physically, how much he loved her. Not tonight, at any rate. Not tonight, thank God! At some time in the future, perhaps, but not tonight.

Later, in bed with Lizzie, holding her tightly in his arms, kissing her hair, her cheeks, her lips, long after she had fallen fast asleep in his embrace, staring up at the ceiling, Lewis recalled the reaction of his late wife, Alice, when he tried to make love to her: calling him a 'filthy beast', an animal, a sexual pervert whenever he had attempted to touch her.

Worst of all, he could not rid himself of the feeling that the vituperative ghost of his first wife still haunted the house. That she was still watching him, planning mischief from afar ...

Filled with apprehension about the party, William went downstairs to find the caterers setting out the food. It was quite a spread. Clara had really pushed the boat out. Red velvet curtains covered the stock shelves, the trestle table holding dishes of poached salmon, mushroom pâtés, cold meats and desserts, covered with a starched white cloth and stacked with cutlery and china.

Two Gasoliers shone down on the dance floor and reflected back the pinpoints of light trapped in the heavy, gilt-framed mirrors with their garlands of greenery and coloured ribbons.

A separate table near the door held the gramophone and a pile of records chosen personally by Nell, a composite selection of the latest dance tunes—tangos, waltzes, foxtrots. The air was filled with a blend of perfumes from the salon: Houbigant's *Quelques Fleurs,* violet oil, green soft soap, jasmine brilliantine, Coty dusting powder, and the subtly intermingled fragrances of hot water and Marcel waving peculiar to the hairdressing profession. Guests had begun arriving by the side entrance to be greeted by Mrs Chalmers wearing Victorian costume, her hair dressed pompadour fashion enhanced with a diamanté tiara, her colour heightened by excitement and the already overheated atmosphere of the room—plus the two glasses of Madeira she'd drunk in quick succession in the privacy of her bedroom.

When Mrs Courteney, a faded beauty yet

still undeniably attractive, entered the room wearing a black lace gown, accompanied by her daughter Gwendoline all in white, Clara received them as if they were royalty, and William knew why.

Well, one may lead a horse to water, twenty could not make it drink, he thought resentfully, stiffly acknowledging the introductions to The Merry Widow and her offspring.

And yet he had to admit that Gwendoline Courteney was a very pretty young woman as he led her on to the dance floor.

FIFTEEN

Nan never regretted leaving Parker Street to live with Lizzie and Lewis. It pleased her to think that Dicky, Beulah and their two children had settled so well in her old home, and the rent they paid her came in useful, providing small treats for her precious granddaughter Emma, now a pupil at The Beaumont Street Infant School, and as pretty as a picture with her softly curling fair hair, rosy cheeks and sparkling blue eyes.

The only cloud on Nan's horizon was that Lizzie's marriage had not so far produced a brother or sister for Emma, and she could not help wondering why not? The couple were obviously devoted to one another, so why hadn't Lizzie become pregnant?

One day, decorum overcome by curiosity, she asked Lizzie point blank if everything was all right between herself and Lewis. 'Tell me to mind my own business if you want to,' she said, 'but I know how much you've hoped for another child. You've said often enough that Lewis would make a wonderful father.'

This was not a subject she would have willingly discussed, even with Nan. But the question had been asked, and Lizzie respected Nan Imerson too much to fob her off with an untruthful reply.

She said simply, 'I love Lewis, and he loves me. There is no lack of affection between us, it's just that ...' Her voice faltered suddenly. Tears sprang to her eyes. 'You are right, of course. We both wanted another child, but it seems unlikely there'll be one. I'm sorry, I can't say more than that.' Blinking back her tears, 'There's really no need, is there?'

Nan guessed at once what Lizzie meant: that to say more would be tantamount to a betrayal of trust between husband and wife.

'I'm sorry too, love,' Nan said heavily.

'I shouldn't have asked. Please forgive me. I'm just a silly, nosy old woman.'

Going upstairs to her cosy bed-sitting room on the top floor, she wondered if she had done the right thing—meddling in Lizzie's affairs of the heart as she had done five years ago. Persuading her to marry an older man for the sake of security and a settled future for herself and Emma.

It never crossed her mind at the time that Lewis might be incapable of consummating the marriage.

William's courtship of Gwendoline Courteney had been a tenuous affair from the beginning, knowing he was not in love with her. Even though she made it abundantly clear that she was head over heels in love with him, and had been from the moment she'd set eyes on him at that benighted fancy dress party when a 'Spanish Grandee' dressed all in black had invited a white-skirted and bodiced 'ballerina' to dance with him the aptly named 'Hesitation Waltz'.

Later on that evening, declaring she'd faint if she didn't get a breath of fresh air, Gwen, as he now called her, lured him away from the party to stand with her on a promontory overlooking Scarborough's South Bay. Gazing at a track of silver moonlight on the sea, she said eagerly,

'Oh, isn't this romantic?'

'Isn't what romantic?'

'Well, you know, moonlight on the sea? And us being alone together at last?'

'I thought you were feeling ill,' he said prosaically, aware of the trap closing in on him; memories weighing heavily on his mind. 'If you're feeling better, we'd best go back to the party.'

'If that's what you really want,' Gwendoline said wistfully, 'but not until you've kissed me, William. Really kissed me, as if you meant it.'

He had the sense to realise the girl had probably drunk more than was good for her and it was time she went home to bed instead of going back to the dance floor. He said lightly, 'I'll fetch your wrap and walk home with you, if you like.'

'But you haven't kissed me! And I do so want you to.' She pulled a face, 'Don't you like me? Is that it? Because I like you, William, more than I can say.'

'It isn't a question of not liking you, Miss Courteney.' He couldn't bring himself to call her by her christian name on so short an acquaintance. Bearing in mind Nell's warning that the party had been engineered by his mother and most probably Gwendoline's mother also for the sole purpose of matchmaking—the son who, in Clara's opinion, needed a wife; the

240

daughter who in Mrs Courteney's opinion, needed a husband. Bring the pair of them together and *et voilà!* William thought, disgusted by his mother's subterfuge and Mrs Courteney's collusion. But they had done more harm than good so far as he was concerned.

Next day, Gwendoline came to the salon wanting to speak to William, saying it was urgent. 'He's engaged at the moment,' an apprentice told her. 'Would madam care to wait?'

Clara emerged from her beauty treatment room that moment, looking flustered, still slightly woozy from the night before, wondering why her son and Miss Courteney had left the party so abruptly without a word of apology. They'd been there one minute, gone the next. Was this a good thing or a bad? Clara asked herself.

William had scarcely spoken two words at breakfast and Gwendoline appeared far from happy, this morning.

'Oh, please do come through to my private sanctum,' Clara said leading the way, not daring to ask Gwendoline if she had enjoyed the party, 'William shouldn't be more than a few minutes. Er, how is your mother this morning?'

'I don't know. I haven't seen her. She was still asleep when I left.'

'Ah, here's William now,' Clara said relieved. Smiling archly, she added. 'If you'll excuse me, I daresay you two young things will want to be alone together?'

Gwendoline came to the point immediately. 'I came to apologise,' she said bluntly, 'for making a fool of myself last night. I can't think what came over me, except ...' her eyes filled with tears, 'that I miss my father so much. We were very close, you see, and I just needed someone to be kind to me.

'And you were very kind, very kind, Will—Mr Chambers—in taking me home the way you did, before I made an even greater fool of myself. Just one more thing before I go, I knew the set-up all along. My mother made no secret of the fact that the party had been planned for the sole purpose of finding me a—suitor; God, of all the ghastly, worn-out phrases, that must be the worst of all.'

Drying her eyes with a lace-edged hanky, she continued shakily, 'I was given to understand you had expressed a wish to meet me, and I was—intrigued—to say the least. Thinking, God alone knows why, that you'd be either effete or bumptious.

'Frankly, I had the shock of my life when I met you face to face and you asked me to dance with you. I knew then that none of the things I had imagined about you were true. I also realised that you were no more interested in me than the Man in the Moon. You made that abundantly clear when I begged you to kiss me and you refused, knowing I was more than a little drunk at the time. A less honourable man would have taken advantage of me—but not you.

'Well, I've said what I came to say. Just one thing, before I go. I really meant what I said about liking you. In fact,' she smiled up at him wistfully, 'I'd go so far as to say that I fell head over heels in love with you last night. But no need to worry, I'll get over it in time.'

Deeply touched by her candour, realising his own loneliness of spirit, his need of someone to care for, William said softly, 'Thank you for coming, Miss Courteney—Gwendoline. Let's meet again soon, shall we?'

And so the die was cast. Their courtship began, although William did not regard it as such at the beginning, merely as a friendship between two lonely people.

There were many reasons for the patchiness of the relationship, the misunderstandings and quarrels that sprang up between them along the way, deriving mainly from Gwendoline's carelessness over money—which had little or no meaning for her apart from a source of enjoyment.

She had always been rich, pampered, cosseted, generous to a fault. She could not understand William's refusal to accept the expensive presents she bought him initially, her little treats and surprises—meant to please him—which produced the opposite effect.

'What's wrong with wanting to dine out once in a while? To see a show? Spend a day in the country?' she demanded. 'For heaven's sake, Will, if it's money you're worried about, forget it. I have so much of the wretched stuff I don't know what to do with it half the time.'

'That's the whole point,' he said. 'You're rich. I'm not. I'm sorry, Gwen, I know you mean well, but it goes against the grain being treated as a—prize poodle. How do you think I feel in the dining room at the Crown Hotel, for instance, ordering food I can't afford to pay for, drinking champagne, sitting in a box at the Londesborough Theatre when I belong in the gods? As for days in the country I'd need to save up for a month or more to afford lunch at one of those hotels you're so fond of.'

'Oh, of course,' she said sarcastically, 'I should have known you'd rather spend time with that strange boy you're so attached to, than me. Well, cooking and eating messes in the kitchen of some hovel near the harbour may be your idea of fun, but it certainly isn't mine!'

William said quietly, keeping his anger in check, 'There is nothing in the least strange about Charlie Thompson, I assure you. The poor kid's had a rough passage in life so far. I regard myself as his custodian, for want of a better word, his guardian if you like. No more than that—his friend. He has only two friends in the world, you see. Myself and an old school pal of mine, Fred Willis, the owner of that—hovel near the harbour.'

'Oh God, Will, I'm sorry,' Gwen said contritely, out of her depth. Then, brightly, 'If it's money he needs—'

William said softly, 'No, Gwen, what Charlie needs is compassion, which money can't buy.'

From that day to this, William's relationship with Gwendoline Courteney resembled a switchback ride in a fun-fair: up one minute, down the next, with Gwen constantly beseeching him to forget his pride and accept her mother's offer of a down payment on a home of their own, fully furnished, if only he would set a date for their wedding. Or, if he didn't want to marry her, why the hell didn't he say so and have done with it? They'd been courting long enough, for God's sake. So what the hell was the matter with him?

William had the feeling of being swept along by events beyond his control, of waiting in vain for some miraculous homecoming of the heart, that sense of spiritual completeness he had known when Lizzie Imerson walked into the front parlour of the house in Parker Street.

Gwendoline had every right to be angry with him, he realised, regarding their longstanding relationship in the light of a courtship leading to the inevitability of marriage in the foreseeable future. Nor did he doubt for one moment that she was deeply in love with him, she told him so often enough, and he would not have been human had he failed to respond to the sweeter, softer side of her nature at times when, returning her kisses, holding her in his arms, inhaling the womanly fragrance of her, he would imagine momentarily that he was in love with her.

Perhaps there comes a time in every man's life to cast dreams aside and face reality. Gwen had become a part of his life now; he knew that as well as he knew that dreams had no substance, those phantom images which came with sleep and faded in the light of day. And yet the phantom girl of his dreams was not and never could be Gwendoline with her dark hair and eyes, her vivid, gipsy face, and high-pitched laughter, richly dressed and expensively perfumed.

Oh no, the phantom girl of his dreams had light brown hair drawn back from the pale oval of her face, smudged violet shadows, like thumb-prints, beneath her eyes; work-worn hands, shabby clothing; perfumed with oatmeal soap and fresh air, a hint of lavender water ...

Facing reality, accepting the inevitable, William asked Gwendoline to marry him.

'You mean that Mummy can go ahead and buy us a house?' had been her initial, disbelieving response to his proposal. 'Oh, Will, how wonderful! God, I was beginning to think that you'd never ask me. And yes, of course I'll marry you!'

In a frenzy of delight, she started making plans right away. She'd wear white, carry a bouquet of orchids. The ceremony would take place in the parish church of St Mary, followed by a reception at the Crown Hotel. She'd have six bridesmaids, including his sisters Nell and Louisa, and they'd go abroad for their honeymoon, to New York. She'd always longed to go to New York, to see the lights of Broadway, to ride on an elevated railway, to have waffles and maple syrup for breakfast.

'We'll be so happy, Will,' she cried ecstatically, 'just you wait and see!'

At that moment, William knew that he had made the greatest mistake of his life so far. That, like Esau, son of Isaac, he had traded his birthright of freedom for a mess of pottage.

Alone in his room that night, contemplating the mess he had made of his life and dreading the future, at least Charlie Thompson had discovered the secret of happiness after his bad beginning, William thought wistfully, envious of the lad's youth and vitality.

Charlie was fine. He'd even found himself a girlfriend to add to his happiness, a plump little lass who thought the sun shone out of him—which it probably did if Charlie's suntanned complexion was anything to go by. On the other hand, his old pal Fred Willis appeared to have lost his appetite for life, his former ebullience and *joie de vivre* disappearing ever since that day he'd gone to Darlington to confront Maudie Thompson and her new so-called lodger, when he'd known for certain that he'd lost the woman he loved beyond recall.

Harking back, William remembered precisely Fred's words on the subject of love: *'The truth is, there's no rhyme or reason when it comes to falling in love. Either you love someone or you don't. It's as simple as that. And I love Maudie, warts and all. What more can I say?'*

Fred had, at least, retained the courage of his conviction, albeit to his own detriment, William considered. Which was more than he could say for himself. So what was the answer?

Deep down, he knew the answer. The question, what to do about it, remained unanswered.

Fred was away from home when the news arrived. William no longer felt it necessary to stay at the cottage to take care of Charlie as he used to. The lad was nineteen now, and well able to take care of himself, a dab hand at cooking and keeping the place clean and tidy. He'd even talked of getting engaged to his girl, Mavis, of buying a cottage on Sandside to move into when they were married.

'I've saved up a nice little nest-egg,' he told William, 'so what do you think, Mister? I suppose we could rent a cottage to begin with, but that wouldn't be the same somehow. I wouldn't feel secure.'

William advised him to follow his instincts, to buy a place of his own, if he was certain of his feelings for Mavis.

Charlie's face radiated happiness, 'Oh yes, Mister,' he said shyly, 'I think the world of her, an' she thinks the same about me. I just can't help wishing—'

'Wishing what? Charlie?'

'Well, you know, that things had been different with Ma an' me, that she'd married Fred when he asked her. I know he did, cos he told me so, an' he was ever so upset when she turned him down. In fact, I don't think he's ever got over it. Seems like all the life's gone out of him nowadays.'

He added wistfully, 'Funny the way things turn out, ain't it? If Ma had married Fred, I might still be in Darlington looking after the shop. I would never have gone to sea, or met Mavis. The trouble with Ma, she never really knew what she wanted after my Dad got killed in the war. Seemed like she was always waiting for someone just like him to turn up. Maybe she was scared, deep down, of—oh, I dunno what. Of growing old, maybe, of losing her looks. I think she thought that Fred wasn't good enough for her. But then nobody was, not even me.'

'Do you still miss her?' William asked.

'I dunno for sure,' Charlie replied. 'It's just that there's a kind of gap in my life; as if I'm two halves of the same person. I suppose it happened when I ran away from home, when I knew that Ma didn't want me back.'

Two days later, to Will's amazement, Charlie turned up at the salon wanting to speak to him, looking distraught.

'What is it, Charlie? What's the matter?' Will asked, taking him aside out of earshot of the customers.

'It's Ma! I've had a telegram. She's ill; asking for me an' Fred. I've gotta go to her, Mister. Please, will you come with me? I don't want to go on my own. I wouldn't know what to do.'

'Where's Fred? Do you know?'

'Not for sure. Somewhere in the New-castle area was all he said. Could be Sunderland, Gateshead, his usual round.'

'I daresay we can find out,' William said briskly. 'Leave that to me. What time's the train to Darlington?'

'There's one at twelve o'clock. I asked at the station.'

'Right then, I'll meet you there in an hour.'

'Thanks, Mister.'

SIXTEEN

There had been a lot of arranging to do in the sixty minutes prior to his dash to the station, the onus of which William placed on Nell's shoulders. Louisa was too slow on the uptake; Clara would have wasted precious time arguing, telling him he could not possibly leave her in the lurch at such short notice.

Rushing upstairs, he'd packed his shaving gear and a change of clothes into an overnight case, scribbled a note to Gwen explaining the situation and telephoned Fred's firm to discover his whereabouts. Not that he came up with a definite answer. The girl on the firm's switchboard gave him Mrs Marble's address in Newcastle as the likeliest means of contact, but Mr Willis might be in one of a dozen places in the area.

Seated with Charlie in a railway carriage, it struck William as odd that they were on a return journey to the scene of his rescue over five years ago. As if the wheel of fate had turned full circle.

It would seem even stranger walking

252

down Parker Street to the corner shop; reliving memories of his first visit; passing the Donens' front door. He wondered who had sent the telegram, but Charlie appeared not to know for certain. 'It was signed, *"A Neighbour"*,' he said hazily, dreading what lay ahead of him.

Maudie must be seriously ill, William surmised, to have asked for her son and Fred Willis, to have prompted a neighbour to send a telegram.

Chances were, Maudie would not even recognise her son when she saw him—*if* she saw him, as the scrap of a kid who had once stood behind the counter of the corner shop in a flat cap and braces. Would never equate the strapping, handsome, clear complexioned man he had grown into with the spotty-faced youth she had so despised in the past.

Entering the corner shop, the girl behind the counter explained that Mrs Thompson was upstairs in bed, too poorly to see anyone except the doctor and her Ma who was taking care of her for the time being until the arrival of her son, who had been sent for.

'I *am* her son,' Charlie said quietly, 'and you are—Ada Smith? Am I right? We were at school together, remember?'

'Huh?' Ada's mouth sagged open, recalling Charlie Thompson as a classroom joke with his frizzy fair hair and spotty complexion, bearing no resemblance whatever to this tall handsome looking bloke confronting her across the counter; wishing she'd been kinder to him in their schooldays. 'Oh, right then,' she added feebly, 'you'd best go upstairs then, hadn't you?'

Ada's mother, Mrs Smith, who lived next door to the shop and had sent the telegram, rose to her feet as Charlie and William entered Maudie's bedroom.

The curtains were closed, the room stank of stale air permeated with disinfectant. Maudie, a shadow of her former self, lay back against her pillows, face wet with perspiration, breathing heavily, eyes shut; hands clawing at the counterpane: mumbling to herself, half unconscious. In desperate need of a familiar hand in the darkness surrounding her.

Standing on the threshold of the room, William's eyes filled with tears as Charlie, gathering Maudie's straying hands in his, whispered hoarsely, 'It's all right, Ma. I'm here now. Your son, Charlie, remember? And Fred will be here soon, I promise. We'll both take care of you, just you wait and see.'

About to leave the sickroom, 'Eh, it's a bad job,' Mrs Smith said to William, 'I've done my best, I'm sure, but I doubt the poor soul will last for more than a few days at the most, and I should know, having nursed my own poor mother through the last stages of cancer.'

She added thoughtfully, 'Funny really, I mean strange, ain't it? That I never cared much for the woman before she was taken ill all of a sudden? Her with all her high-flown ways an' all them so-called lodgers of hers, an' the way she treated that son of hers. An' I daresay I'd have gone on not caring if it hadn't been for Emily Donen, at number twenty-three, who organised a rota of neighbours to take turns in looking after Mrs Thompson day and night, whether we wanted to or not. Most of us didn't, an' that's the truth of the matter. But we did just the same, for Emily Donen's sake. Now I'm glad, not sorry, that we rallied round to help a neighbour in distress.'

Mrs Smith smiled faintly, 'A grand woman, Emily Donen, an' that daughter of hers, Lizzie Gilbert. Though I don't suppose you ever met them, did you? Being as you're a stranger here, though your face seems familiar somehow. Now, let me think.' Wrinkling her forehead, 'Of course, now I remember! You once lodged with Mrs Thompson a long time ago, didn't you? You're the one who ran down the street as if the devil was after you one morning when I was clearing away the snow from my doorstep, aren't you? The one who worked for that old German barber in Skinnergate, an' took up with Lizzie Gilbert's sister, Bessie?'

Ignoring the string of questions, 'What does the doctor say?' William asked.

'There's not much more he can say, is there? He gives her stuff to ease the pain, an' a nurse comes in twice a day to make her as comfortable as possible. Us lot, the neighbours, do the shopping an' cooking, not that she eats much the poor dear, but we can't let her starve, can us? An' we takes turns to look after the shop, to keep a bit of cash coming in to pay the bills. I mean the doctor charges half a crown a visit. Shocking, ain't it? Eh, it's a bad job all round. By the way, I wouldn't have known that lad of hers. He's come on a bit, I must say. Just as well he hopped it when he did. That last bloke she took up with was a proper bugger. Huh, he took off smartish when Maudie started bein' poorly. Didn't want to know her then.'

Mrs Smith went downstairs. Alone in the living room, William remembered the first time he'd entered this overcrowded parlour with its gimcrack ornaments and brightly burning fire, Maudie's ebullient presence, the fortune-telling incident, the way she had edged closer to him on the sofa.

The tall vase of peacock feathers was still there beside the hearth, he noticed, recalling her words: *'Peacock feathers are supposed to be unlucky, but I don't believe in that kind of superstitious nonsense. People make their own luck, that's what I think'.* Poor Maudie, whose 'luck' had all but run out.

Now, as a matter of urgency, he must try to contact Fred Willis. On his way downstairs, he heard the ping of the shop bell, the sound of voices, and hung back a little until the customer had gone. At least he'd assumed it to be a customer on her way out, but he was wrong. The bell had pinged for Ada after her stint behind the counter. Someone else had taken her place.

William's heart lifted. A feeling of relief, of pure joy swept over him. 'Hello, Lizzie,' he said.

'Hello, William.' She smiled uncertainly. 'I heard Charlie had been sent for.'

'I came with him, to keep him company.'

'That was kind of you. Not a very happy homecoming for him, I'm afraid.'

'No, it isn't.'

'Anything I can do to help?'

'Well yes, perhaps. I need to contact someone rather urgently, by telephone. A friend of mine, Fred Willis. Maudie's been asking for him, I gather.'

'My parents had a telephone installed recently,' Lizzie said. 'I'll lock up here for a few minutes and come with you, if you like, to—explain things to Mother—to save time. There's really no time to waste, is there?'

'Thanks, that would be a great help.' Trust Lizzie, he thought, to come to the heart of the matter without fuss or prevarication. And how lovely she looked. 'If you're sure your mother won't mind my intrusion?'

'I hardly think so. After all, what happened is all in the past now. A lot of water has flowed under the bridge these past five or six years.'

'Flowed?' William smiled. 'You mean—trickled? I wonder if that rusty bicycle frame is still there?'

'I shouldn't be at all surprised. Fancy you remembering that.'

'I remember everything about this place and the time I spent here,' he said quietly as Lizzie locked the shop door. He hadn't meant to say it, but he did, 'I really need to talk to you, Lizzie, to set straight certain misunderstandings between us, to explain certain actions of mine.'

'I know. But this is neither the time nor the place. In any case, is it really necessary, after all this time?'

'It is to me. Not just necessary but

important. Vitally important. You see, Lizzie, you've never been out of my mind for a moment these past years, knowing your poor opinion of me. Just an hour or so of your time is all I ask.'

'I don't know. I'm not sure,' Lizzie protested, remembering at the same time her old longing to apologise for her lack of sensitivity and common sense on the night of the Ox incident. 'I'll let you know. That's all I can possibly say for the time being.'

Emily Donen, alone in the house, welcomed him graciously into her hall to make use of the telephone. An hour later, William had succeeded in contacting Fred in a pub in Sunderland—where else?—where he was apparently imbibing a late liquid lunch.

Vaguely disorientated at first by the urgent message, he'd sobered up immediately when he realised the nature of the call.

'All right, Billy Boy, I'll come right away. Be with you as soon as I can. But it ain't all that bad with Maudie, is it? What I mean is, she will get better, won't she?'

'I'm sorry, Fred, believe me,' was all William could say as he hung up the receiver.

Thanking Emily for the use of the

instrument William counted out what he deemed to be a sufficient amount to cover the cost of the calls he had made, erring on the generous side to make certain she wouldn't be out of pocket, on his account. Then he turned towards her in surprise when she said softly, 'For what it's worth, Mr Chalmers, I never imagined for one moment it was my daughter Bessie you were in love with. I knew all along it was Lizzie from the moment she walked into the room that Sunday afternoon, remember?'

'How could I ever forget?' William said. 'But she was a married woman, a mother. And yet I knew, the moment I set eyes on her, that she was the one and only woman in the world for me. And nothing has changed to alter that opinion, Mrs Donen, believe me. I'm still in love with her, and I shall go on loving her all the days of my life.'

'I *do* believe you,' Emily said compassionately, 'but everything has changed so far as Lizzie is concerned. She is now happily married to a man capable of giving her the security she needed for herself and her child after the tragic death of her first husband. So I'm not merely asking but begging you to stay away from her. Not to unsettle her with reminders of a past she would do much better to forget.'

'I've already asked Lizzie to spare me an hour,' he admitted, 'and she knows how I feel about her.' He was speaking quietly, urgently, 'The last thing I want is to unsettle her or remind her of things she'd sooner forget, but the past has a way of haunting the present unless it is laid to rest once and for all; not forgotten but come to terms with. That's all I ask, to make things right between us.'

'For whose sake? Your own or hers?' Emily asked heavily, fearful of the reappearance of William in her daughter's life, thinking no good could come of it. 'You say Lizzie knows how you feel about her, that you will go on loving her all the days of your life. Frankly, I mistrust that kind of high-flown nonsense. The kind of love you're on about belongs in fairytales; it has little or nothing to do with reality. I don't want you filling my girl's head with that kind of rubbish, leading her to the mistaken belief that you could have given her the world on a plate. Real life isn't like that, and neither is love.'

'I'm prepared to believe that,' William said, thinking of Fred Willis and Maudie Thompson, of poor Charlie at his mother's bedside. He added wearily, 'All I ask is that you are prepared to believe that, loving Lizzie as much as I do, I would do nothing to hurt or harm her in any way.'

Fred's train arrived at Bank Top Station at seven o'clock. Anticipating the time of arrival, William was on the platform to meet him. The man presented a sorry spectacle: bleary-eyed, unkempt, suit wrinkled, tie askew.

'Have you eaten?' William asked. Fred shook his head. 'Then come with me.'

'Where to?'

'The buffet,' William said briskly, leading the way.

'Oh gawd, mate, thanks,' Fred murmured, 'I could do with a drink.'

'Forget the drink! What you need is a good meal inside you. Sit down. I'll do the ordering. Sausage, egg and chips do you?'

Staring at the plate of food in front of him, the rounds of bread and butter, the mug of hot, strong tea, 'I can't sit here eating with Maudie wantin' to see me,' Fred protested.

'Come off it, Fred. You were prepared to sit here drinking,' William reminded him.

'Yeah, but—'

'But nothing! Now you listen to me, Fred. No way are you going anywhere near Maudie the state you're in. Get that food inside you to begin with. You're going to need all your strength, believe me. When you've finished your meal, we'll go to the house. You can have a wash and brush up before going in to see Maudie.' He paused. 'She has lucid moments now and then.'

'Lucid moments? I don't understand. You mean she's been off her head? Delirious?' Fred was eating hungrily now, talking with his mouth full, frowning at William across the table, trying to make sense of the situation. 'But she'll snap out of that, won't she, when she gets better?'

This was the moment William dreaded, this awful moment of truth. He said quietly, 'I'm afraid Maudie isn't going to get better. She's in a pretty bad way, old son. She has—cancer.'

Slowly, Fred lay down his knife and his fork, his shoulders began to shake, tears ran down his cheeks, 'Christ, man,' he uttered despairingly, 'why didn't you tell me sooner? Why bring me here to sit stuffing my face, knowing all the time ...' His voice broke in a sob.

'To give you a breathing space,' William explained gently. 'Because you needed food to offset the effects of that liquid lunch of yours. Because I gauged your reaction to the bad news when you heard it; to give you time to pull yourself together, for Maudie's sake.'

Leaning forward, he placed a comforting hand on his friend's shoulder, 'What she needs now is strength, not weakness; that's why she asked for you, I reckon. To make her peace with you before it's too late. So when you go in to see her, I want you clean and smart and in control of yourself the way you used to be in the old days. Fair enough?'

'Fair enough, Billy Boy,' Fred said hoarsely, wiping away tears with the back of his hand. 'No need to worry, I shan't let you down, nor Maudie neither. I just wish that things had been different between us, that's all. When I asked her to marry me an' she turned me down flat, that really hurt. But all these years, I've never stopped loving her, nor ever shall.'

'Then why not tell her so?' William smiled ruefully, 'I imagine that's what she really wants to hear right now.'

'And to think the last time I saw her I as good as called her a fat pig. I'll never forgive myself for that. I was just so bloody jealous of that new lodger of hers.'

'You'll have to forget all that now,' William said patiently, thinking of Lizzie, beginning to realise the impossibility of living in the shadow of the past to the detriment of the future. 'Life moves on, and so must we.'

'Easy for you to say, old pal,' Fred responded drearily, 'but you've never really been in love, have you? Not really in love? What I mean is, that lass you've been courting these past five years ain't the be-all and end-all of your existence, is she? Perhaps I'm speaking out of turn. If so, forgive me. It just strikes me as being one of them "on off" affairs that don't really matter a damn one way or t'other, to either party. Not like Maudie an' me. Well, all I can say, if you end up marrying that Gwendoline Courteney, you'll live to rue the day.'

'You think I don't know that?' Rising to his feet, leading the way from the station buffet through an underground bypass to the street beyond. 'But it's you, Fred, not myself, I'm concerned with at the moment. I'll sort out my own problems when the time comes.'

'You will be staying on, won't you?' Fred asked anxiously, on their way down Parker Street.

'For as long as possible,' William said, 'but not at the house. There isn't room. I'll book in at the North Eastern Hotel. Well, here we are, old son. Remember, a wash and brush up and a change of clothes first before you see Maudie.'

'Ain't you coming in?'

'Not tonight. My case is in the hall, I'll just pick it up and be on my way. Maudie doesn't know I'm here. No reason why she should. It's you and Charlie she asked for, not me. And Fred, that lad will be looking to you for support. I know you won't let him down.'

Fred swallowed hard, 'I'll try not to, Billy Boy.'

SEVENTEEN

Unable to sleep, William found himself churning over the events of yesterday; the shock of seeing a once beautiful woman devastated by illness; his meeting with Lizzie and her mother; Emily Donen's words, *'The kind of love you're on about belongs in fairytales. I don't want you filling my girl's head with that kind of rubbish'*.

Getting up in the early hours, he lit a cigarette and stood at his bedroom window looking down at the empty street below; the gas-lamps spilling pools of light on wet pavements, thinking of the many, seemingly disparate facets of his life, leading to the inevitable conclusion that he had reached a watershed and was desperately seeking a solution to his problems. Thinking first of Lizzie, now happily married and with a secure future ahead of her, then of Gwendoline, the girl he'd proposed to on the spur of the moment whom, he now realised, would face a far from happy and secure future with a man who did not love her as she deserved to be loved: whole-heartedly, without reservation.

But perhaps this was neither the time nor the place to attempt to come to terms with the future in face of the present circumstance—a terminally ill woman fighting for life with every breath she drew.

Stubbing out his cigarette, his own problems scarcely amounted to a hill of beans, William realised, compared with the suffering of poor Charlie Thompson and that of Fred Willis, called upon to witness the decline of a towering presence in both their lives.

When he had bathed, shaved and breakfasted, he walked to the shop, knocked on the side door and stood there nervously awaiting a reply. Soon, Fred appeared in his shirtsleeves, eyes bleary from lack of sleep, yet reasonably in control. 'Come up to the kitchen, I've just put the kettle on for a cuppa,' he said, keeping his voice down. 'Mrs Smith is keeping an eye on Maudie. A nurse will be here soon to make her comfortable, an' Charlie'll stay with her while I get a bit of shut-eye. It's been one hell of a long night.'

William knew the feeling. 'Here, let me make the tea, and how about a bite of something to eat?'

Fred shook his head. 'Naw, I ain't hungry, though I daresay Charlie wouldn't say no to a couple of rashers an' a fried egg. I sent him off to bed early last night. The poor kid looked all in, an' there weren't much point in both of us sitting up. Besides,' he added, 'I kinda wanted to be alone with Maudie, an' I'm glad. She *knew* me, Billy, she recognised me.' His voice shook slightly with emotion. 'She opened her eyes, looked at me, smiled and said, "Hello, Freddie. I knew you'd come to see me."

'I damn near broke down, but I didn't. I told her I'd come because I loved her, and always would. Then I took hold of her hand, an' kissed her, an' she said, "Not very beautiful now, am I?" I told her she'd always be the most beautiful woman in the world to me, an' I meant what I said.

'Then ...' tears filled Fred's eyes, 'I asked her to marry me, an' she smiled an' said—yes.' His tears spilled over and ran down his cheeks. Yet, curiously, he was smiling, his face aglow. 'I know it sounds daft, but that was one of the happiest moments of my life, knowing she wanted me. If only ...' His smile faded, the glow diminished. He uttered brokenly, 'How the hell can I face losing her now?'

William's heart went out to his friend, knowing the question he'd asked was unanswerable. That no words of comfort, however well meant, would even begin to alleviate Fred's suffering. He said briefly, 'Drink this, then go to bed; try to get some sleep. I'll wait here for Charlie, cook him some breakfast; make myself useful, if possible. Though truth to tell, I feel pretty damn useless right now.'

Later, walking the length of Parker Street, passing the Ox public house, crossing the Skerne bridge into the market square and making his way to the High Row, William thought he'd be better off spending the rest of his brief sojourn in Darlington at the King's Head. He certainly had no wish to pass another sleepless night at the North Eastern, which he'd found strangely depressing. Nothing to do with the hotel itself, which was clean, adequately furnished and respectable, in keeping with most railway hotels, but more to do with the tragedy that had taken place there over five years ago, when Tom Imerson committed suicide in the pub yard.

Having booked in at the King's Head for an unspecified length of time, he treated himself to a half-pint of ale in the bar. A different barmaid was on duty, a friendly lass who told him, when he asked after

269

Beulah Cammish, that she had left some time ago, that she was now Mrs Donen, and the mother of two young children with a third on the way. 'Why? Was she a friend of yours?' the girl asked nosily, liking the cut of William's jib.

'No, not really. I just met her in here a couple of times when I lived in Darlington.' He smiled, making conversation. 'I knew she was thinking of getting married. Somehow I never visualised her as the mother of what promises to be quite a large family.' Fatuous words, but he felt in need of conversation to take his mind off the painful events taking place above the corner shop in Parker Street.

'Where are you living now, then?' the barmaid enquired, polishing glasses. 'Scarborough? Oh, lucky you! A friend and I spent a week there last summer. Bed, breakfast and an evening meal in a boarding house on the North Side. It was really smashing, with all them dancehalls and new-fangled movie shows. I wept buckets when I heard that Rudolph Valentino was dead. My friend and I saw him in *The Sheikh* in a funny little picture house where the usherette squirted disinfectant over our heads during the interval. Gawd! Talk about sneeze. As if we were lousy or summat.'

William smiled and finished his drink.

About to move away from the counter, the barmaid called after him, 'Are you staying here? If so, perhaps we'll meet again later?'

'Perhaps,' William prevaricated, unwilling to commit himself to any precise course of action for the time being, his movements dependent entirely on the needs of others.

And yet, in all conscience, he could not stay away from home indefinitely without a word of explanation to his mother to account for his desertion at this, one of the busiest seasons of the year in the salon. A telephone call would suffice he reckoned, standing on the pavement fronting the King's Head Hotel, if perchance Nell, not his mother, answered the call. Otherwise, Ma would not let him get a word in edgeways, so he'd far better write her a letter. In which case he'd be spared her histrionics for the time being at least; knowing full well they were bound to happen sooner or later. But not *now*, God willing, in his present state of emotional insecurity, in a limbo-land of uncertainty regarding his own future, let alone that of Charlie Thompson and Fred Willis.

Feeling suddenly desperately hungry and in need of sustenance, William turned his footsteps unerringly towards Zisslers' hot pie shop in Skinnergate, to relive that sublime moment when, standing in a shop doorway to eat them, biting hard into the succulent pastry containing the richly seasoned pork-filling beneath the crust, uncaring of the gravy running down his chin, he had experienced for the first time in his life, the meaning of freedom.

He now knew that no such thing as freedom existed, that every man worth his salt, carried with him a burden of responsibility towards the happiness and well-being of others apart from himself: that a sublime moment of happiness could never be reprised; never come again as it came before, except, perhaps, in dreams, which had little or no bearing whatsoever on reality. A fact succinctly pointed out to him by Lizzie's mother, Emily Donen, which he now reluctantly, accepted as the truth. Above all he cared about Lizzie's peace of mind, which he would never willingly destroy.

Passing the pie shop, he retraced his steps to the High Row, uncertain what to do next to kill time. Glancing across the road, it occurred to him to renew his acquaintance with Madame Marcia.

Delighted to see him, she invited him through to her private sanctum. 'What on earth are you doing here?' she asked, thinking he'd lost something of his sparkle since their last meeting. 'If you want your job back, it's yours. I mean it. Most of the girls you worked with have left now to get married, and I'm seriously short-staffed at the moment.'

'No, I'm sorry. Thanks for the offer, but I'll be leaving soon.' He explained the circumstances of his visit as succinctly as possible, adding that this was a case of necessity, not a planned visit.

'You've changed, William,' Marcia commented, 'but then so have a lot of things. Take the Jessingtons, for example, though I daresay you've heard what happened? The scandal was widely reported at the time.'

'No, not a word.'

'Oh, my dear. Poor Myra Jessington. I never thought I'd feel sorry for her, but I do now. It all started when that wretched husband of hers was caught with his fingers in the till, so to speak. Apparently he'd embezzled thousands of pounds from the firm of which he was a director. But worse was to follow. A young girl from a poor class family named him as the father of her child, and blabbed her story to a newspaper reporter, claiming how badly she'd been treated by him; saying that he'd offered to pay her a hundred pounds to have the child aborted and keep her mouth shut into the bargain.

'Then the fat really was in the fire, as you can imagine! How Myra coped with the shame of it all, I don't know. Of course the

273

property had to be sold for a start in part restitution of her husband's embezzlement and in payment of the lawyer's fees. The upshot was that Sir Miles was sent to prison for ten years to mull over his misdeeds, and Myra folded her tents like the Arabs and as silently stole away.'

Marcia sighed, 'Her ladyship came to see me before she left town to join up with some repertory company she'd been involved with before her marriage. The poor woman played ingénue roles then, God alone knows what kind of roles she'll play now.'

'*Femmes fatales?*' William suggested, remembering his early morning encounter with Lady Myra at Jessington Hall.

Marcia smiled, 'It was always a case of what's sauce for the gander is sauce for the goose,' she commented drily, misquoting the saying deliberately, 'and who could blame her? She knew very well that Miles had a string of mistresses a mile long; a bitter pill for an attractive woman to swallow. I know because she told me so herself, in this very room. Which reminds me, I have a client due in five minutes.' She rose to her feet, hand extended, 'It's been lovely seeing you again, William, and remember what I said. If ever you want your old job back, just drop me a line.'

'Thank you, Mrs Hunter, I'll remember.'

274

Taking his leave of her, William recrossed the road to the King's Head and went up to his room to unpack the few belongings he'd brought with him. At a loose end, not wanting to return to Parker Street till later on in the day, afraid of getting in the way, neither use nor ornament; thinking he'd be far more useful cooking a meal for Fred and Charlie at suppertime, he lay down on the bed and fell asleep. He awoke suddenly to the realisation that someone was knocking at the door.

'Just a second. I'm coming.' Getting up, he brushed back his hair with his hands and straightened his tie. A porter was on the landing. 'There's a lady to see you, sir,' the man said, 'in the reception area.'

Mystified, William shrugged into his jacket and hurried downstairs to find Lizzie standing forlornly near the front entrance. The last person on earth he had expected to see. His heart lifted momentarily then sank just as quickly, realising why she had come by the sad expression on her face as he hurried towards her.

'It's Mrs Thompson,' she said quietly, without preamble. 'She died at two o'clock. The end came very suddenly; quite peacefully. She simply—fell asleep. Charlie and Mr Willis were with her at the time. I thought you'd want to know.'

'Oh God, if only I'd been there,' William said hoarsely.

'You couldn't have done anything more than you have done already,' she reminded him gently. 'Travelling with Charlie the way you did, and getting in touch with Mr Willis—Fred. He told me you'd met him at the station. The way you looked after him, talked sense to him; made him pull himself together for Mrs Thompson's sake. He said he'd have gone to pieces without you. So no regrets, William. They'll need all your strength now to help them through the days to come.'

'It was kind of you to come,' William said gratefully. 'Please sit down, Lizzie. I'll order some tea and scones.'

'No, thanks all the same, but I can't stop. I must be on my way home to give Emma her tea, and cook my husband's supper, or they'll be wondering what's happened to me.'

'Yes, of course, I understand.' At that moment, William longed to draw Lizzie into his arms, to tell her again how much he loved her, and knew that he must not, for her sake, not his. 'Before you go, how did you know where to find me?' He hadn't told anyone he'd changed his mind about staying on at the North Eastern.

'Oh that?' Lizzie said, 'My sister Elsie told me. She was looking out of the hat shop window at the time she saw you entering the King's Head, luggage in hand. She simply put two and two together, and so did I.'

'I see. Then I owe Elsie a debt of gratitude for bringing you here, however briefly, to prove how much kindness there is still left in this sad old world of ours.' Holding out his hand to her, 'Well, goodbye Lizzie, and God bless you,' he said softly.

Clinging to his hand momentarily, she murmured. 'Just one thing, I'm sorry for what I said to you that night at the Ox, and afterwards. I should have known better. I was angry and humiliated at the time, knowing deep down that you were right. Please forgive me for being so blind, so stupid, not to realise that you had my best interests at heart all along?'

Then suddenly, swiftly, she was gone, hurrying away from him along the High Row, leaving him bereft of her shining presence in his life to face the terrible reality of his return to Parker Street—to administer to the needs of the living in a house mourning for the newly dead.

EIGHTEEN

The church was packed for Maudie's funeral service. Neighbours turned out in full force to pay their last respects to a woman whose shop had become a focal point of their lives, a convenient port of call for whatever they'd run short of during the day. And even when the shop closed for the night, people thought nothing of knocking on the side door to ask for an ounce of baccy or a packet of Woodbine cigarettes.

The congregation, composed mainly of women, did not immediately recognise the chief mourner as Maudie's son, Charlie; that gangling, odd-looking kid who had served customers wearing a flat cap and braces. They'd all felt sorry for poor Charlie standing behind that shop counter all day looking like a spare part; as spotty as a Dalmation and forever at his Ma's beck and call.

Treated him like dirt, she had, had been the consensus of opinion when he'd run away from home five, going on six years ago, and no wonder. Rumour had it that the lad had been beaten black and blue by his Ma's latest lodger at the time. A brute of a man if ever there was one. What was his name? Trevor summat-or-other?

Any road, what did it amount to now with poor Maudie dead and gone and Charlie home in time to attend her funeral? If it really was Charlie walking behind her coffin? If so, he'd certainly come on a bit now he'd grown into a man. And what a man! High, wide and handsome.

And who were the other two blokes? The one with a ginger moustache and the one walking beside him, a bit of a toff by the look of him; older than Charlie but just as handsome in a quieter, more refined kind of way.

The one with a ginger tash looked in a bad way, they reckoned, walking unsteadily and blubbing openly, poor devil. Of course, one woman remembered, he was some kind of corset salesman, a frequent visitor to the corner shop before that Trevor moved in to queer his pitch.

Rumour had it that he'd asked Maudie to marry him and she'd turned him down flat. But here he was, large as life, a bantam rooster of a man; a bit on the short side in the leg department, and with receding red hair. But he couldn't be all that old. Perhaps he hadn't take care of himself properly in the past; probably the reason Maudie had given him the brush-off?

Eh dear, what a mix-up to be sure, but the wreaths were lovely, and the parson was saying nice things about the dear departed; a warm-hearted human being, a loving wife and mother. As if *he* knew. Chances were that Maudie Thompson had never been inside a church more than twice in her life. Once to get married. Once to get buried.

Mind you, she'd been a good-looking woman during her lifetime. A bit too good-looking for her own good at times. But that husband of hers thought the world of her until he'd been killed in the war. A really nice man, Jim Thompson, and a damn fine grocer, building up that corner shop the way he had.

So what would become of the business now Jim and Maudie had gone to their higher reward? Would Charlie return to Parker Street to live? He'd be a fool not to, one woman thought, wishing she'd been left a house and a shop in Parker Street, though she couldn't quite see the present-day Charlie Thompson standing day long behind a counter the way Jim had done. In which case, he'd probably put the house and shop up for sale once the funeral was over, and his mother had been laid to rest in the Carmel Road cemetery.

Meanwhile, 'Guide me, O Thou Great Redeemer'. A fine, resounding end to the service ...

The sense of loss, anti-climax, was almost unbearable after the funeral when William, Fred and Charlie returned to the house to find it empty, robbed of the vivid presence of Maudie Thompson.

At William's suggestion, the chief mourners including Emily Donen, Lizzie, Mrs Smith and her daughter Ada, and the rota of neighbours who had looked after Maudie so well during the last weeks of her life, had been invited to partake of suitable refreshment in a private room at the King's Head. An unorthodox departure from the usual wake held at the home of the deceased, he'd realised, but less stressful for Fred in particular, whose reaction to the death of the woman he loved had been terrible to witness.

Charlie, on the other hand, proved to be a tower of strength. It was he, not William, who had requested the removal of his mother's body to the undertaker's mortuary to lie there at peace preceding her funeral. It was for Fred's sake, the state he was in: sitting at her bedside, talking to her as if she was still alive. Telling her over and over again how much he loved her; that they'd get married the moment she was better.

'What are we gonna do about him, Mister?' Charlie asked William, when they had taken Fred upstairs and they were alone in the sitting room, near an empty grate.

'I don't know, Charlie,' William admitted despondently, trying to make sense of the situation. 'I suppose, in the present circumstances, all we can possibly do is to take him back to Scarborough with us—if you intend going back to Scarborough, that is?'

'Yes, of course I do! The last thing I want is to stay on here in Darlington. I've been giving it a lot of thought. I reckon I'll have to sell up. Ma told me to do the best for myself. She was very weak at the time, but she knew what she was saying.'

Charlie bit his lip. 'She asked me to forgive her for all the things she'd done wrong; told me she was proud of me. Said I'd grown into a fine man, just like my father.'

Trying hard not to cry, 'Another thing she said: "Tell William I'm sorry for the way I treated him". Then she began to ramble a bit. Does what I've told you make sense?'

William nodded. 'Oh yes, Charlie, a great deal of sense. Now I'd best be on my way to the King's Head. Try and get some sleep, son. Tomorrow we'll decide what's to be done about selling the shop. I'll go with you to the estate agents, if you like?'

'Thanks, Mister. I dunno what I've had done without you.'

An unexpected hiatus occurred when Fred, more in control of himself after a good night's sleep, begged Charlie not to sell the property his mother had left him.

'But what else can I do with it? What use will it be standing empty?'

'That's the whole point,' Fred said eagerly. 'No need for it to stand empty if—'

'If *what*, Fred?' Charlie frowned.

'If I stayed on here to keep it going.'

William entered the arena at that moment having let himself in by the side door in time to hear Fred's hoarsely uttered words: 'You see, Charlie, I belong here, close to your mother. Oh, I realise I know next to nowt about the grocery trade. But then, I knew even less about ladies' underwear when I became a corset salesman.

'The fact is, lad, I have a proposition to put to you. An exchange, if you like. My cottage in Scarborough in exchange for a house and corner shop in Parker

283

Street. Well, Charlie, what do you think of the idea?'

'I dunno for sure,' Charlie said hesitantly, more concerned about Fred's welfare than a mere exchange of properties. Fearing that Fred's obsessive desire to remain close to Maudie might well result in a nervous breakdown. Turning to William for advice, 'What do *you* think, Mister?'

Drawing in a deep breath, 'This is a matter to be settled between the pair of you and no-one else,' William responded. 'All I can say is if you, Fred, intend turning this house into a kind of shrine in memory of Maudie, you'd best stick to your job as a corset salesman. There's no room in business for sentimentality, besides which you'll need to restrain your fondness for alcohol, otherwise you'll not stand a chance of success. You'll need your wits about you.'

'On the other hand you, Charlie, could do worse than exchanging something you don't want for something you do and still hold on to your nest-egg. As I see it, it boils down to a matter of trust between friends backed by a bit of sound legal advice so you'll both know exactly where you stand contractually speaking. You see my position? I don't want to take sides. You must make up your own minds.'

Early next day, William returned to Scarborough alone. Charlie and Fred needed more time to talk over their plans for the future. Charlie was still not entirely convinced Fred would be all right on his own, running a business he knew nothing about. He'd have liked William to stay on for a bit longer but what he'd said about not wanting to take sides made sense. Now it was up to him to make his own decisions, to prove himself a man.

He knew the house and shop were worth more than Fred's cottage, but money didn't enter into it as long as Fred realised what he was letting himself in for. And would Fred look after himself and the house properly without help? Despite her many faults and failings, Maudie had been intensely houseproud. In the long run, Charlie persuaded Fred to keep on Ada Smith to help in the shop and someone to come in two mornings a week to clean up for him.

When these matters had been thrashed out to their mutual satisfaction, they went into town together to have the necessary documents drawn up by a firm of solicitors in Skinnergate.

Mentally and physically exhausted by the exigencies of the past few days, the last thing William expected was the full-scale row with his mother that erupted the minute he set foot across the threshold.

'Oh, so you've decided to grace us with your presence once more, have you?' Clara uttered icily. 'All this time, and not a word to me, your own mother! You simply disappeared, like a thief in the night, without so much as asking my permission.'

'I'm sorry, Mother,' William said wearily, 'there wasn't time for explanation. Charlie's mother had been taken desperately ill and the train to Darlington was due to leave within the hour.'

'Huh,' Clara said venomously, 'I might have known that *he* would take priority over your own flesh and blood. Answer me one question, William, and I demand to know the truth! Are you in love with him? Is that the reason why you have played fast and loose with Gwendoline Courteney's affection all these years? The truth now, remember!'

William's anger broke through his weariness. Confronting his mother, ablaze with anger, 'How dare you even suggest such a thing?' he uttered scathingly. 'Very well then, Mother, you asked for the truth, now you'll have it! To begin with, it was your cockeyed idea, remember, to bring Gwen and me together at that stupid fancy dress party of yours.

'Think about it, Mother. Did you ask my permission to interfere in my life so blatantly? For your information, I was deeply in love with someone else at the time. A woman, not a man, to satisfy your curiosity concerning my sexual proclivities, which I regard as disgusting, to say the least.

'As for Charlie's mother. She died of cancer a few days ago. Now, to further satisfy your sickening curiosity, I have no intention of marrying a woman I'm not in love with. It wouldn't be fair to either Gwendoline or myself to enter a loveless marriage engineered by yourself and that manipulative mother of hers.

'Tell me, Mother, the truth now, since you are apparently a stickler for the truth. Did you ever stop to consider my future as a kept man, married to a woman far richer than myself? No, of course not. Why should you? You've never been able to see further than the nose on your face. But no need to worry, I'm home now and I'll work for you till the end of the summer season. In short, I'm giving you six weeks' notice to find a replacement. Now, if you'll excuse me, I'm going upstairs to my room to wash away the dirt of this unpleasant homecoming.'

'My God,' Nell said later, 'I could hear

the row going on downstairs. Not what was said, but the sound of raised voices. I switched on the stock room wireless pretty damn quick, I can tell you, to cover the racket. What was it all about? No, don't bother to tell me, let me guess. Ma's been on the boil for days now, spoiling for a fight. Can't say I blame her entirely. It was a bit much, walking out the way you did without asking. I tried to explain, but she wouldn't listen. She almost hit the ceiling when she knew you'd gone off with Charlie Boy.'

'I did write to her,' William said impatiently.

Nell continued, setting the supper table, 'Gwenny's not best pleased either, I should warn you. You should have seen her face when I gave her that note you left her, so you'd best be prepared to eat a large slice of humble pie the next time you see her.'

'I'll be seeing her tonight,' William said, dreading the encounter. 'I might just as well tell you. You're bound to find out sooner or later anyway—I intend breaking off our engagement.' He added, 'What's more, I've given Mother six weeks' notice. Mrs Hunter offered me my old job back, if I wanted it. I didn't at the time, but I do now.'

Clattering down a handful of cutlery

on the dining-room table, 'You've done *what?*' Nell regarded her sibling with an expression of disbelief and grudging admiration intermingled. 'Well, all I can say is you certainly know how to put the cat among the pigeons. A case of practice making perfect, I suppose. But where will it all end? That's what I'd like to know. Talk about "Off again, on again, away again, Finnigan". Have you the faintest idea what you really want from life, or are you simply prepared to fritter it away chasing rainbows?'

William smiled reflectively. He said, 'I'll let you know, if ever I find the rainbow's end.'

After supper, which Clara had eaten alone in her room, William walked to Cliff Bridge Terrace to visit Gwendoline.

'Oh, it's you, is it?' she threw at him, opening the front door. 'My reluctant lover, no less! I suppose I should feel flattered you've even remembered my existence since you've obviously had far more important things on your mind recently than our wedding plans.'

Knowing the moment of truth had finally arrived, William said heavily, 'Not *our* wedding plans, Gwen, *your* wedding plans, in which I have no part to play. I'm so sorry, believe me, but I can't marry you

289

under false pretences. The truth is, I'm in love with someone else, another woman. The only woman in the world for me.'

'I see. So why the hell didn't you say so before? Before I made a complete fool of myself the way I have done?'

'I'm so sorry, Gwen,' William reiterated, deeply aware of the humiliation he had caused her, not wanting their long-standing relationship to end on a sour note. He had after all thought enough of the girl to ask her to marry him, and he would in all probability have gone ahead with the wedding, had he not met Lizzie again.

'Oh, sorry, sorry, sorry!' Gwen mimicked. 'It's always been a case of "sorry" with you, hasn't it? Now I know why. Well, I shan't be in the least sorry to see the back of you. And to prove it, here's the bloody engagement ring you gave me!'

Tearing the ring from her finger, she threw it down on the hall carpet in front of him. 'Now get the hell out of here. I pray to God I'll never set eyes on you again!'

Leaving the ring where it had fallen, William walked away from the house with a deep feeling of remorse that he had inflicted hurt on a fellow human being. But far better, he thought, a moment of truth rather than a lifetime of regret.

NINETEEN

Rearranging a row of medical reference books, Lewis Gilbert resisted the temptation to delve into a volume containing a chapter relevant to the ageing process in man. No need, he knew that chapter by heart, having read it many times before. Especially the paragraphs on impotence; linked, in the author's view, to underlying psychological problems of the past. In which case the sufferer should seek the help and advice of a qualified psychiatrist to establish the nature of the problem.

Lewis needed no psychiatrist to tell him the underlying reasons why he had failed Lizzie so miserably as a husband. It had to do with his first wife's scarcely concealed disgust of any kind of physical intimacy; her utter refusal to bear his child. "We are human beings, not farm animals", had been her battle-cry throughout the years of their marriage. A condemnation which rung in his mind repeatedly whenever he tried to make love to Lizzie, who so desperately wanted a child by him, a brother or sister for Emma.

He had never for one moment believed

that, loving her so much, he would prove incapable of ever consummating their marriage, of impregnating his wife: and giving her the child they both wanted so much.

Not that she ever uttered a word of blame or regret that this was so. Not Lizzie. She had simply said, quietly, night after night, lying in the circle of his arms, her head against his shoulder, 'I love you, Lewis, and I always will.'

He knew that she meant what she said, but was that good enough for a girl like Lizzie? Making do with second best, a husband old enough to be her father. An impotent husband to boot.

He hadn't mentioned the letter he'd received from his brother Lance in America, asking him to consider taking charge of his Greenwich Village antiques shop when he and his wife Della opened another business in Boston in the new year.

Lance had written glowingly of the accommodation on offer, a spacious brown stone house above the shop, very like his present set-up. A family house. Of the challenge involved in making a fresh start with Lizzie, little Emma and Nan Imerson—if the old lady wished to come with them. Old lady? Lewis thought. Nan was scarcely more than his own age, possibly a year or so younger.

Even so, the offer held certain attractions for a man in Lewis's present state of mind. Recently, he'd come to regard Attica as little more than a dusty repository of secondhand literature and faded prints, and of equally faded hopes for the future, Lizzie's in particular. Removed from the baleful influence of his dead wife, Alice, facing a new challenge in a new country, who knew what might happen? But he needed time to think things over before telling Lizzie about the letter. She'd seemed off-colour lately, unlike her normal happy self.

Perhaps what she needed, what they all needed, was a holiday at the seaside to blow away the cobwebs. Before he told her about the letter and asked her to make one of the most important decisions of her life so far; realising as he did, Lizzie's love of her hometown and the strong family ties linking her to her birthplace which she might find impossible to sever. Above all, he wanted her to be happy.

Things had gone from bad to worse between William and his mother when he told her that he had broken off his engagement to Gwendoline.

'Are you determined to drive me mad?' Clara wailed in despair. 'Have you no sense of honour, of responsibility towards myself or Gwendoline? No, of course not, selfish beast that you are! Well, what have you to say for yourself? Don't just stand there looking as if butter wouldn't melt in your mouth.'

'All I can possibly say,' William replied, tight-lipped, 'is that I deeply regret your poor opinion of me, but far better a broken engagement than a lifetime spent with the wrong woman.'

'It would serve you right if she sued you for breach of promise.'

'Talk sense, Mother. You can't get blood out of a stone. Anyway, you'll soon be rid of me. September will soon be here, then I'll be on my way.' He had already written to Mrs Hunter. Now every day that passed was one day nearer to his return to Darlington, and closer proximity to the woman he loved.

Fred had taken to shopkeeping like a duck to water. In no time at all he got the hang of ordering supplies from the various travelling salesmen who paid him regular weekly visits, advising him which lines to re-order—mainly tinned goods, tea, sugar, sweets and cigarettes, bacon, eggs and starch.

Bread was delivered daily by a local bakery. Taking the initiative, he added pork pies to the order, half a dozen at first, then a dozen, encouraged by the quick sale of these readymade comestibles to housewives in need of summat different to pack in their husbands' bait-boxes.

Every Sunday, as regular as clockwork, he would walk to the cemetery to place flowers on Maudie's grave.

The woman who came in twice a week to clean up for him, a plump pleasant-faced neighbour, Mrs Gladstone, changed the bedding which she took home with her to wash and iron, brushed the carpets and lumped out the proddy mats to the yard to be shaken. One day, 'If you don't mind me saying so, Mr Willis, I'd have shot of them things if I was you,' eyeing the peacock feathers with distaste. 'Unlucky things, peacock feathers!' And so they had ended up in the dustbin. Then he had packed and put away some of the brass ornaments and pictures to save Mrs Gladstone unnecessary work.

Pride of ownership, of being his own master rather than a wage slave, a peripatetic pedlar of women's underwear, had imbued Fred with an overwhelming desire to make a success of his newfound independence; not just for his own sake but Maudie's and Charlie's.

The exchange of properties between himself and Charlie had presented few problems, if any, since Charlie had stalwartly refused to take into account the price differences between a two up, two down fisherman's cottage in Scarborough and a well-situated six-roomed house and corner shop in Parker Street, Darlington.

When the solicitor pointed out to him that he might reasonably request the additional sum of five hundred pounds from Mr Willis, in respect of fixtures, fittings and stock relevant to the shop alone, not to mention the size of the premises, Charlie had told the man succinctly that he couldn't care less about the financial aspects involved in the exchange, even to his own detriment.

Afterwards, 'Thanks, lad,' Fred said awkwardly, 'I'd have been hard pressed to stump up five hundred quid.'

Charlie said simply, 'I'd be hard pressed to repay you, Fred, for the way you have looked after me all these years. The roof over my head, the food you've put into my mouth with no thought of repayment; that first job of mine as a "donkey boy" on the sands, remember? Then the good word you put in for me with the captain of *The Pride of Scarborough*. But more than that, the way you—cared for my mother in the final stages of her life. You made her so happy, telling her how much you still loved her; asking her to marry you the way you did.'

It was then, on the pavement in Skinnergate outside the solicitor's office that Fred, close to tears, showed Charlie the wedding ring he'd bought for Maudie a few hours prior to her death, as a symbol of his eternal love for her.

Now, to Fred's satisfaction, Charlie and his fiancée, Mavis, planned to marry in Scarborough's parish church. They had invited him to attend the wedding—an invitation which he gladly accepted.

One afternoon in August, walking along the beach to clear his mind after a particularly unpleasant lunch spent in the company of his mother and sisters, William came unexpectedly, breathtakingly across Lizzie and Emma paddling in the sea close to the harbour mouth. Lizzie's skirts were tucked up about her ankles, the child laughing up at her, daring her to come closer, being deliberately provoking. Emma dodged away from her mother, venturing further into the sea in her protective waders, jumping over the waves rolling in on the shore and ignoring her mother's warning to come back before she got out of her depth.

William saw the danger. He knew the strength of the tide about the harbour mouth and the way the beach shelved down suddenly from the lifeboat slipway. The inevitable happened. Suddenly the child took fright as the sea-swell swept her off her feet, flinging her backward into the tide, churning her into the strong undertow ebbing beneath her.

Emma was screaming now, calling out 'Mama, Mama!' Panic-stricken, Lizzie began wading into the water, skirts water-logged, hampering her progress. Hastily pulling off his shoes and jacket, William strode into the sea. Crowds had gathered on the shore to watch the drama as, reaching the child, lifting her up in his arms, he carried her safely back to the beach to a burst of spontaneous applause from the onlookers.

'She's very wet and very frightened,' William said briefly, handing her to Lizzie. 'I should get her into a hot bath, then to bed as quickly as possible if I were you.' He smiled encouragingly, 'She'll be fine.'

Lewis and Nan had left their deckchairs and hurried to the water's edge to find out what was happening, in time to see a tall young man wading from the sea holding Emma in his arms. Lizzie, her skirts wet, hair in disarray and tears streaming down her face, was stumbling towards the man, arms outspread to receive the child he was carrying.

'My God,' Lewis uttered hoarsely, pushing through the crowd to get closer to Lizzie, calling her name. Not that she heard him.

Standing close to the stranger, looking up at him, she murmured, 'Thank God you were there, William. How can I thank you for being there when I needed you so much?'

In a blinding moment of realisation, Lewis knew beyond a shadow of doubt that his wife was in love with that man, and he with her. The signs were unmistakable; the look in Lizzie's eyes as he handed the child into her care, a tenderness reflected in his own eyes as he smiled at her. As if they were alone on the crowded beach, bound together by an invisible bond of understanding—and love.

Deeply shaken by his brief encounter with Lizzie, hurrying home to change into dry clothing, William thanked God that he had been in the right place at the right time to save her child from drowning. It could so easily have happened—a little girl out of her depth, caught in a strong current dragging her relentlessly towards the open sea.

Thank God he had been there in time to prevent that happening. He remembered the way she'd clung to him, the feel of her arms about his neck as he'd whispered words of encouragement to her, telling her not to be frightened, that she was perfectly safe now.

Never would he forget the way that Lizzie's child had clung to him so trustingly, or her mother's words: *'Thank God you were there, William, when I needed you so much'.*

He knew now that Lizzie had forgiven him. If only he'd possessed, ages ago, the courage and common sense to end his relationship with Bessie before telling Lizzie he loved her, how differently things might have turned out.

Strangely, he had given no thought to fatherhood before. But then, before today, he had never experienced the feel of a child's arms about his neck—Emma's trust in him as he'd carried her safely ashore. He had known, at that moment, an overwhelming tenderness for the little girl, as well as her mother. An added dimension to loving.

Jimmy Blaney still cut little ice with the Donen family, although even Jack had to admit the lad appeared to have his head screwed on right. The appendage on his top lip had developed into a handlebar moustache of impressive dimensions. Neatly waxed at the tips, it gave him a certain panache in keeping with his new role in life as stage-manager of the Theatre

Royal. Whilst Bessie, at his instigation, had been promoted to the front of house box office.

Jack and Emily had consented to their engagement on condition that their prospective son-in-law provided a suitably furnished home for Bessie before the wedding. This despite Bessie's tearful protestations that they'd have to wait years to get married. Jack and Emily remained adamant, knowing Bessie's propensity for rushing headlong into affairs of the heart and secretly doubting Blaney's suitability as a steady husband for their romantically minded daughter.

To their amazement, Jimmy had proved his worth as a suitor, having saved up enough money for a house in Victoria Road—considerably bigger than theirs in Parker Street—a fumed oak bedroom suite; tables and chairs, a horsehair sofa, several secondhand Axminster carpets from Leckonby's saleroom, plus a gas cooker, and a job-lot of cooking utensils—the last to Bessie's dismay, since her cooking skills were limited to hard-boiling eggs, burning toast, and making lumpy custard. At which point, Emily had derived perverse pleasure from teaching the feckless Bessie the rudiments of cookery, with the constant reminder that the way to a man's heart was through his stomach.

301

'But Jimmy ain't all that interested in food anyway,' Bessie lamented, 'well, not in stew an' dumplings. He'd rather have a cod an' a pennorth or a hot Zisslers' pork pie any day of the week. Jimmy's got brains, in case you hadn't noticed. He'll go far, mark my words.'

'Not if you feed him on fish and chips and pork pies, he won't,' Emily said calmly. 'In any case, the fish and chip shops, and Zisslers are closed on Sundays, in which event he'll be glad of a plateful of stew and dumplings, I daresay.'

But Bessie knew that what she'd said about Jimmy was true. He *would* go far. He had his eye on the future, the development of the Hollywood Movie Pictures Industry, ahead of the time when theatres would become redundant. To which end, on their Wednesday afternoons off together, he had taken to dragging his fiancée to a local flea-pit adjacent to the theatre to watch silent movies to the accompaniment of a pit-piano and onscreen captions depicting the actors' dialogue.

One such afternoon, seated on the back row of the stalls, watching a movie featuring the latest Hollywood sensation, Marjorie Starr, Bessie leant forward breathlessly, pushing away Jimmy's exploratory hand. Not quite believing her eyes at first, then half rising to her feet to take a closer look at the screen, certain at last that her eyes had not deceived her, 'That's our Madge,' she cried out excitedly, uncaring of the eyes turned in her direction in the darkened cinema, 'That's our Madge!'

Deeply embarrassed, 'For heaven's sake, sit *down*, Bess,' Jimmy hissed, petulantly. 'What the hell are you on about?'

'I've just said, haven't I?' Bessie hissed back at him, resenting being hauled back to her seat by a tug of Jimmy's hand on her skirt. 'Marjorie Starr, the latest Hollywood sensation, just happens to be my sister, Madge Donen, so there!'

TWENTY

Quickly, they had taken Emma back to the lodgings where Lizzie bathed her and put her to bed. The child, inclined to tears and fretfulness after the shock of her immersion, soon fell asleep, watched over by her mother until Lewis suggested that she, too, should take a hot bath and try to get some rest.

'I'll be all right,' was all she would say, looking at Emma asleep in her trundle-bed near the window. 'I wouldn't want her to

303

wake up and find herself alone.'

'She wouldn't be alone,' Lewis said patiently, 'if you'll take my advice. You really should get out of those wet skirts.'

'Oh, are they wet? I hadn't noticed,' Lizzie said vaguely.

'Lewis is right,' Nan said, appearing in the doorway. 'You can't just sit there, dripping wet from the knees down. Now, get along to the bathroom, get out of those wet things, give them to me and I'll take them down to the landlady to hang out.'

Reluctantly, Lizzie did as she was told, moving slowly like a woman in a dream, with one thought in mind—how close she had come to losing her child. If it hadn't been for William's presence on that crowded beach ... William had a knack for showing up at stressful moments of her life; at Tom Imerson's funeral, in the Ox, at Maudie Thompson's corner shop, and in the foyer of the King's Head Hotel when she had gone there to impart the news of Maudie's passing. Above all, this afternoon when she had realised for the first time the depth of her feelings towards him—akin to love. Not that she knew the full meaning of the word, except that in the fraught and fragile moment when he had placed her child in her arms, she had been aware of—what exactly? A touch of half-forgotten magic, perhaps? Memories linked to moonlit nights long ago in the springtime of her life when she had felt that, reaching up her hands, she might gather into them a scattering of stars and moondust, along with the scent of lilacs in blossom ...

When Nan returned from her foray to the landlady's private quarters on the ground floor, bringing with her a tray of tea things, having pegged out Lizzie's sodden underwear to dry on the washing-line in the yard, 'I just thought,' she said cheerfully, 'that what we all need most, right now, is a good strong cuppa.' Setting down the tray on the dressing table, 'Especially Lizzie, when she's had her bath. I wonder what's keeping her, by the way? Perhaps I'd better go and see if she's all right?' She added more concerned, 'You do realise, don't you, Lewis, that the poor girl is in shock? Not entirely responsible for her actions for the time being?'

Lewis said wearily, his mind in turmoil. 'For God's sake, Nan, drop the pretence! I need to know the truth. I have a right to know. The man who rescued Emma, who *is* he? She called him by name, remember? Tell me, Nan, is Lizzie—in love with him?'

'No, of course not,' Nan reassured him, speaking the truth as she knew it. 'He's just someone she met a long time ago, that's all. Her sister Bessie's young man, as I recall.'

She added quietly, 'Look, Lewis, I've known and loved Lizzie since her childhood, as dearly as if she was my own flesh and blood. She's as incapable of double-dealing as I am of—flying to the moon!'

'Then why didn't she tell me about him before?' Lewis persisted.

'Why should she? There was nothing to tell. He's been here in Scarborough going on six years now. She only came in contact with him again through Mrs Thompson, the woman who died recently. He went to Darlington with her son. You knew all about that, didn't you?' She paused, 'Emily Donen organised a rota of neighbours to help look after the poor soul. Lizzie helped out in the shop. That's where she met William again. Here, have some tea. I'll go and see if she's all right.'

'So you've met this—William, have you?'

'No, I've only heard about him. I'd never even seen him before today.'

Lizzie was coming out of the bathroom as Nan walked towards it. She was wearing a dressing gown and slippers, her hair loose about her shoulders. 'I've pegged your wet things out to dry, and there's a pot of tea in your room,' Nan said lightly. 'Emma's

306

still asleep. Lewis is with her. When you've drunk your tea, I should get into bed if I were you; stay there till morning. I'll ask Mrs Burton if I can bring your supper up to you.'

'Thanks, but I'm not hungry. You and Lewis go down to the dining room at suppertime. I'll stay with Emma. Have you had a cup of tea, by the way?'

'No, but I'm not bothered. I'll just nip along to my own room for a sit down. I expect you and Lewis would like to be alone for a while, to talk things over.'

Lizzie puckered her forehead. 'What things? I don't understand. Is anything the matter? Something you're not telling me? Emma is all right, isn't she? You think we should send for a doctor? That's it, isn't it?' Lizzie's voice was rising hysterically.

'No, of course not. She'll be as right as rain in the morning.'

'That's what William said.' Pulling herself together, speaking naturally, 'I'm sorry, Nan, it's just that she gave me a fright. I thought for one awful moment that I was going to lose her. And, try as I might, I couldn't get to her. Everyone else was just standing there doing nothing until William arrived on the scene. Oh, Nan, I shudder to think what might have happened if—'

'There now, love, calm down. We've all

had a bit of a fright one way and another, but no real harm done. I reckon we'll all feel better in the morning.'

No real harm done? Nan thought about that later. Lying sleepless in her bed, tossing and turning, she wondered if what Lewis suspected was true? If Lizzie was in love with William Chalmers?

'Sea View' was a tall narrow building in the old town area of Scarborough, in close proximity to the seafront and harbour. For its present owner, Mrs Burton, it provided a source of much-needed income since the death of her husband, a deputy harbour-master, ten years ago. Now, her paying guests brought in, during the summer season, their own food to be cooked and served by herself, with the help of two part-time women who came in daily to clean the rooms, make the beds, prepare vegetables, clear the dining room tables after breakfast, dinner and supper, and do the washing-up.

Not an easy way of supplementing her late husband's pension and her own meagre widow's pension, but the income from her visitors kept her head above water, and she made certain they received good value for money.

Normally, most folk wanted bacon, eggs, sausages and fried bread for breakfast, cold ham, tongue, or crab and salad for supper. She had categorically refused to cook three hot meals a day and posted reminders in the guest rooms to that effect. She had, after all, only one pair of hands, four burners and one small oven. If their stomachs were rumbling after a night out at a show or a dance, then they'd best treat themselves to a parcel of fish and chips on the foreshore, leaving her in peace to get a bit of a rest before the onslaught of breakfast.

Of course one became involved in the affairs of other people, some more than others. The Gilbert family for instance, and Mrs Imerson, though how she fitted into the picture, Mrs Burton hadn't quite worked out yet. All she knew was that the Gilberts' little girl, Emma, had been involved in an accident of some kind this afternoon. Moreover, it struck her as decidedly odd that Mrs Gilbert, young and pretty, was married to a man old enough to be her father. A nice enough man, certainly, still handsome in an elderly kind of way, but no fit mate for a lovely young woman in the prime of life?

Ah well, Mrs Burton surmised, it took all kinds to make a world. And it was none of her business, anyway. But she'd put her foot in it good and proper when, assuming that the older couple were man

309

and wife, Mrs Imerson their daughter, she had called Mrs Imerson Mrs Gilbert and said she'd best move the trundle-bed into the young lady's room since the little girl would want to sleep with her mother, not her grandparents.

Emma woke up as chirpy as a cricket next morning, none the worse for her wetting, wanting to know if she could have a boiled egg and soldiers for breakfast?

Lizzie admonished the child gently. 'It was naughty of you not to come to me when I called you. You might have been—drowned.'

'What's drowned? You mean getting all wet? But the nice man told me to hang on to him, an' I did, ever so tight, an' *he* wasn't cross with me, so why are you?' Hop, skipping and jumping about the bedroom, '*Can* I have a boiled egg and soldiers for my brekfust? *Please,* Mama!'

'I expect so,' Lizzie capitulated, 'if you'll stand still a minute and let me brush your hair.' She smiled, 'We don't want you in the dining room looking like a ragman's horse.'

Emma giggled. 'Then can we go on the sands? An' can I have a donkey ride an' an ice cream cornet?'

'We'll see. If you promise to behave

yourself, and stay close to Papa, Nana and me.'

That same morning, William received a letter from Marcia Hunter containing not altogether welcome news. She had decided to sell the salon, to retire in view of her forthcoming marriage to an old friend of her late-husband's.

Reading the letter slowly, fearful at first that this meant the ruination of his September plans, his return to Darlington, and the loss of the job Marcia had promised him, he realised thankfully that this was not so. She had written:

'I shall rely heavily on you to manage the business in my absence. As you can imagine, I'll be kept fully occupied, in the immediate future, removing my belongings from my old home to the new, not to mention planning my wedding and so on.

'Now I have a proposition to put to you. I can think of no better owner of the salon than yourself, if you would consider entering into a mortgage agreement on the premises; the salon and fittings included, to be paid by monthly, half yearly or annual instalments, whichever you prefer. Largely dependent, of course, on your successful management of the salon.

'We shall need to discuss this further, in

*great depth, when we meet in a few weeks
from now. I look forward to seeing you
again. Meanwhile, I trust that you will
give due consideration to the contents of
this letter, and your future prospects.
Yours ever,
Marcia Hunter'*

Food for thought, so far as William was
concerned. Possibly the greatest challenge
of his life so far. Eventually owning his
own hairdressing salon on Darlington's
High Row, if he was prepared to work
his guts out every hour God sent to own a
lot of empty spaces, devoid of the presence
of the one person on earth capable of filling
these empty spaces with love and laughter
... But life must go on.

One light on the horizon was Charlie's
wedding, due to take place before his return
to Darlington. Charlie had asked him to be
his best man, an honour which William
had turned down reluctantly in favour of
Fred, pointing out to the bridegroom that
he had a greater claim to the privilege.
He understood the lad's dilemma in not
knowing which of them to choose, thinking
the world of both of them as he did.
Smiling, he'd said, 'I'll be your second
best man. How's that?'

'You'll never be second best to me,
Mister,' Charlie replied. 'I couldn't have

two best men, could I?'

William laughed, 'Not without confusing the parson. But I'll look after Fred; make sure he doesn't forget the ring.'

'Could we all stay at the cottage together on my last night? Just like the old days?' Charlie asked wistfully.

'I don't see why not. On one condition.'

'What's that?'

'You'll play "The Sheikh of Araby"!'

Perhaps this seaside holiday hadn't been such a good idea after all, Lewis thought, the letter from his brother weighing heavily on his mind. How to reply to it? Time was of the essence, and time was fast slipping by. He'd been a fool not to show Lizzie the letter the day he'd received it. He had simply wanted a breathing space to weigh up the pros and cons, to consider the matter from every angle before burdening his wife with the final decision regarding their future.

Selling his shop and the house would present few, if any problems, he knew. A prime site in the centre of a busy industrial town would be quickly snapped up, at a more than adequate market price. Even so, selling his property remained the least of his worries. There were far more important issues to take into account, which he had so far evaded. Why? Because, deep down, he desperately wished to take advantage of his brother's offer of a new beginning, a fresh start for himself, Lizzie and little Emma, far removed from Attica, the dusty smell of secondhand books. Above all, the baleful influence of his dead wife, Alice, which had somehow soured his relationship with Lizzie.

Now, to his dismay, another man had appeared on the scene to undermine his never very robust self-confidence.

One day on the beach, when Lizzie had taken Emma to watch a Punch and Judy show, Nan asked Lewis if he was feeling all right. Always inclined to speak her mind, to tackle problems head on, 'If you're still fretting over William Chalmers,' she said forthrightly, 'I should forget it if I were you. The holiday won't do any of us much good if you carry on the way you are doing, as if you had the weight of the world on your shoulders. You've scarcely smiled or strung two sentences together since Sunday. What's up with you?'

'I'm sorry, Nan. The fact is ...'

Unburdening himself to her came as a relief. Nan listened intently as he told her about the letter from his brother. When he had finished speaking, she said, 'You should have told Lizzie straight away.'

'I know. But I didn't,' he said wearily.

'I wanted to work things out in my own mind first. You see, Nan, things haven't been quite normal between Lizzie and me since our marriage, for reasons I'd rather not go into. Deeply personal reasons.'

He paused momentarily, then continued, his voice harsh with emotion, 'Loving her so much, I can't help thinking that what we both need is a new beginning away from Attica—'

'Away from memories of your first wife, you mean?' Nan interrupted sagely. 'Well yes, I can see why that might be an advantage. On the other hand, America's a hell of a long way to go to get rid of a ghost.'

Startled by Nan's perception, 'You've known all along, haven't you?' Lewis said.

'Yes,' Nan admitted. 'I've felt her influence, too, believe me. I know that Lizzie has not had a fair crack of the whip at Attica, which was never really her home in the first place. I must shoulder my fair share of the blame for that, wanting Lizzie to marry a man who loved her as she deserved to be loved; whom she loved and respected equally in return.'

She added, 'Another thing I know beyond a shadow of doubt. Loving you as much as she does, and because she married you for better or worse, Lizzie will sail with you to America. But whether she'll take to the idea of leaving behind all she has known and loved is anyone's guess.'

Understanding the man's dilemma, forced against her will to recognise her own feelings towards him—a caring, handsome man of roughly her own age—she said quietly, knowing that so far as he was concerned she was nothing more than Emma's grandmother, Lizzie's former mother-in-law; a rootless woman he'd taken pity on for Lizzie's sake at the time of their marriage, 'You've already reached your decision, haven't you? And Lizzie won't stand in your way. But you must tell her what's in your mind, give her time to get used to the idea.'

TWENTY-ONE

Charlie's wedding was a joyous occasion. Mavis, a fisherman's daughter, had grown up at the heart of a loving family into which her bridegroom had been accepted as one of their own ilk: a man of the sea, hard-working, warm-hearted—a grand lad who would make their Mavis a good steady husband.

Watching the ceremony, William's heart

filled with pride that the scrap of a boy he had brought home with him that long gone Christmas Eve had made such a fine, decent thing of his life. Now Charlie would never be alone, cold and hungry again, thank God, and in time to come he would have sons of his own to care for; a happy, purposeful future ahead of him with a loving woman beside him to give point and direction to his existence. Unlike himself.

Clara had tried to dissuade him from leaving home as the time of his departure drew near. Things would be better in future, she promised, climbing down from her high horse—perhaps they would be for a while, he thought, until the next emotional explosion occurred. And he was right. His mother went off the deep end when he told her his plans had reached the point of no return. He had no wish to change them and to leave Marcia Hunter in the lurch.

'Oh that's right. Put other people first, as usual. What about leaving *me* in the lurch? Your own mother!' Incensed, Clara let rip hysterically, 'Just don't imagine you can come running back to me for help if you end up head over heels in debt. The trouble with you, William, is you have no sense of responsibility. Faugh! Even as a child, you never knew what you wanted or what was good for you. Well, I wash my hands of you from now on. Go your own way, and much good may it do you!'

He had packed his belongings quietly and taken them down to the cottage prior to Charlie's wedding. Next day, he and Fred would travel to Darlington together. Better to slip away unnoticed than cause more fireworks. Unkindness was not in his nature. The pity of it was, he had always loved his mother as, he suspected, she loved him deep down. They had simply been incapable of communicating with one another.

As the train jogged towards Darlington, William wondered if Clara's dogmatic attitude to life was borne of fear? Fear of failure, of growing old? Widowed at a comparatively early age, had she deliberately cast herself in the role of a father rather than a mother figure? Never at any time during his childhood could he remember her holding him in her arms, kissing him goodnight.

'You're very quiet, Billy Boy,' Fred observed from his seat opposite, 'is anything the matter—apart from the obvious?'

'No, not really. I'm just a bit on edge about the future, that's all.'

'Taking on that posh hairdressing salon

on the High Row, you mean?' Fred chuckled softly. 'Now you know the way I felt taking on Maudie's corner shop. At least you know all about hairdressing. I knew damn all about being a grocer. The tins of condensed milk those women in Parker Street get through in a week, you wouldn't believe! Count yourself lucky, old pal, that you know your profession inside out. As for me, I still haven't quite got the hang of that bloody bacon-slicer.'

It was good to laugh with his old pal, to make light of the future ahead of both of them. Even so, he could not bring himself to admit, even to Fred the real reason for his return to Darlington; to once again be close to the woman he loved ...

Next morning, Elsie Donen was clearing the hat shop window in readiness for a new display of millinery, when she saw William cross the road from the King's Head to Madame Marcia's salon next door. A nugget of information she took pleasure in relaying to her parents at suppertime.

'You must be mistaken,' Emily said, hoping to heaven she was. Things were quite bad enough without William Chalmers showing his face again. The state Lizzie was in, everything at sixes and sevens; life as she knew it about to change forever when that liner sailed for New York a few weeks from now.

The house which had once seemed too small to shelter a family of six, suddenly seemed far too big now Dicky had left home. True, she saw him most days, but the house still seemed empty without his ebullient presence. His children were at the inquisitive, into everything stage, lacking their father's charm; saucy like their mother. Emma remained Emily's favourite grandchild. The thought of losing her and Lizzie was more than she could bear at times, but what else could she do other than keep her thoughts to herself? She had to be strong for Jack's sake, and Lizzie's. This was her role in life, what her family expected of her.

'I'm not mistaken. I know what I saw,' Emily snapped, put out by her mother's brief dismissal. 'In any case, I asked one of the girls who works there, and she said he's in charge of the shop now that Madame Marcia's getting married and going away to live, so there!'

'All right, that's enough. I'm not interested!'

'Bessie will be, when I tell her,' Elsie said snidely. 'It might put her off getting married when she knows her old boyfriend's back in town.'

Jack spoke up from his chair near the

fire. 'You heard what your mother said, my girl. Stir up trouble, and you'll have me to reckon with. So shut that silly mouth of yours and do something useful for a change!'

Elsie stared at him dumbfounded, burst into tears and ran upstairs to her room, flinging herself on the bed. It isn't fair, she thought. Nothing was fair. There was Bessie about to get married, with a big house all ready for her, her wedding day to look forward to; Lizzie with a new life ahead of her in America; Madge, a Hollywood movie star, and here she was, stuck with a job she hated with nothing to look forward to. Not even a gentleman friend to call her own.

As Lewis had surmised, Attica sold quickly at a fair price and as a going concern, thereby saving the necessity of getting rid of the stock separately. When items of china, linen and silverware had been crated for the journey and surplus furniture sent to Leckonby's saleroom, he'd rented furnished accommodation to tide them over until the journey to Southampton on the twentieth of December.

Throughout the transition, Lizzie had been dogged by a feeling of unreality like a sleepwalker, expecting to wake up any minute to the sweet realisation that none of this was true, just part of a nightmare. The loss of her home, fear of an unknown future ahead of them in a strange country far removed from her own family—apart from Nan who was going with them to New York.

She had not at first believed what Lewis said was true, the day he had told her, after their holiday in Scarborough, that he desperately wanted to take advantage of his brother's offer of a new beginning, a fresh start in life in America. Then he had shown her the letter, and the nightmare began.

'Well, if it's really what you want,' she said dully, handing back the letter to him with trembling fingers.

'Not without your consent, Lizzie,' Lewis reminded her gently. 'You know how much I love you? That I would do nothing to hurt or distress you in any way?'

'Really? Is that the reason you didn't tell me about the letter the day of its arrival? To give yourself time to make up your own mind first before even bothering to tell me about it?'

'You know that's not true, Lizzie,' Lewis uttered despairingly.

'Do I? Frankly, Lewis, I'm not quite sure I can tell the difference between truth and lies any more. All I know for certain is that I promised before God on our wedding day to love, honour and obey you, in which case I have no other choice than to follow you to the ends of the earth, if necessary. Just give me time to get used to the idea, and don't expect me to rejoice.'

He had never seen Lizzie like this before, as if some inner illumination had been switched off at source. He said, 'I should have told you, I know that now. But I didn't lie to you. And you are right, I did want to think things over, to weigh up the advantages or otherwise of a new challenge.

'The truth is, I'm tired of the shop and the house. I'm sorry, love, but I see it now in terms of failure. My own failure as a husband. We've never talked about it before; my inability to father a child. Please, let me explain—'

'Please don't, Lewis,' Lizzie interrupted him, speaking in a low voice charged with emotion. 'There's no need to explain why. I reached certain conclusions a long time ago, and I've known for some time that you haven't been entirely—happy. I couldn't help noticing. I understood and accepted the underlying reason for your unhappiness. What I could not fully understand or accept was your withdrawal; the lack of laughter in our lives, your disinterest in the shop—and Emma. Yes, Emma! Suddenly you were too tired, too wrapped up in yourself to play games with her anymore, to take her to the park to feed the ducks.

'And that day on the beach in Scarborough, you preferred sitting in a deckchair whilst we went paddling together! Has it ever occurred to you, Lewis, that had you been there at the time, she might never have ventured out so far to sea?

'Now I know why you were content to sit there, with Nan. Mulling over this America bombshell, I daresay, whilst my daughter was in danger of drowning?'

'I'm so sorry,' Lewis said wearily, 'I never meant my unhappiness to rub off on you or Emma. I simply saw my brother's letter as a means of escape from our present circumstances, a dusty old shop filled with secondhand books; a ghost-ridden house above.'

'So why the long face?' Lizzie asked. 'I've already told you that I'm prepared to follow you to the ends of the earth, if necessary.'

'Even against your own better judgement?'

Lizzie's face softened suddenly, 'No, not entirely,' she said quietly, ashamed of her outburst. 'I told you on our wedding night how much I loved you and always would, if you recall? And I meant what I said. It's just that I can't bear the thought of parting with my past life so easily. Never seeing my parents, my brother and sisters ever again.'

'Don't forget that Nan is coming with us,' Lewis reminded her gently.

'I know, and I'm glad. But Nan has nothing to keep her here. Tom was all she had apart from me and Emma. Then you came along.'

'What do you mean?' Lewis frowned.

'Nothing. Except she thinks the world of you, or hadn't you noticed? I am right in thinking that you told her about the letter before you told me?'

'Yes, but that wasn't a deliberate decision. She sensed I was worried and asked me why. You and Emma had gone to watch the Punch and Judy show. We started talking, and I told her about the letter.'

'And what did she say?'

'That I should have told you about it in the first place.'

'She was right. You should have,' Lizzie said dully. 'That's what really hurt, knowing you didn't trust me enough to confide in me. What were you afraid of, Lewis? That I'd pour cold water on the idea? I thought you knew me better than that.'

'Lizzie, please! Don't be angry. Don't shut me out.'

She smiled sadly, 'The boot's on the other foot, isn't it?'

'There was more to it than that,' he said hoarsely. 'If you must know, I had more on my mind than the letter. That man on the beach, the one who rescued Emma, I'd got it into my head that you were in love with him. You called him by name, so I knew you'd met before. You said, "Thank God you were there, William, when I needed you so much".'

'I see. Which begs the question, where were you, when I needed you?' Lizzie said quietly, going upstairs to bed.

Bessie would have preferred a June wedding. November was such a dull month. But Jimmy was anxious to move into their house and she couldn't wait to wear a wedding ring and be called Mrs Blaney.

She just hoped it wouldn't hail, rain or snow on her wedding finery. No plain grey costume and prayer book for Bessie. No fear! She wanted white satin, a 'tarara', veil and a bouquet of red roses from Strike's the florists.

'You'll have a job to get hold of roses in November,' Emily said impatiently. 'You'll have to make do with chrysanthemums.'

Then came the fuss over the reception, held traditionally in the front parlour of the bride's home. Bessie wasn't having any of that. She wanted a posh do at the King's Head, a sit down meal of chicken plus trimmings, not sandwiches and sausage rolls in the front room. In the event she'd been obliged to settle for a boiled ham meal in the upstairs room of a restaurant overlooking the High Row when she found out how much it would cost to eat at the hotel.

Elsie hadn't cottoned onto the idea of a brown velveteen bridesmaid's dress, albeit a rich chestnut brown, nor of having her thunder stolen by a miniature bridesmaid in the shape of Emma carrying a basket of flowers. And why couldn't *she* carry a basket of flowers? To which Emily replied tartly that she could carry a chamber-pot trimmed with a purple ribbon for all she cared, and the sooner the wedding was over and done with, the better. At which point Bessie had burst into tears, complaining bitterly that nobody cared about her wedding day at all. Elsie was jealous because she hadn't found herself a husband: the only member of the family Pa cared tuppence about was Madge—who couldn't care less about him. As for Emily, her favourites had always been Lizzie and Dicky. She'd always been treated as a fool. Well, she hadn't turned out such a fool after all, seeing she'd found herself a chap who worshipped the ground she walked on, a man of her own age, not a bloke old enough to be her father as Lizzie had done.

Emily knew deep down that what Bessie said was true and apologised for her remark about the chamber-pot. Of course she cared about Bessie's wedding, but it was an event overshadowed by her forthcoming separation from Lizzie and Emma. If only she felt certain that Lizzie was happy, but her mother's instinct told her she was not; that all was not well between her and Lewis.

Oh, drat the man! What had come over him to uproot his family at his time of life? The niggling thought occurred that she and Nan were partly responsible in wanting Lizzie to remarry for security reasons after the tragic death of her first husband. What price security now that Lewis had sold his business and decided on a new life in America? Lizzie had simply said that he felt in need of a change of lifestyle, a new challenge.

'But what about *you*, Lizzie? What do *you* want?' Emily asked her.

'Does it really matter what I want?' Lizzie replied sadly. 'Lewis is my husband.'

'Of course it matters! Marriage is meant to be a partnership, not a form of slavery. I don't understand what's come over you lately. When Tom Imerson died, you fought tooth and nail to repay the debt

328

owing to that moneylender; worked every hour that God sent to maintain your independence, your self-respect. Now look at you, not an ounce of fight left in you! You should have told that husband of yours to forget his pie in the sky notions of a new lifestyle, a new challenge, at his age!' Emily added hoarsely, 'For pity's sake, love, wake up. It's still not too late to change your mind about America, but it will be three weeks from now, when you're aboard that liner!'

Thankfully, Bessie's wedding day dawned reasonably fair and clear, for November.

Upstairs in her room, the bride, seated at her dressing table, staring at her reflected image in the swing mirror, removed her overnight curl-rags and buzzed up her fringe becomingly beneath her diamanté tiara—hired for the occasion from Madame Marcia's salon.

So William Chalmers was back in town, was he? Well, she'd given him short shrift right enough when she'd hired the tiara and told him succinctly that the following Saturday, at one o'clock, she'd enter St Cuthbert's Church as Bessie Donen and emerge from it as Mrs James Blaney, so he'd best put that in his pipe and smoke it!

Closing the salon at one o'clock precisely, William hurried across the market square to await the emergence of the wedding party from the church. His heart set on seeing Lizzie again, albeit from a distance.

The last thing he'd envisaged was that a little fair-haired girl, breaking away from the group of guests assembled on the church steps to have their photographs taken, would run down the path towards him, calling out her own version of his name: 'Willum!' and fling herself into his arms with childlike abandon. Wanting him to lift her up the way he had done that day on Scarborough's south beach, clasping her arms about his neck and nestling her face against his shoulder.

William did just that. Lifting the child in his arms, holding her close to his heart. Glancing towards the church steps where the wedding guests were assembled for the photographer, he saw Lizze standing there, pale-faced, unsmiling, staring at him and the child in his arms. Then, hurrying down the path towards him, 'Why are you here?' she asked breathlessly.

'I wanted to see you, to talk to you if possible.'

'It isn't possible. Please, people are looking at us. Come along, Emma, you're going to have your photograph taken. The man's waiting.'

'Don't want to,' Emma said, keeping tight hold of William's neck.

'Of course you do,' he said putting the child down, smiling at her. 'You know the saying, "it wouldn't be a show without Punch".'

The child giggled. 'Will you watch me having my phottie taken?'

'Of course. Go along now, and remember to smile or you'll break the camera.'

As the little girl trotted off, 'Please, Lizzie,' William murmured, 'Just ten minutes of your time. I'm at the High Row salon.'

'I can't promise. I'll see. I must go now, my husband's waiting for me.'

Standing in the porch, witnessing the little drama at the church gate and noticing Lizzie's heightened colour as she came towards him, Lewis knew that what he'd suspected was true. Lizzie was in love with William Chalmers.

TWENTY-TWO

Lizzie went to the salon ostensibly to return Bessie's hired tiara. A legitimate excuse. Even so, she'd felt guilty entering the shop. An assistant came forward. Taking her courage in both hands. 'May I see Mr Chalmers?' Lizzie asked. 'He's otherwise engaged at the moment,' the girl said, 'but you can wait in his private room, if you like?'

After the excitement of the wedding and the departure of the bride and groom, Lizzie had spent a bleak Sunday cooking meals for her family. The rooms Lewis had rented as a stop-gap until their journey to Southampton were overcrowded with the landlady's furniture, lacking the space she'd become used to at Attica, especially the light and airy kitchen. Here, she felt trapped, imprisoned.

Throughout that seemingly endless day, Lizzie's thoughts centred on her meeting with William. Nan said, 'You look tired out, love. Why don't you have a rest? I'll see to the dinner.'

'I couldn't rest if you paid me.'

'Why? What's on your mind? Or need I ask. It's William, isn't it? His being there at the church yesterday?'

'Lewis has got it into his head there's something going on between us.'

'And is there?'

'No, of course not. It's just that I can't stop thinking about him. I can't bear the thought of going away without saying goodbye to him; thanking him properly for saving Emma's life.'

'Well, you know where he is, and Bessie did ask you to return that tiara of hers.'

'I don't think Lewis would approve,' Lizzie said, slicing carrots.

'Then why tell him? Returning a tiara doesn't amount to a secret assignation exactly, now does it?'

'I suppose not. Thanks, Nan.'

She was standing in Marcia's beauty room looking at the weird assortment of contraptions, when William came in. 'Thank God you're here,' he said. 'I lived through hell yesterday, wondering if you'd come.'

'I had to come,' she said simply, casting aside the restraints which had held her prisoner for such a long time now, wanting to be held by him, knowing that her love for him could no longer be hidden or denied. An overpowering feeling of inner joy and intense happiness she had never known before, intensified by the touch of his lips on hers, his hoarsely whispered words against the softness of her hair, her cheeks, her throat, telling her over and over again how much he loved her.

Then, because of conscience, her inbred sense of right and wrong, she withdrew from his embrace. 'I shouldn't have come. I knew what would happen. The truth is, I wanted it to happen. I couldn't have borne to say goodbye without letting you know how much you mean to me.'

'Goodbye? I don't understand.'

'We—my husband, Emma, Nan and I are emigrating to America two weeks from now. It's all arranged. We're sailing from Southampton on the twentieth of December.'

He looked at her disbelievingly, his heart in his eyes, 'But you *can't*, Lizzie! I won't let you. You belong *here* with me!' Clasping her shoulders, drawing her back into his arms. 'We can't be parted now, not ever again, knowing how we feel about each other.'

'I'm sorry, William, it's no use. Please don't make things harder for me than they already are.' Tears filled her eyes. 'Do you imagine that I want to go away, to leave everything I know and love behind me? My family, my home—and you?'

'Then *why?*'

'Because I'm a married woman. What kind of person would I be if I cast aside my marriage vows so easily?' Facing the reality of the situation, torn between right and wrong, she held William's hands in hers, looked up at him, committing to memory every line of his face, his eyes, mouth, nose and strong jawline; the way his dark hair fell forward onto his forehead, 'In a sense

I have already betrayed my husband in coming here to see you, in wanting you to hold me, to kiss me—which I'll remember, with joy, all the days of my life.'

'This—husband of yours,' William said slowly, needing to know the truth. 'Are you—in love with him?'

'In love?' Lizzie pondered the question, uncertain how to answer. She said softly, 'Not in love, but I do love him. He's a good man, kind and honourable. My mother once told me that there are degrees of loving. I didn't know what she meant then, but I do now.'

'Hello, Billy Boy! What's brought you here? I thought you'd forgotten where I lived. Come upstairs to the fire. Cor, it's cold enough to freeze a brass monkey out there.' Fred led the way to the sitting room, 'I've just had my supper, but there's some left over if you're hungry?' He grinned.

'No, I'm fine thanks.' Entering the room, William shivered slightly, half expecting to see Maudie, large as life, come through from the kitchen. And this was what his life would be like from now on, he thought, forever turning his head expecting to see Lizzie walking behind him, entering a room, or meeting her face to face at the next street corner. Only he knew now that this would never happen, just as Fred knew

335

that he would never see Maudie again in this life.

'Sit down, man, before you fall down,' Fred suggested quietly, 'and tell me what's up.' He had never seen his pal like this before, grey-faced and shaking like a leaf. 'What you need is a good stiff drink! Here, get this down you,' handing him a sizable tot of brandy from a bottle on the sideboard. 'Oh, not to worry, I haven't started boozing again. I just keep a drop handy to help me over the worst patches now and then; usually around this time of night when I start thinking back over the old days, wishing I'd done things differently whilst I still had the chance. Not that it makes a damn bit of difference now Maudie's dead and gone. But never mind about me. What about you?'

This was the first time William had talked about Lizzie in depth to anyone apart from her mother. Strange really, he reflected, gazing into the fire, that his love for her had, of necessity, remained a secret part of his existence.

His words came slowly at first, borne of inhibition. But he needed to talk and Fred proved himself a good listener in what William would look back on as a firelit confessional.

Getting up, 'I'm sorry, Fred,' he apologised awkwardly, 'I had no intention of staying so late, burdening you with my problems.'

'You haven't. In any case, what are friends for? I'm just pleased you came, that you did me the honour of confiding in me. I only wish I could say or do summat to help you. You see, mate, I know how it feels to lose someone you love. But where there's life there's hope. In your shoes, Billy Boy, I'd pursue that lass of yours to the ends of the earth and back, rather than lose her the way I lost Maudie. I gave up too easily when it really mattered.'

Never in his life before had Jack Donen felt so lonely, so expendable. The house seemed empty, too quiet now that only himself, Emily and Elsie were left beneath a roof that had once sheltered an entire family.

Losing Madge had been bad enough. Soon he'd be losing Lizzie and little Emma to a continent which appeared to him as a whirlpool, swallowing his children into a vortex of no return.

Madge was doing fine in America according to Bessie, who had raved on about her appearance in some film or other showing at one of those new-fangled cinemas. Understandably, Bessie had been more than a little put out by his stubborn refusal to watch Madge's indeterminate image superimposed on the so-called 'silver screen'. Emily had understood. Knowing her husband as well as she did, he could not have faced the realisation, the ultimate proof that his favourite child no longer loved or needed him as she used to long ago. There was, after all, a world of difference between a little lass called Madge Donen and a Hollywood actress called Marjorie Starr. Besides which, Jack had his pride. If Madge had wanted to keep in touch with her family, she would have done so of her own accord. If not, so be it.

Making ready for bed one night, 'What's happening to us, Emily?' Jack asked his wife.

Braiding her hair with quick, deft movements born of practice throughout the long years of their marriage, she said, 'It's something called life. Children growing up, moving away, making their own way in the world. And that's as it should be. After all, bringing them into the world was our choice, not theirs. Now all we can do is to learn how to let go of them as graciously as possible, with no regrets.'

'You make letting go sound so easy,' Jack said hoarsely, close to tears.

'I didn't say it was easy, but it *is* necessary.'

'Necessary to sit back and say nowt about losing Lizzie and Emma? You should have let me give that Lewis Gilbert a piece of my mind. I never did cotton on to that chap from the start, wheedling his way into our family, making sheep's eyes at a lass young enough to be his daughter. I hold you and Nan Imerson responsible for that. All that stuff and nonsense about wanting her to marry for security. Well, what price security now, eh? A man of his age dragging our Lizzie and Emma off to America to make a fresh start. Huh, a fresh bloody start! Doing what exactly? Managing a business he knows damn all about. And what if his brother decides to sack him if he doesn't make it pay?'

'Don't, Jack, love,' Emily said wearily, slipping into bed beside him. 'We've been over this time and time again, but picking a quarrel with Lewis isn't the answer. It could only make things worse, not better. Think how Lizzie would feel, going away knowing you and her husband were at loggerheads with one another.'

'What I'm trying to say is Lizzie needn't go away at all if she doesn't want to. What's to prevent her staying here with us? There's plenty of room now Besie's flown the nest.'

'You're talking nonsense, Jack, and you know it. Lizzie would never renege on her marriage vows: "For better or worse", remember?'

'The pity of it is,' Jack said gruffly, 'that she didn't marry a man of her own age—that young hairdresser bloke, for instance.'

'William Chalmers, you mean? But you didn't think much of him either, as I recall. You said he seemed a bit prissy.'

'Happen I did then, but I don't now. I think he has the makings of a real man. After all, he did save Emma's life, and you told me yourself about that incident when he laid out the landlord of the Ox with his bare fists—which must have taken some doing considering the size and brute force of Sid Belcher. Now, according to Elsie, he's in charge of that hairdressing salon on the High Row with a view to owning it one day, I daresay.'

'You may well be right, Jack, but the fact remains that Lizzie is married to Lewis, and whether we like it or not we must accept that she is duty-bound to go with him to America. We must learn to let go of her.'

Inured throughout the years of their marriage to his wife's superior education and knowledge, on this occasion he muttered a heartfelt, 'As graciously as possible, be damned! The trouble with you, Emily, is you have your feet on the ground and your head in the clouds. No way am I prepared to let go of Lizzie and Emma without a fight—a head to head confrontation with that husband of hers, the selfish bastard! So now you know.'

Meanwhile, sick at heart, Lewis had turned to Nan for counsel regarding his wife and William. Deeply shaken by the incident outside the church on Bessie's wedding day, he needed to know the truth about their relationship.

'It's Lizzie, not me, you should be asking,' Nan said impatiently. 'I've told you before, the girl's upset. Frankly, I'll be glad when we're on our way. This hanging about is getting us all down.'

'I'm beginning to wish I'd torn up that letter the day it arrived and told my brother I wasn't interested in his proposition.'

'But you *were* interested. In any case it's a bit too late now to start having regrets, isn't it?'

Lizzie said much the same thing when Lewis talked to her later. 'What's done is

341

done,' she said wearily. 'Ignoring problems doesn't make them go away. You'd have been miserable wondering if you'd done the right thing or not.'

'And have I done the right thing?' he asked wistfully, wanting her approval, a return to their old happy relationship. 'I have the feeling you don't want to go with me to America? That you no longer care for me as you used to. Please be honest with me, darling. Are you—in love with William Chalmers?'

Her moment of truth had arrived. 'Yes,' she said softly. 'I do love him. But my feelings for you haven't changed. I do still care for you as I used to.'

'But you never really loved me as much as I loved you? You married me not loving me. I see that now.'

'You're wrong, Lewis. I did love you. I told you so often enough, remember?'

'Despite the fact that I wasn't man enough to consummate our marriage? Or did you feel sorry for me? They say that pity is akin to love.'

'*They* say? Who are *they?* This is between us, you and me, no one else in the world! You've been good to me, Lewis. I liked, respected and trusted you from the day we met, when I came about that job as your housekeeper. Later, when you asked me to marry you, I said I'd try to make you a good wife—for better or worse. Sexual relations didn't enter into it—'

'In other words, you didn't want me—physically?'

'I suppose not,' Lizzie conceded thoughtfully. 'Wanting you physically never really occurred to me at the time. All I wanted was a continuance of the quiet happiness you had brought into my life and Emma's. Worthwhile marriages have been based on far less, I imagine.

'I'm sorry, Lewis, but you must remember that I'd been married before; had borne a child by my first husband. I've never said this before and I shouldn't be saying it now, but I derived no particular pleasure from physical intimacy with a man who had become a stranger to me on our wedding night.'

Drawing in a deep breath, she continued, 'You asked me if I'm in love with William Chalmers, and I said yes. Don't ask me why, because I don't know the answer. In any case, does it really matter why?' She smiled sadly, 'Perhaps I've cast him in the role of a knight in shining armour because he saved Emma's life. One thing's for sure, I'll never see him again once we set sail for America.'

Determined to have his say, during a farewell party organised by Emily on the eve of her loved ones' departure to Southampton, Jack confronted his son-in-law in the kitchen.

Closing the door firmly behind him, 'Well, I hope you're pleased with yourself, Lewis Gilbert,' he muttered hoarsely. 'A man of your age going off to America to make a new life for yourself.

'But what about my daughter and grandchild? I suppose it never occurred to you how Lizzie would feel being torn away from her roots? God dammit, man, you've only to look at her to see how unhappy she is! As for Emma, the poor kid hasn't a clue what's happening. All she knows is she's going to somewhere called "Merry Car" on a big boat.

'The fact is, I never wanted Lizzie to marry you in the first place. A man old enough to be her father. You should have had more sense than to expect she'd be happy with a dried up stick of a bloke like you! Well, all I can say is if you were half the gentleman you pretend to be, you'd never have started this caper to begin with! Why the hell couldn't you have gone on peddling those secondhand books of yours? Why ruin the lives of an entire family? Because that's exactly what you have done.'

344

TWENTY–THREE

Southampton docks were shrouded in mist. A foghorn sounded its dreary intermittent warning to shipping approaching the peninsula confluent with the drowned estuaries of the rivers Itchen and Test. A dangerous place to be on a day such as this with visibility almost nil beneath heavy clouds and occasional downpours of rain.

Yet aboard the liner *Southern Queen* bound for New York, there was a festive atmosphere as the passengers went aboard to claim their cabins.

The size of the vessel frightened Lizzie. She had never imagined a ship of these dimensions. She felt dwarfed by the towering funnels looming high above the superstructure, the bulk of the stern, the intimidating sweep and strength of the bows, the thickness of the hawser cables mooring the ship to the shore. Nor had she imagined the chaos of departure, the clanking of porters' barrows stacked with luggage, the crush of people surrounding her: fellow passengers and those who had come to wish them *bon voyage*.

She saw, in her mind's eye, a scene

from the outbreak of war when the ship had been commissioned as a troop carrier. Uniformed figures, soldiers with packs and rifles mounting the gangplank, standing at the ship's rails, staring down at the sea of upturned faces below, looking their last at the shoreline of England as the hawsers were cast off and the ship headed for the open sea. Uncertain of their return to their native land, leaving behind them all they knew and loved: families, home and friends. The familiar sights and sounds of home: this earth, this realm, this—England. Just as she was destined to do now.

Yesterday, they had travelled from Darlington to London where they stayed overnight in a small hotel near King's Cross before embarking on the second leg of their journey.

Numb with misery, she could not now clearly recall taking leave of her loved ones. She had simply been aware of faces blurred by her tears, being held close in loving arms; the faint scent of her mother's perfume, the silkiness of Emily's fur collar brushing against her cheek. The gruffness of her father's voice, only she could not for the life of her remember what he said to her as she entered the compartment and the train pulled away from the platform. She had simply stood at the open window waving her hand, trying hard not to cry until the people she loved best in the world slowly diminished in size as the train ate up the distance between them and they gradually disappeared from view.

With every turn of the wheels on that seemingly endless journey to London, she had thought of William. Unpacking the sandwiches her mother had given her for the journey, she thought of William. Playing 'I Spy' with Emma, she thought of William. Entering the London hotel; lying sleepless, night long, beside Lewis, she thought of William, dreading the morning's journey to Southampton.

Now she was here, walking beside her husband, wondering if this was the way Anne Boleyn had felt on her way to the executioner's block? Too proud to weep; rigid with fear of the unknown.

Lewis was being kind to her, far kinder than she deserved. Carrying Emma in his arms; realising the extent of her physical and mental exhaustion. Nan also, mounting the gangplank laden with hand-luggage. She apparently harboured no misgivings about the future ahead of her. Lizzie wondered, not for the first time, if Nan was in love with Lewis. Could not help thinking how much happier he might have been with a woman of her calibre, age and experience. No torment, no jealousy, simply a warm loving relationship between

347

a kind-hearted man and a loving woman who would give him a Daisy powder before he even realised he had a headache.

The liner was due to leave harbour at three o'clock that afternoon, by which time the fog had lifted and the passengers gathered together at the ship's rails.

Gas-lamps had sprung into bloom on the dockside, illuminating the faces of the crowd beneath. A band somewhere was playing 'Keep the Home Fires Burning'.

Standing near the rail, Nan and Lewis beside her, holding Emma in her arms, eyes blurred with tears, Lizzie saw the faces of the crowd below as through a glass, darkly.

Forever after, she would thank God for the clear, unsullied vision of the child in her arms.

Pointing a chubby finger towards a well-known face in the crowd, 'Look, Mama,' Emma cried gleefully, 'it's Willum!'

Brushing aside her tears, gazing down at the one person on earth she had longed to see and would want to go on seeing for the rest of her life, Lizzie was aware that the gangplank was on the verge of removal any second now. Turning to her husband, she whispered hoarsely, 'Tell me what to do, Lewis! I'll abide by your decision.'

He said quietly, courageously, 'You'd

best hurry, my love, before it's too late.'

With moments to spare, Lizzie stumbled down the gangplank into William's arms, outspread to receive both herself and her child. Her heart sang with joy that she was safely home at last, her feet on England's shore where they belonged; secure in a greater love than any she had known before.

The fog had cleared completely. The night sky was littered with stars. Standing together near the rail, hearing the wash of the sea against the ship's sides and aware of the faint sound of music and laughter from the ballroom. Nan and Lewis derived comfort from each other's presence. Stunned by the enormity of what had happened, the suddenness of Lizzie's departure; that dramatic race against time down the gangplank split seconds before its removal.

'What else could I have done?' Lewis asked, looking up at the stars, glad of the cold, cleansing wind on his face and the quiet understanding of the woman beside him. 'Loving Lizzie so much, I had to let her go. If only there had been a little more time.'

Nan smiled wistfully. Laying her hand on his, she said gently, 'No need for regret. In answer to your question, so far as I'm concerned you did the right thing at the right moment. The question is, what are you going to do next?'

'I don't know. I haven't had time to think about it yet,' Lewis admitted, turning up his coat collar against the knife-edged wind scouring the decks. 'Frankly, Nan, you are my main concern at the moment, having embarked on a voyage to New York which you would not have undertaken in the first place had it not been as a travelling companion for Lizzie and Emma. I'll pay for your ticket home the moment we land in the USA.'

'Oh, really? Very kind of you, I'm sure,' Nan countered tetchily, tongue-in-cheek. 'And what if I have not the remotest intention of being shipped back to England like excess baggage?'

Lewis frowned. 'I'm sorry, Nan, I don't quite understand. You can't possibly mean that you would want to stay on with me in New York?'

'And why not, for heaven's sake? Use your head, man! You'll need someone to look after you, cook for you; someone to keep the home fires burning. So why not me?'

Why not, indeed? Lewis thought—a woman of Nan's calibre. A woman he had always liked and admired for her down-to-earth approach to life, her kindness and common sense.

'Besides,' Nan said, 'I have nothing to go back to. No home, no ties apart from Lizzie and Emma—whom I intend seeing again one day. So you're not the only one in need of a new challenge. I'm looking forward to getting stuck into some real work for a change, making my life count for something. And I'll not be a hanger-on, a burden to you. I'll work hard and expect to be paid a proper wage. That way I'll keep my independence.'

Lewis smiled. 'Sounds fine to me, if that's really what you want?'

'It is.'

He said, 'The night of the farewell party, Jack Donen made me realise how wrong I'd been, how selfish in uprooting Lizzie and ruining the lives of an entire family. He didn't mince matters, believe me.'

'Well, diplomacy has never been Jack's strong point, he left all that to Emily— pouring oil on troubled waters and keeping the peace. The trouble with Jack is he never got over losing Madge. He thought the world of that lass. He was never quite the same after she went away, especially when they lost touch with her—or rather when she lost touch with them. Poor Jack, I can understand why he dreaded losing touch with Lizzie and little Emma in much the same way.'

Nan sighed, 'Now, I don't know about you, but I'm frozen stiff and ready to call it a day. I could sleep on a clothes' line.'

She loved the close confines of her cabin with its porthole window, the gentle throb of the ship's engines, the soothing lullaby of the sea. The thrill of occupying her own space, however limited, and of a new life ahead of her; a new challenge. A new beginning.

Ready for bed, her long ash-blonde hair neatly braided, and wearing a brand new winceyette nightgown and matching blue robe, she heard a knock on the cabin door.

Opening it a crack, she saw a steward in the corridor holding a tray containing a plate of sandwiches, a cup and saucer, milk jug and teapot.

'There must be some mistake,' she said. 'I didn't order anything.'

'No, ma'am. Mr Gilbert did. He thought you might be feeling a bit peckish since you didn't have much to eat at dinner.'

'How thoughtful of him. Thank you, young man, and he was quite right.' She laughed delightedly, 'Must be all the sea air that's given me an appetite.'

She hadn't realised how hungry she was until she bit into the delicately cut triangles of bread and butter containing smoked salmon, egg and cress, cream cheese and anchovies, which she ate in bed, accompanied by several cups of Earl Grey tea.

Talk about luxury. She could get used to this kind of life, Nan thought, settling down and falling asleep as soon as her head touched the pillow.

William had watched, his heart in his mouth, as Lizzie raced down that gangplank. Had pushed his way through the crowds of well-wishers lining the dockside like a man possessed to get to her, ready to catch her if she stumbled at the last minute, heart pounding like a drum, scarcely able to believe what was happening. It had all taken place so quickly. Then suddenly she was in his arms, Emma sandwiched between them, and Lizzie was laughing and crying at the same time, her head flung back, looking up at him, gasping for breath, unable to speak. No need of words. Words would come later.

Understanding Lizzie's need to bid farewell to her husband and Nan, William moved away from her into the shadows as a mark of respect for the tall, elderly man whose unselfish devotion to his wife had made possible her liberation, or so he imagined. A man whom Lizzie had described as kind and honourable, who was now standing near the ship's rail looking down at her and Emma, his hand raised in a final gesture of farewell until the faces of those aboard the liner were blurred by darkness and distance, no longer discernible in the enfolding gloom of a sleet-scurried winter twilight.

Shouldering his responsibility towards Lizzie and Emma and realising their immediate need of rest and refreshment, William found a small hotel a stone's throw away from the dock area. He booked rooms for them, signed the register and ordered tea, sandwiches and cakes for three. Asked about luggage, he produced one small overnight case containing his shaving gear, pyjamas and dressing gown. Not that the receptionist asked to look inside it, though she probably thought it odd that so small a receptacle contained gear enough for two adults and a six- or seven-year-old child. Ah well, that was the hotel business for you; people flowing through it at a rate of knots, especially in a place like Southampton.

'Thanks, William,' was all Lizzie said, after tea. 'Now, if you don't mind, I'd best put Emma to bed. She's half asleep already. Not that she has anything to wear, poor kid. Still, I daresay she'll sleep just as soundly in her petticoat, and I'll sleep just as soundly in mine.'

Later, on a shopping spree in the town centre, William purchased a mini nightgown for Emma and a larger one for her mother, plush toothbrushes and tooth powder, several bars of Vinolia soap; face flannels, talcum powder, a loofah and an earthenware flask of Devon violets perfume, which on his return to the hotel, he placed on the landing outside Lizzie and Emma's bedroom, along with a note asking Lizzie to have dinner with him, if she felt like it. Otherwise, hopefully, they'd have breakfast together next morning.

He added a PS: *'I shall never ask more of you, Lizzie, than you are prepared to grant me of your own free will'*.

He was in the drawing room when she came downstairs around seven, refreshed after her rest, delighted with the presents she had found outside her door. There was a roaring fire in the grate, a decorated Christmas tree near the bay window, colourful paperchains looped around the walls. Emma was still asleep, she told him, and she mustn't be away too long in case she woke up and felt frightened in a strange place. 'I just wanted to see you, William,' she said quietly. 'To thank you for coming all this way. The last person on earth I expected to see. The one person on earth I *wanted* to see. Thank God Emma saw you when she did, otherwise it might have been too late. We wouldn't be here now, we wouldn't be going home tomorrow.' She smiled, 'Why did you come? For all you knew, the ship might have sailed and I might have been too far away to get you in time. Oh, God, I daren't even think what might have happened if that gangplank hadn't been there!'

'But it *was* there, darling, and so was I. Did you really think I'd have let you go so easily? I'd have followed you to America if necessary, just to be near you.'

'But what about your job? Your livelihood, your future?'

'There could be no future without you, Lizzie. My sister Nell once asked me if I knew what I wanted from life, or if I would fritter it away chasing rainbows. I said I'd let her know if ever I reached my rainbow's end. Now I have. You are my rainbow's end. You and Emma. All I've wanted for such a long time now. My reason for living.'

There was more he wanted to say; questions he needed to ask, but he knew instinctively that this was neither the time nor the place to ask her what had happened aboard ship before it sailed. Lizzie would tell him in her own good time when memories were less raw, less painful.

To question her now would be both unkind and insensitive.

'I'd best be getting back to Emma now. Goodnight, William, and bless you. See you in the morning.'

'Goodnight, my love. Sleep well.'

'Promise me you'll have dinner?' she said. 'I don't want you to go to bed hungry.'

He chuckled, 'Very well then, I promise to eat all my greens like a good boy.'

At that moment, he'd have settled for a couple of Zissler's hot pork pies eaten in a shop doorway with gravy running down his chin, as the young William Chalmers had done a long time ago. But a world of difference lay between the immature youth he was then and the man he was now. A family man!

On his way from the dining room, at the reception desk, he ordered chicken sandwiches, milk and biscuits for little Emma, to ensure that, in events of the little girl waking up hungry, there'd be food and drink on hand to sustain her.

The poor kid, he thought compassionately, it wouldn't be easy for a child of her age to come to terms with the dramatic changes in her life. The loss of a familiar father figure and a beloved grandmother in the wake of her recent separation from the equally familiar and well-loved people she had grown up with.

How he would fare as a substitute for Lewis Gilbert, he had no idea. Far better not to even try, William decided. At least the child appeared to like him—the man she called 'Willum'—who had saved her from drowning. Never would he expect her to call him Papa. That accolade belonged to Lewis Gilbert alone. And so be it.

Making ready for bed, William pondered the many pitfalls ahead of him so far as the Donen family were concerned. Lizzie's brother Dicky, for instance, had threatened to thrash him within an inch of his life if he ever showed his face in Parker Street again. Her sister Bessie hated the sight of him. Emily Donen had warned him to keep away from her daughter and not to fill her head with romantic nonsense; daydreams destined never to come true.

The fact remained that they *had* come true. With patience and understanding he hoped, in time, that he would overcome the Donen family's mistrust of him for Lizzie's sake, though he might well have added fuel to the bonfire in coming between man and wife the way he had done; besmirching her reputation.

The gossips of Parker Street would have a field day when Lizzie returned home without her husband, he realised, as they had done when her sister Madge had fallen pregnant by a married man. At least he had partially settled that score on her behalf. He'd been quite handy with his fists in those days, he thought. But the battles that lay ahead of him now relied on diplomacy, not force for their solution.

A daunting prospect. There would be a long hard road ahead for himself and Lizzie, fraught with prejudice, mindless gossip and misunderstanding—the home-wrecker and the faithless wife. It would take a great deal of courage to weather the storm. A great deal of love.

TWENTY-FOUR

Dicky, Beulah and their offspring would be spending Christmas Day with the Cammishes. Such matters had to be given due consideration to prevent jealousy. Beulah's mother could be a might touchy if she thought the Donens were seeing more of the grandchildren than she was.

Jack didn't mind one way or the other now that Lizzie and Emma were safely home again; a small miracle for which he felt himself partly if not wholly responsible, in view of his confrontation with Lewis Gilbert. Not that he'd mentioned the incident to Emily whose joy at Lizzie's return had been overshadowed by William's role as knight-errant in the affair: the person to blame for coming between a man and his wife, to Lizzie's detriment.

'I am not inviting him to spend Christmas Day with us, and that's final,' Emily said. 'The very idea!'

'But we can't let the lad spend Christmas Day on his own,' Jack objected. 'After all, Christmas is supposed to be a time of peace on earth, goodwill towards men.'

'Oh? And what's come over you all of a sudden, Jack Donen? Is there something you're not telling me?'

He might have known that Emily would ferret out the truth sooner or later. 'The fact is, the night of the farewell party, I had a word or two with Lewis Gilbert about dragging Lizzie off to America against her will. I think he got the message.'

'You did—*what?*' Emily stared aghast at her husband. 'After I'd warned you not to interfere?'

'Someone had to,' Jack said stubbornly. 'You know as well as I do that Lizzie didn't want to leave home. Now she's back where she belongs, and if that's my fault, I'm glad, not sorry. Blame me for what happened, not young Chalmers. God dammit, woman, he was the one who brought her back home to us! And as long as I'm the master of this house, I reckon I should have some say in what goes on under my own roof. So you'll invite young Chalmers to Christmas dinner, like it or lump it!

'Have you forgotten the way you stood by Madge when she was in trouble? Well, now it's up to you, to both of us, to stand by Lizzie in the same way. To my way of thinking, she should never have married Lewis Gilbert in the first place, a man old enough to be her father. Now, if our lass has found happiness with a decent young man she's obviously in love with, what right have we to stand in the way of her happiness?'

He continued quietly, 'I've always bowed to your better judgement, so far. But think on, my lass, I'm still the breadwinner of the Donen family, the father of our children, and I expect to be treated as such from now on, is that clear?'

'Abundantly clear,' Emily conceded, rejoicing inwardly at her husband's re-awakened interest in family affairs. 'So I'll invite William Chalmers to spend Christmas Day with us, if you insist. Then, of course there'll be Bessie and Jimmy, Lizzie and Emma, Fred Willis from the corner shop, Elsie and her young man—what's his name? Percy Peregrine? Well, anyway, what's in a name?'

Counting up on her fingers, 'So there'll be you and me, Lizzie, Emma and William, Bessie and Jimmy, Fred Willis, Elsie and Percy, to cater for on Christmas Day.'

Emily's face crumpled suddenly, her eyes filled with tears and she said hoarsely, 'Oh Jack, I miss Nan Imerson so much. More than you'll ever know. She was my best, my dearest friend in all the world. I can't help wondering where she is now and what she'll be doing on Christmas Day.'

Aboard the *Southern Queen*, standing on deck with Nan beside him, Lewis spoke quietly of Lizzie's future, haltingly of the reasons why divorcing him should not prove difficult and his intention to secure her future financially. Matters he would take care of on their arrival in New York. He had already written to her explaining the steps she should take to end their marriage, enclosing certain evidence of his medical condition.

'Oh, my dear, I wish none of this was necessary,' Nan said, understanding the depths of his despair at losing Lizzie and Emma, admiring at the same time his desire to smooth her path in life.

'No more than I do,' he said wryly, 'but her happiness means everything to me.'

'And what of your future? Buying and selling antique furniture. A bit different

362

from buying and selling secondhand books, I imagine?'

He smiled, 'No need to worry on that score. Antiques of every kind have always interested me: paintings, china, silverware as well as furniture. I even have some knowledge of early American furniture, though I'll need to do some research. That's part of the challenge, learning something new at my age.' He paused, 'By the way, Nan, I haven't thanked you for wanting to stay with me, to take care of me. You don't know how much it will mean to me having you there to share the—adventure. How much it has meant to me having you here on this voyage. Thank you, my dear.'

Bessie and her husband had had a royal time of it on their honeymoon, despite the bad weather: invigorating walks along the Scarborough sands and wind-scoured promenade to 'jog down' breakfast in readiness for a hefty lunch; afternoons in bed prior to dinner in the romantically candlelit hotel dining room.

Oh, how she'd enjoy bragging about it to Elsie. It had come as something of a shock to find that her sibling had found herself a gentleman friend, albeit a dried-up stick of a man rejoicing in the name of Percival Peregrine. A solicitors' clerk, balding slightly, with furrows carved into the bridge of his nose from his pince-nez spectacles; a newcomer to Darlington whom Elsie had met on the High Row on her way to work. A passing acquaintance until one morning when, removing his headgear as a mark of respect, he had invited Elsie to a lantern-slide show at the town hall. On philately of all things; a passionate hobby of his apparently. Not that Elsie had a clue what the word meant at the time. In her state of euphoria at being invited anywhere at all by a member of the male sex, she'd have gone to a lantern-slide show on the mating rituals of Amazonian tree frogs if necessary.

Not that Elsie cared tuppence about Bessie's opinion in any case, and he had been invited to Christmas dinner—so there!

'Why? Is he an orphan?' Bessie had commented offhandedly. 'Hasn't he a home to go to? I'd take care, if I was you, getting involved with a bloke you know next to nothing about.'

'Like you did, you mean?' Elsie retorted snidely. 'When you started chasing William Chalmers? At least *I* didn't have to chase after my young man. In any case, it was Lizzie William wanted all along, not *you*, only you hadn't the sense to see it at the time. Not that I blame him. What man in his right mind would have wanted a fat, stuck-up girlfriend like you? An' if you don't take care, you'll bust your stays.'

'There's a reason for that,' Bessie purred softly. 'I happen to be expecting, if it's any of your business!'

Not to be beaten, 'Huh!' Elsie countered hostilely, 'At the rate you're going, you'll need a crane to get you to hospital.'

Christmas dinner would quite definitely be a fraught occasion, Emily realised, wishing she had the courage to cancel the whole affair. Bessie and Elsie at loggerheads as usual, Lizzie and William seated at the same table as Bessie, who had never forgiven him for his treatment of her in the past.

On the whole, she was glad that Dicky, Beulah and their riotous offspring would be absent from the front room table. The tension would have been unbearable with her son's trio on the rampage.

Jack begun to wish he hadn't been so adamant about inviting William and placing such a burden on his wife's shoulders. For the first time, Emily seemed reluctant to cope with a family gathering, incapable of keeping the cart on the wheels.

'Look, love,' he said, 'why not call the whole thing off?'

But Emily wouldn't hear of it. 'No,' she said firmly, 'it's too late now. Just as long as Bessie doesn't start throwing her weight about.'

'What's really bothering you?' Jack asked.

'If you must know, it's Bessie's holier than thou attitude towards Lizzie. I thought she'd be more understanding of poor Lizzie's situation. There is such a thing as family loyalty.'

'You leave Bessie to me,' Jack muttered darkly. 'I'll give her a good talking to.'

'You'll do no such thing! Besides, what good would it do? She's so full of herself she wouldn't even listen.'

At dinner, revelling in her new-found status as a wife and mother-to-be, Bessie bragged unceasingly about the champagne she'd drunk on her honeymoon, her husband's splendid new job, their house in Victoria Road. Adding with a snide reference to Lizzie's misfortune, that she felt sorry for women less successful than herself in choosing a husband; having to make do with second best.

Watching Lizzie intently, Emily realised that the girl had almost reached the end of her tether. She also noticed the clenching of William's hands on the tablecloth. Mr Peregrine tried to concentrate on eating as he speared a sprout on his plate, paying undue attention to its correct positioning on the fork before conveying it to his mouth. Fred Willis's method of attack was more direct: a whole potato, a portion of goose and two sprouts on his fork at the same time; yet Emily knew he was listening to Bessie's monologue with both ears, itching to get a word in edgeways in defence of his pal William.

Eventually, 'Champagne, eh?' he said engagingly to Bessie. 'You must have spent your honeymoon at the Crown Hotel, then, or the Royal. Which was it?'

'I really can't remember offhand,' Bessie said loftily, wondering what had possessed her mother to invite such a common little man to Christmas dinner.

'Blooming heck,' Fred responded chirpily, 'fancy not remembering the name of your honeymoon hotel. But then, I daresay you were too pissed to care much anyway where you was staying—a lovely young lass like you with a first-class, not a second-rate husband in tow!'

Having fired his broadside, Fred returned to his food as innocently as a child.

Emily covered her mouth with her hands, trying hard not to laugh. Bessie subsided like a pricked balloon. Mr Peregrine, looking shocked, wished that he had not wasted good money on a stamp album as a Christmas present for Elsie in the unlikely event that he would ever wish to set eyes on her again after today, in view of this disastrous encounter.

Jack thought darkly that Bessie had deserved her comeuppance, and the sooner this shambolic Christmas Day was over and done with, the better. But there was worse to come.

When the front room table had been cleared, the washing-up done and the table relaid for tea, the party repaired to the back parlour. There, they sat in constrained silence in front of a roaring coal fire cracking walnut and Brazil nuts in an atmosphere more conducive to a wake than a celebration. The only redeeming feature was the presence of little Emma whose childish delight in the Christmas tree and the many presents she'd received knew no bounds as she played blissfully with her new-found treasures, unaware of her Aunt Bessie's hostility towards her mother and her beloved Willum.

She was playing happily with her toys when the door opened suddenly and her Uncle Dicky strode into the room.

Emily looked up startled, wondering why he had come.

About to speak, his face darkened suddenly when he saw William. 'What the hell's he doing here?' he spat out.

368

'I warned him what would happen if he showed his face in Parker Street again. Well, don't just sit there. Get up! You're coming outside with me.'

William got up, 'I have no quarrel with you,' he said calmly.

Lizzie was also on her feet, looking distraught, 'For heaven's sake, Dicky,' she cried out in alarm, 'go home. You're frightening Emma!'

Jack stood up. 'Don't be a fool, son,' he said, laying a restraining hand on Dicky's arm. 'I'll not have you making a scene in my house.'

'There isn't going to be a scene *in* your house,' Dickie muttered. 'I'll settle this outside.'

'I don't think so,' William said levelly.

'Oh, I get it! Too much of a coward, are you? Well you need teaching a lesson, my lad. Wrecking my sister's marriage; having the brass nerve to worm your way in here after all the trouble you've caused.'

Wringing her hands, 'For God's sake, Jack, *do* something,' Emily cried shrilly, 'before someone gets hurt.'

The room was now in chaos. Everyone except Bessie and Elsie were on their feet grouped about the protagonists, the men attempting to restrain Dicky. Then Fred Willis spoke up, 'I'd think twice about tackling my pal William,' he said jovially.

'I was at the Ox when he laid out the landlord. Gawd, I'll never forget it if I live to be a hundred. Sweetest thing I ever saw. A bloke twice your size, old son. Went down like a ton of bricks, he did. Out like a light! Just because he said summat nasty about your sister Lizzie, as I recall.'

'What Fred said is true.' Lizzie picked up the thread. 'I, not William, was the coward. I should have told you, Dicky, that he fought Sid Belcher to defend my reputation. William didn't like the idea of my working in a public house. I wouldn't listen, though I knew he was right. That's when the fight started. I should have cleared up the misunderstanding straight away, but I didn't. I was too stubborn, too pigheaded.'

Drawing in a deep breath, 'If I'd been honest with myself and you that night, none of this would have happened. I told William he was either drunk or crazy when he told me he loved me. I know better now. He has never stopped loving me. Now we intend spending the rest of our lives together, no matter what the world or anyone in it thinks of us.'

'I had no idea,' Dicky muttered hoarsely. 'I'm sorry. What more can I say? Shake hands, Will. Show there's no ill feeling?'

'Sure thing. For what it's worth, I

admired what you did. Standing up for your sisters, I didn't blame you. Any decent man would have done the same.'

Bessie burst into tears, 'I'm sorry too,' she admitted, throwing her arms about Lizzie. 'Please forgive me. I didn't mean all those nasty things I said to you. Another thing, we only had champagne once—on our wedding night. The rest of the time we drank pale ale.'

Emily breathed a sigh of relief. Jack put his arm about her shoulders. When things had quietened down a little, she said, 'You didn't say why you'd come, Dicky.'

'Oh, that? Beulah wondered if you had a tin of condensed milk handy?'

'Condensed milk? No, I haven't. I never use the stuff, and where you'd find any on Christmas Day, I haven't any idea.'

Fred said happily, 'Once a grocer, always a grocer! You come along with me, Dicky old son. I've a cellar full of condensed milk. Mind you, I wouldn't open my shop for just anyone on Christmas Day. But seeing it's you ...'

Mr Peregrine said awkwardly, 'Well, I might as well cut along, too.'

Elsie said surprisingly, 'Yes, you might just as well if you don't like me or my family. And you might as well take your stamp-album with you. Who wants to spend a lifetime sticking stamps into a book anyway? I'm sure I don't.'

Much later, kissing Lizzie goodnight on her doorstep, William said tenderly, 'I'm so proud of you.'

'And I of you, darling. The way you handled Dickie—'

'I didn't handle him. *You* did,' he reminded her.

'It has been an odd kind of day, hasn't it?' she said quietly.

'Very odd. But some good came out of it, and that's all that matters. However long it may take, whatever the pitfalls ahead of us, we have a future ahead of us now. With you and Emma beside me, loving me, having faith in me, I'll work my fingers to the bone to give you all the happiness you deserve.'

'I already have more happiness than I deserve,' she said simply. 'If only ...'

'If only what, my love?'

'Oh, nothing, just that I wish everyone in the world could be as happy as we are. But that would take a miracle, wouldn't it?'

'What are you trying to say? You can tell me.'

'I couldn't help noticing how tired my mother looked today. For the first time my parents seemed—old—to me; defeated somehow. I can't put it into words exactly, but I couldn't help remembering the way they used to be in the old days, with all their loved ones under one roof. The five of us, Dicky, Madge, Bessie, Elsie and me. Life seemed so vibrant, so purposeful then, with Ma ruling the roost—a tower of strength. Now that tower seems to be crumbling after all she's been through lately, what with Dickie and Bessie leaving home, Madge disappearing without a word, and all my troubles to contend with. And now dear Elsie's gentleman friend not coming up to scratch. Poor Elsie, my heart bled for her when he left her in the lurch the way he did.'

'Taking his stamp album with him,' William reminded her. 'Not much of a loss, in my view. Indeed, I have high hopes of Elsie finding herself a more suitable gentleman friend one of these days, since she had the good grace to acknowledge that her family meant far more to her than he ever could. A step in the right direction, I'd say.'

Lizzie smiled, 'Shall I be seeing you tomorrow?' she asked wistfully.

'Not just tomorrow, but every day of your life from now on,' William reassured her. 'Until the end of time and beyond.' He remembered a dream where he was

walking on the meadowlands of space
with Lizzie at his side, a dream now
come to fruition—holding the woman he
loved safely in his arms at last.

EPILOGUE

She had managed to escape her captors by pleading a headache and needing an early night alone in her room. Then, changing into her oldest clothes, wiping every vestige of makeup from her face and slipping past the desk clerk unnoticed, she ventured out into the street beyond.

She had forgotten how cold England was in winter. But there were things she hadn't forgotten—the two-tier High Street, for instance, the covered market, closed now and shuttered for the night, the open square beyond, and the grey bulk of St Cuthbert's Church.

She had come to England with her American agent plus an impressive entourage including a studio publicist, personal maid, camera crew, chauffeur and bodyguard. Marjorie Starr was 'big' in the States, but as yet not so well known in England. They wanted her photographed at the Tower of London, at the gates of Buckingham Palace, outside Westminster Abbey, on top of a double-decker bus; dining at the Ritz, strolling down Regent Street—'they' being her studio bosses who ruled her life; told her what to do, what to wear, what to eat, where to live.

The publicity shots would tie in with the preview of her latest picture on its overseas release. Apart from the stills, a series of newspaper interviews had been arranged for her, boosting the angle of a poor little English girl who had made good in Hollywood—the tinsel city of dreams come true. Then her agent, Jake Feldman, had come up with the idea of taking their golden girl to Darlington, to revisit the scene of her youth; take shots of her in all the old familiar places; outside her old school, for instance, the church where she was christened; the house where she was born. A really swell idea, he'd enthused. But Marjorie Starr didn't think so.

Crossing the market square towards Skerne bridge, she pondered the facets of her life so far. The realisation of all she had let slip through her fingers since the day she'd left that note on her dressing table for her uncle and aunt to find when she'd left New York to seek her fortune in California.

She had behaved despicably. A man had been involved, a young freelance writer anxious to get into the movie industry. *'You should come with me'*, he'd told her. *'With your looks you'll soon find a job'*.

Deeply ashamed, she hadn't dared write

to her parents. They'd have been shocked that she was living in a two-room apartment in a suburb of LA, sharing a bathroom with six other people including an out-of-work musician of Russian extraction with a penchant for vodka and a habit of singing 'The Flea' in the early hours of the morning.

Crossing the bridge, watching gas-light flickering on the turgidly moving water beneath, she thought of her affair with Miles Jessington, the illegitimate child she'd given birth to as a result of her liaison with a man who had spoken convincingly of love. Love? She doubted if he had ever known the meaning of the word. She had been too carried away by his wealth, charm and charisma at the time to doubt his veracity when he'd told her he loved her.

Even so, she hadn't learned her lesson. In New York she'd embarked on a passionate affair with a penniless young writer whose name she could now scarcely remember. She had believed him, too, when he told her he loved her; had gone with him to California, visualising a glorious future ahead.

Six months later, she woke one morning to find a note pinned to the empty pillow beside her; the cupboards and drawers of the bedroom stripped of his belongings.

The note read, '*Sorry. Going home!*'

The glorious future had at least materialised. She'd been working as a waitress in a diner on Sunset Boulevard when a talent scout, struck by her beauty, had offered her a screen test at the major Hollywood studio he represented. Next thing she knew, she'd been offered a movie contract, taken in hand by the studio bosses and had her name changed to Marjorie Starr. Now here she was. *Where* exactly, she wondered, staring down into the slow-moving water. But of course she knew where, within a stone's throw of her roots, within an arm's length of real love: the kind she had known as a child; the incomparable love of her family.

Continuing her journey in the cold night air, passing the Ox at the lower end of Parker Street, she recalled the way her mother had walked proudly beside her when she was pregnant with Miles Jessington's child; daring anyone to utter a word against her. The way her father used to kiss her goodnight, at bedtime.

How could she have let so much love slip through her fingers so uncaringly, in pursuit of what? Fame and fortune? Money, which didn't amount to a hill of beans bereft of—love.

Love, the most precious gift in the world, yet the hardest of all to find—unless one knew exactly where to look for it.

Drawing in a deep breath, raising the knocker of 23 Parker Street, she awaited a reply to her summons. The door opened, light from the passage spilled onto the pavement and her mother stood there, framed in the doorway, peering into the darkness of the street beyond. 'Who is it?' Jack called out to his wife from the kitchen.

Eyes streaming with tears of joy, holding Madge safe in her arms, drawing her into the house, 'Someone for you, Jack,' she called back to him unsteadily.

Never till her dying day would Emily forget the look on her husband's face as, emerging from the kitchen, catching sight of Madge, he hurried towards her, arms outspread to enfold her close to his heart at last. As if the long years of their separation had never happened.

'Oh my lass, my little lass,' he uttered over and over again. Then the three of them, went together into the firelit kitchen.

At the King's Head hotel, finding her mistress's bed empty, unslept in, Marjorie Starr's personal maid hurried along the landing to announce dramatically to the assembled throng supping champagne in a private reception room, 'She's gone! Miss Starr's gone!'

'Huh? Whaddayou mean, she's gone?' Jake Feldman asked bemusedly. 'Gone? Where to for Chrissake?'

'How should I know? I'm her maid, not her keeper. I found this note on her bedside table.'

Standing up, swaying slightly on his feet, 'Here, give it to me,' Feldman said, tearing open the envelope. 'I don't understand. It just doesn't make sense.'

The note read simply: *'Going home!'* It was signed, Madge Donen.

The publishers hope that this book has given you enjoyable reading. Large Print Books are especially designed to be as easy to see and hold as possible. If you wish a complete list of our books, please ask at your local library or write directly to: Magna Large Print Books, Long Preston, North Yorkshire, BD23 4ND, England.

This Large Print Book for the Partially sighted, who cannot read normal print, is published under the auspices of

THE ULVERSCROFT FOUNDATION